Born in Pontypridd, Pat attended the Girls' Grammar school there. After leaving school she worked as a solicitor's clerk and secretary to a surveyor. Interested in poetry, short stories and plays since she was young, Pat also enjoys reading, crochet and belongs to a Celtic hand weaving group.

Pat's other interest is Celtic languages, particularly Welsh, which her daughter and three granddaughters all speak fluently.

Chasing The Rainbow is her first novel.

Don't look for these islands in any atlas. They exist only in my head as do the characters, but I've lived with them all so long that they are real to me.

Patricia Thomas

Chasing The Rainbow

by

Patricia Thomas

Published by
Mediaworld PR Ltd
Best Books Online

To my family and friends - with love

*'Better to spend your days
Chasing the rainbow of your dreams
Until you come full circle,
Than to waste your life wondering.'*

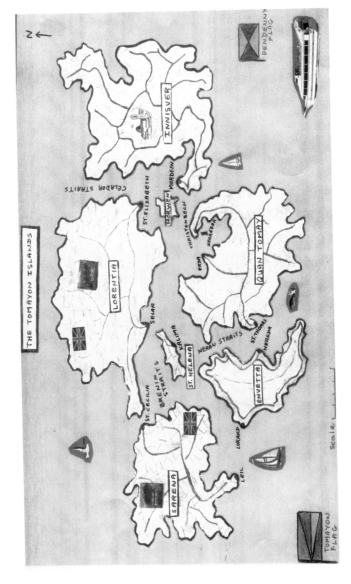

THE TOMAYON ISLANDS

N ←

SARENA

LORENTIA

ST. CECILIA
BRENIN'T'S STRAITS

SELAR

ST. HELENA
VALIMA

ST. ELIZABETH

NORWIEN
MORDEN
CHRISTEN BECH

ZERREBAR

BRIA

INNISVER

CELADOR STRAITS

QUAN TOMAY

NERAN STRAITS
ST. THOMAS
NERADA

ENVETTA

LORANS
LEIL

PENDEANNY
FLAG

TOMAYON
FLAG

Scale

Chapter 1

January

Dear Mum and Dad,

I arrived safely in Bath and am settled in my new flat. It's in a very nice area on the outskirts of the town. There are three bedrooms, one of which is very tiny, but it will be big enough if you want to come and spend a weekend with me, as long as you don't put on any weight! My flat mate is Nadia Laridon who comes from St. Helena, not the island where Napoleon was imprisoned, but one of the Tomayon islands. Nadia says the climate there is gorgeous, fairly constant the whole year, the temperature ranging from 60°-70° in the winter, rising to 80°- 90° in the summer time. Doesn't it sound heavenly? Especially after the weather we had last summer. Mind you they do sometimes have very heavy rainfall and a few weeks in the autumn when it is very windy.

Before you rush for the atlas, (it's in the spare bedroom on top of the wardrobe by the way), you'll need a magnifying glass to find them. They're only a very small group of islands and are in the index under Tomay. The two large islands and one small one are a colony, or dominion, of Great Britain and soon to be granted independence. Do you know the difference between a colony and a dominion? I don't.

Anyway the islands are ruled over by two different families, the Pendennys and the Draymers. The main dream of most of the people is that when independence comes, all the islands will be united again as they once were centuries ago. Nadia's father is the Tract Holder of one small island for the U.K. It's only a tiny island according to Nadia, about the size of the Isle of Wight. This title was granted to an ancestor of hers on condition that he raised an army to guard the Brenin Straits from attack by the native people. This title can't be passed to a female (sex discrimination rearing its ugly head) and as Nadia has no brothers, the island will revert to the British Islands on the death of Nadia's father, or some say that her husband could claim the title, but either way, Nadia isn't too bothered.

I think Nadia and I will get on all right living together. She is a lovely looking girl, with long black, naturally wavy hair and dark blue eyes. I do sometimes envy her her looks and money, but she is a really nice person and as she's always been used to having money, it's no big deal to her. She's engaged to be married and has the most gorgeous pink sapphire ring - yes pink. I didn't know you could get them in that colour either, but by all accounts you can get green and yellow ones too. Her fiancé, Vonryn, never heard that name before, lives on one of the islands, so unless I get invited to the wedding, I'm not likely to meet him. I've seen his photograph and he's very good looking and rich as well. Life isn't fair is it?

I seem to have fitted in well at the office and they don't seem to resent the fact that I've been brought in from another office to take charge, thank goodness. I had to organise a cheese and wine party the other evening to promote tourism in the Tomayon Islands. Nadia has been over here liaising with different tourist boards in an endeavour to attract more visitors to them. By all accounts the islands were stopping off places for the sailing ships to replenish their water supplies but now, in this jet age, places like these have lost their importance. They want to develop tourism in the islands, but without destroying them and altering the way of life too much, so it has to be done very carefully. They don't want high rise concreted monstrosities overlooking the sea shore everywhere, also a lot of young people will want to work in the hotels instead of on the farms, and if tourism should fail and the land isn't being worked productively, it could be a disaster in the making in the long term. Once she knew I worked for a travel agent, she asked me if I could persuade my boss to hold an evening to do a promotion. There's a large upstairs room above the office space and as we'd advertised it well, we were hoping for a good turnout. Two hours before it was to start, in fact just as we were about to leave the flat, I had a phone call. The man who was going to give the talk had a tummy bug and couldn't do it. He apologised profusely for letting us down, but said it would be so embarrassing if he had to rush off in the middle of giving his talk to go to the loo. I was just starting to panic, having visions of giving the talk myself. Luckily all the slides were set up ready and the man said we were very welcome to make use of them if we could find a replacement speaker, also his notes were with the slides.

Nadia said that she'd phone a friend of hers, a Michael Vandrell, she was sure his father would step into the breach. Somehow or other they persuaded Mr Vandrell senior to do it and he was on the doorstep of the office waiting for us when we got there. He was quite attractive, in his fifties I should think, but to be honest I didn't take a lot of notice, as we were so busy getting everything organised and Mr Vandrell, or Richard as he asked us to call him, wanted to look at the original speaker's notes and see what slides there were.

When we opened the doors, we were relieved to see quite a few people waiting outside on the pavement, and soon the room began to fill up rapidly. It was apparent that even if we didn't entice people to the Tomayon islands, they were busily picking up other brochures and looking to see if there were any bargain holidays on offer. Richard had looked at the notes and said that he couldn't possibly use them. He seemed a trifle worried. Nadia asked him if he was sure, but when he gave her the notes to read for herself she could see what he meant. She handed them over to me to read and my heart sank. We were both grateful that our original speaker had come down with a tummy bug; he'd have bored people to death! His notes read as if he were about to give a geography lesson and that would put people off going there straightaway. Richard started his talk by saying that the audience would have to make allowances for him as he was just a stand in and that although he hadn't been to the islands for many years, he had it on good authority that they hadn't changed much.

The first slides showed lovely white beaches under cloudless blue skies and hillsides dotted with groves of citrus trees. He said that in the spring and summer the islands are ablaze with colour, firstly from the wild spring flowers that carpeted the hillsides and then the bougainvillea, poinsettias and hedgerows of oleanders. You could almost smell the wild thyme and rosemary as he talked, and I was ready to book a holiday myself there and then. He did, however, warn people about the hot wind that came in the autumn and said if possible to avoid that short period and also warned that because of the hot all-year-round climate, there would be more insects than at home, but there was nothing poisonous.

If I win the lottery this week, we'll all go on one of the cruises that call in ports on the outer shores of the islands. I missed the next part of Richard's talk. I was daydreaming about hot summer days lazing in the sun and warm dark evenings. I could see myself sipping an exotic drink on a balcony under a black sky dotted with myriads of silver stars, illuminated by a large golden moon. I came back down to earth when I heard him ask if there were any Welsh people present. There were a few of us from Wales, and we dutifully raised our hands. Richard then went on to ask did we realise that a Welsh man was to blame for the feud between the two ruling families, although he might also have helped to keep two of the islands independent from the U.K. The man's name was Morgan Draymer and he'd arrived in the islands during the reign of Elizabeth I. This Morgan Draymer was a bit of a chancer. He owed money everywhere and to escape his creditors, he signed on a sailing ship as a deck hand, jumping ship when it called in at one of the islands that Elizabeth had annexed for England. Nothing was heard of him for a while, but records showed that he was fighting against the English and doing quite a good job of it. He became a favourite of the Vaga (their word for King) and became betrothed to the eldest of the Vaga's twin daughters; at least he said she was the eldest. That didn't go down too well with Ranulf Pendenny, who had been second in command after the Vaga and expected to marry the eldest daughter and rule the islands after the Vaga's death. Ranulf Pendenny claimed that it was his bride-to-be who had been born first and not Morgan's, and that after their marriage he would hold the islands until such a time as any future son of his reached maturity and was able to take control. The Vaga had to decide once and for all who was to succeed him. He himself wasn't sure which of his daughters had arrived in the world first, and if it hadn't been for the intervention of a Christian missionary on the island, one of the twins would have been killed at birth as it was considered unlucky to have twins.

Morgan and Ranulf had a double wedding in the Cathedral at Christenbech and straight afterwards, the Vaga decreed that they both had to go to the island of Envetta, (The Rainbow Island). The islanders also call this island the unfriendly isle as the terrain in the centre of the island is mountainous and dangerous. Even in the summer time storms can blow in from the sea quickly without any warning and in the winter it is a no go area. The two men were set a task to bring the Vaga back one of the rare gemstones that could be found in Envetta, and the first one who did so would be his heir.

What happened on Envetta is not known, but Morgan must have won, because to this day his descendants are the rulers of Envetta and Quan Tomay and Ranulf Pendenny was granted the title Larn (Lord, to us). It caused a lot of bloodshed though, as once the Vaga died, Ranulf Pendenny moved to the island of Innisver and proclaimed that he was the ruler of that island and the lawful Vaga.

Anyway that's enough of a history lesson, but the evening went down well and a fair number of island holidays were booked, and even those who didn't want to go to the islands booked holidays elsewhere. On re-reading this letter, I seem to have talked a lot about the islands, sorry if I've bored you. I'll phone you next week.

Love, Kathryn xxxxxx
P.S.   Richard's son, Michael is very nice.

Chapter 2

April

Dear Mum and Dad,

I hope you're both sitting down when you read this letter. Your only daughter is engaged to be married! I know I haven't mentioned seeing anyone in my phone calls, but there was nothing much to tell until last night when he proposed to me. I know you're sure to think that we haven't known one another long enough and that's why I'm taking the coward's way out and telling you in a letter and not on the phone. Michael felt we shouldn't get engaged until he personally asked Dad for my hand in marriage. I told him that that was terribly old fashioned and that you wouldn't mind. His full name is Michael Vandrell and I hope, once you get over the shock, that you'll be happy for me.

You thought it wasn't going to happen, didn't you Mum. I've seen the way you've steered me towards all my old friends in the High Street when I'm home, stopping to peer in numerous prams at healthy, but to me unremarkable, babies. The only part you won't like is that I'll not be coming back to South Wales to live, but at least you've got Tom and Mary nearby, and my niece and two boisterous nephews. I don't know when we're getting married, or where, but rest assured, you'll be the first to know. I realise you've always wanted to see me walk down the aisle of St. John's Church swathed in yards of tulle, and carrying a bouquet of red roses, and I know it wasn't the same when Tom married Mary. Somehow a son's wedding is different to a daughter's. Wherever it is, you'll still be there, and Dad will make sure he has a plentiful supply of tissues to mop up your tears.

I met Michael the night of the holiday promotion. I think I

mentioned him in a P.S. in an earlier letter. If you recall it was his father who stepped in and gave the talk when the other speaker was taken ill. Michael is twenty-four years of age, tall, very dark, and handsome - at least I think so. Anyway you won't be ashamed to be seen with him when I bring him home to meet the family and you can judge for yourself. We'll be coming down for a few days mid week in about two months. If it's all right with you, probably in the last week of June. I'm giving you plenty of warning so that you can spring clean your spotless house from top to bottom, and so that you can nag Dad into redecorating any room that hasn't seen a lick of paint for the last six months. I'm only teasing, but I do know the way your mind works.

To save Michael from the Spanish inquisition when we visit, I'll ramble on, giving you all the gen. I know about him and his family. You can then pass all the info on to the Tafia Mafia before we arrive.

I bumped into Michael regularly after that first meeting and fell for him hook line and sinker on our first date, but I didn't know whether he felt the same. Nadia belongs to a club for exiles from the islands. It's surprising how many there are living in this country and descendants of those who came here years ago. Michael's mother was born on the islands and Michael's grandfather was Governor General there a long time ago. I thought Michael was gorgeous the first time I clapped eyes on him. I didn't think he'd notice me with Nadia there, but they'd known one another for a good while before I met him, and luckily it was me that Michael fell in love with and not her. Anyway, Nadia is already engaged and is very much in love with Vonryn. Did I tell you that she's returning home for good shortly? She can't wait to return. It has been ages since she's seen Vonryn. I don't think I could bear to be apart from Michael for that long.

Before you ask, Michael isn't going to move in with me once Nadia returns home. We're going to do things properly, the whole white wedding thing. I can just about manage to pay the rent on my own, although it won't leave me much cash to spare. I'm going to take my time choosing a new flat mate as I'd rather be a bit short of cash than have the wrong person sharing with me. I'm really going to miss Nadia. In the short time we've lived together in the flat, we've got very close.

Michael hasn't got a job at the moment. Don't worry, he isn't some longhaired layabout, which should be obvious from the fact that his grandfather was Governor General, but he has enough money so that the urgency to find work isn't there. We're moving in exalted circles now, I can tell you. To be honest, I sometimes wonder if I can fit in. I can hear Dad saying that our family is as good as theirs any day, but they're from a different world. Michael's a qualified solicitor, the same as his father. His father was living and practising law in Bath, but the family have just moved to the Isle of Wight. They haven't bought a house there, just leased one for a few months. Michael's father has taken early retirement, or so he says, but Michael thinks he'll soon get bored. I haven't met my future mother-in-law yet; only Michael's father, and I like him very much. Michael and he are very similar in appearance, although Michael says that he looks like his mother. Mrs Vandrell has moved down to the Isle of Wight first and Michael's father is winding up a few things in Bath before he follows on down.

After we've visited you, we'll be going straight down to the Isle of Wight. They're celebrating their silver wedding so they'll be having a small get together for friends and presumably any relatives that might be in this country. Michael says it will give me a chance to meet some of his relatives. I am a bit nervous about meeting them en masse. It's strange really, but Michael doesn't know much about his family on his mother's side. He sees his mother's half brother, James, quite regularly as he and his family spend part of the year on the islands and the rest with his in-laws just outside Bath. Both his paternal grandparents are now dead and he has never met his other set of grandparents. Apparently Michael's mother didn't get on with her father, and although Mr and Mrs Vandrell didn't elope, there was some trouble, for they've never gone back to the islands since they were married. It's strange, but on the few occasions when his maternal grandparents have been in the U.K. and Mr and Mrs Vandrell have gone to see them, Michael always seemed to miss meeting them. He doesn't know whether it was deliberate or not. His parents rarely mentioned the islands, and although Michael used to ask his paternal grandfather about why they never went back, the old man would always fob him off with some vague answer. Mrs Vandrell's other two brothers never visited, but kept in touch over the years by telephone, or when Justin was in London, he'd meet his sister. Michael said he always received expensive birthday and Christmas presents from them, and it was only as he grew older that he wondered about why he'd never met any of them. His mother always spoke to him in her native tongue, so I suppose deep down she must think that one day he might go there. Michael wonders whether his grandparents will come over for the silver wedding as it is a special occasion. I know deep down he is hoping that they will. We'll just have to wait and see.

The weekend after next, I'll be on my own in Bath, so Mum why don't you hop on a train and spend the weekend with me? There's a good train service to Bath from Cardiff. I can show you my engagement ring. It should be ready then as we're having it made. Michael and I are going to London to chose the stone and the type of setting tomorrow. When you come down we can go and look at wedding dresses to get some idea of what I'd like. Michael will be on the Isle of Wight that weekend and as I said earlier Nadia is returning to Tomay. She's been invited to the silver wedding party, so we'll meet up again on the Isle of Wight. Nadia has an important meeting to attend and has to cast her vote on something that can't be done by proxy; otherwise she would have stayed in the U.K. until after the party.

We've had a member of parliament staying with us, not our parliament, the British Islands Parliament. Being a colony/dominion of Great Britain, their Parliament is on similar lines to ours, only much smaller. Her name is Ruth Graham and she's about your age, I should think. It's not the sort of thing you ask people, especially women. She'd never left the islands before and decided to take a vacation and visit Europe. Nadia's father suggested that she stay here whilst she was in Bath and then she and Nadia could fly back together, as they will both be attending the meeting.

Although the three of us were complete strangers to each other a short while ago and the difference in our ages, we've become good friends and I'm going to be really lonely once they leave. Ruth has done really well for herself. She was born in a little fishing village on one of the British Islands. I think she said she was about fifteen when her father was drowned at sea and her mother died not long afterwards. She went to work as a maid in the local priest's house. He helped to raise funds to send her to University, where she read law. I don't know what it is about the law, but everyone I come into contact with these days seems to be involved with it. It will be handy if we ever need free legal advice. I think she fell in love with the priest. She seemed to radiate a certain glow when she talked about him even after all this time, although I may be mistaken. Priests can marry, there's no law against it like with Roman Catholics. Anyway she never married, so it might be unrequited love, or she wanted to put her career first. I'm too nosy for my own good sometimes, but I'm so happy myself that I want everyone else to be the same.

As usual I've rambled on, but please do try and keep your lonely daughter company that weekend.

Lots of Love, Kathryn xxxx

Chapter 3

The sun was setting as the light aeroplane landed in Christenbech airport on the island of Quan Tomay. The airport was no more than a runway with a small wooden customs shed. The sky was diffused with all the colours of the spectrum, through red to gold and lavender.

"It's good to be home, even if it is only for a short time." Nadia said, as they passed quickly through customs, the bulk of their luggage having been checked at the main airport on the British Island of Lorentia, and arrangements made for its collection and dispersal to their respective homes. Outside, the air felt balmy and warm in comparison with the cooler British weather they'd left behind.

Nadia and Ruth had booked accommodation in the Julyan's Hotel, which was only a short taxi ride away from the airport.

"I'm not changing for dinner tonight," Ruth remarked. "I'll have something sent to my room. How about dining with me Nadia, or have you arranged to meet Vonryn. I know it's been many months since you've seen him."

Nadia smiled and then sighed. "No, I won't be seeing him until the meeting tomorrow. His father hasn't been well and my father invited Vonryn, the Vaga and his parents to spend a little time on St. Helena. They'll fly here first thing in the morning, it's only a 20 minute flight." She sighed again. "I was hoping our first meeting again would be more romantic than the sight of one another across a boardroom table. Still I've been patient all these months, I can wait a little longer."

"When is the wedding?" Ruth asked.

Nadia looked pensively at her engagement ring. "To be honest Ruth, I don't know. I love Vonryn, he loves me, or he says he

11

does, and our families are happy, but when I told him that I was going to Britain for months, he didn't try to dissuade me, or even make the effort to come over to see me. It was I who made a journey home to see him. I sometimes wonder if he really loves me, or if the Vaga has put pressure on him to marry me so that St. Helena will become part of his little empire."

Ruth looked skeptical. "I don't want to be rude Nadia, but St. Helena isn't that important anymore. It was years ago of course due to its location." Ruth paused, "I hope I haven't offended you by speaking this way."

Nadia laughed. "I'm not offended. Why on earth should I be? Of course the island isn't important strategically anymore. The only ones who covet it are Drystan Pendenny and Hallam Draymer. As you know the British leased the island to an ancestor of mine, Henry Laridon and his male descendants, so that they could guard the Brenin Straits. My father is the last of the male line and when he dies, I, as a mere woman, can't become Tract Holder, but it might be argued that Vonryn could as my husband, and that wouldn't suit Drystan Pendenny. I think he'd prefer the British to have it. I know Drystan wanted me to marry his grandson Philip, but I fell in love with Vonryn and if that means Hallam Draymer gets control of St. Helena so be it. My father owns his house and lands so no one can take them from him. I don't really care. Oh take no notice of me Ruth, I'm tired and I'm longing to see Vonryn again. Everything will be fine, I'm sure."

Before showering, Nadia remembered her promise to telephone Kathryn as soon as she arrived. When she looked at her watch and worked out the time difference, she wondered whether she ought to wake her, but Kathryn had been most insistent that Nadia phone to say she'd arrived safely. She then quickly showered and changed into a long sleeved cotton dress that almost reached to the floor. It was something she'd normally wear to the beach, but it was comfortable and the deep blue colour matched her eyes. She quickly brushed her hair and twisted it into a ponytail.

Ruth's identical bungalow was nearby, though hidden slightly by the jacaranda trees that shaded the lawn. Ruth opened the door and they both burst out laughing for Ruth was wearing a similar dress, only apricot in colour.

"I've already ordered for you Nadia. I hope you don't mind; just some soup, chicken salad and half a bottle of white wine. If we're still hungry we can phone room service for something else when they bring the coffee."

A little while later Nadia pushed the plate away. "I couldn't eat another thing," she said. "It was just enough and I enjoyed the wine. What was it? I don't think I've ever tasted it before."

"I ordered it especially," Ruth replied. "I wasn't even sure if they would have any. It's made in Leil, which is a small fishing village on the westerly side of the island of Sarena. It's made from Zarin fruit, but there is a secret ingredient which gives it that distinctive flavour."

"I nearly asked you what the secret ingredient was Ruth, but obviously if it's a secret you wouldn't know."

Ruth poured some more wine into their glasses. "A handful of people in Leil know. Obviously it has to be more than one person; otherwise the secret would die. About twenty-five years ago a big wine producer tried to bribe someone to tell the secret and even went so far as trying to get a Government edict that it was in the country's interests to know the formula so that it could be marketed on a more commercial basis. Luckily the priest was able to prevent it becoming law. I never found out how, but he must have had friends in high places."

Ruth sipped her wine. It was obvious that she was many miles away.

"Tell me about him Ruth." Nadia said. "I thought the name Leil rang a bell and then I remembered overhearing something you told Kathryn about your background."

Ruth was quiet for a moment. "There's not a lot to tell really. My father died at sea, and my mother died not long afterwards and I was left an orphan. It was all a very long time ago." As she continued with her story, Ruth seemed to have forgotten that Nadia was present.

"I was fifteen at the time, doing well at school and studying for a scholarship to enable me to go to University. I think that was why my father had gone fishing that day. He was so proud of the fact that his daughter was clever enough to go to University. He never should have gone, but he was determined to earn every penny he could for me, as the scholarship money wouldn't cover everything. I felt so guilty for a long time afterwards. I even thought about giving up studying. I can remember the day he died as if it were yesterday. I was young and thoughtless and didn't understand the danger. I wanted him to go. You see every penny he earned was my gateway to freedom.

My mother had read the weather signs correctly. The day was too calm and the sky, although blue, was tinged with a yellow streak on the horizon. A sudden storm blew up and on that rocky coastline the boat didn't stand a chance. If others had been fishing nearby they might have been able to help, or they might have all been drowned too. Of course all the other boats had foreseen the danger and stayed in harbour. Anyway, six months later, my mother died. She'd been an invalid for years, a weak heart and I think the shock of my father's death and the strain afterwards was more than she could cope with."

Nadia put a comforting hand on Ruth's arm. "I'm going to ring room service for some coffee and a brandy. It will make a good nightcap."

After the waiter had brought the coffee and brandies, Ruth continued her story.

"The whole village rallied around. It was a very close-knit community. The money wasn't there for university and in our grief we'd forgotten about the scholarship examination. I was found a job at the Presbytery. Father John was there at the time. He was a kindly old man, short and fat, with a red face that shone as if he had polished it. He gave me a room in the house and I helped his housekeeper and he encouraged me to start studying again. He helped me in so many ways."

"But I thought you were in love with the priest, the way you looked when you mentioned his name." Nadia interrupted then, realising what she'd said, looked embarrassed.

Ruth smiled sadly. "Is it that obvious after all these years. Oh I loved Father John. He was like a second father to me, to the whole village in fact. Always kind, but he could be quite stern. No, it was Father Luke that I fell in love with. Father John was on the point of retiring and Luke came and took his place. He was like a breath of fresh air through the village. It was Luke that started the wine co-operative, found an old recipe that gave the secret ingredient I was telling you about - where he got the recipe from I don't know, but he did. It was he that thwarted the wine company who wanted the recipe to be made public. He fell in love with me too, but he was determined that I should go to University. Without the scholarship, I thought it would be impossible, but he managed to find the money from somewhere, and career-wise I've never looked back."

Ruth yawned and stood up. "Don't think me rude Nadia, but I'm so tired, and the brandy has just about finished me I must go to bed, we've a busy day tomorrow."

Nadia kissed the older woman on the cheek. Ruth did look tired. Her eyes were red as if she'd been crying and the lines on her face seemed to be etched deeper than before.

"One more question Ruth," she pleaded. "What happened after you'd qualified. If he loved you and you loved him what went wrong? Didn't he ask you to marry him?"

Ruth opened the door to the corridor. There was sadness on her face and about her eyes. She smiled ruefully. "No. All the time in college we corresponded and I went home in some of the holidays but we never spoke of our love, although we both knew. When I qualified, I went back. It was a beautiful day. The sea was calm beneath a turquoise coloured sky and the brightly coloured fishing boats were unloading their catch at the quay as the bus turned the corner. The smell of fish was so strong, it was overpowering. I'd always hated that smell. I went to the presbytery, but there was no one at home, so I went to the church. He was there conducting a wedding, a very small one, only the bride and groom and two witnesses. I sat quietly in the back of the church until it had finished. I don't think anyone saw me, because I crept in and sat behind a pillar thinking to surprise Luke after the ceremony. It was strange, but when the wedding was over, they all left through the side door, which led into the presbytery garden, and not through the main church door. Something stopped me following them, I don't know what. I stayed a while in the church and then once again knocked on the presbytery door. Luke seemed pleased to see me, although very preoccupied. I'd travelled miles that day to tell him that I'd got my degree. He didn't ask me in; just congratulated me on my news and it was obvious that he couldn't wait to get rid of me. I didn't have any pride that day. I told him that I loved him and wanted to be his wife. When he said no, I couldn't believe it, for I knew he loved me, his eyes told me the truth although his words said the opposite. He said that he couldn't leave his people in Leil and that I wouldn't be happy living there and that I wasn't to waste my education. I decided to go for a walk and think things through. When I got to the quay, the bus was still there. It was the end of the line and the driver always took an hour's dinner break. I sat on the wall, the pain I felt was a physical pain. I had never known such a hurt, not even when my parents died. Anyway, the driver came out of the café and on an impulse I got on the bus and left. I knew, you see, that when Luke said something he meant it, all my pleas that day would have fallen on deaf ears. Luke knew the time the bus left and he could have come down to stop me but he didn't. I've never returned to Leil."

"I'm sorry Ruth. I shouldn't have asked. I've opened too many old wounds with my curiosity."

"Don't be silly." Ruth was once again the self assured woman that Nadia admired. "It's history. Tiredness and brandy is making me maudlin. What we both need now is a good nights sleep ready for tomorrow's meeting. I'll see you there."

Ruth shut the door and going to the refrigerator took out a miniature brandy. Drinking wouldn't help, she wasn't stupid but Nadia was right, too many old wounds had been reopened. She slept uneasily that night, tossing and turning from one side to the other, for her mind was too active, reliving her years in Leil, looking for answers that would finally lay to rest the ghost of Father Luke.

At seven o'clock she arose, donned her swimming costume and towelling robe, and went out to locate the pool. There was no one around, but sounds of activity could be heard coming from the main building. This was a single storey edifice, built in local cream coloured stone. It was an attractive looking building with French windows that opened out onto a wide verandah. The hotel was small, catering at the most for about seventy guests.

"It will have to be enlarged if tourism is to be developed in the islands," Ruth mused. The bungalows were dispersed within the grounds and the oleander bushes and jacaranda trees afforded each bungalow a degree of privacy and welcome shade from the hot sun. All bungalows were identical and again built of local stone. Each was decorated and furnished simply, and could accommodate two guests, but there was a sofa bed in the lounge area which could be used for a third guest if the need arose.

The early morning sun was pleasantly warm on her skin as Ruth skirted the immaculately kept lawns, where sprinklers were spinning around directing fine sprays of water on to the thirsty grass. The pool was sited well away from the main building surrounded by a tall hedge. All around were deserted sun loungers and gaily striped umbrellas to shelter the guests from the, sometimes unbearable, midday sun. On an impulse, and wondering if she was heading for her second childhood, she climbed the steps to the chute and laughing to herself, she swooshed downwards into the cool water. As she surfaced and started to swim vigorously across the pool, revelling in the feeling of freedom, she noticed a man coming through a gap in the hedge.

She groaned inwardly when she realised it was Gregory Rollins, the Governor General of Lorentia and Sarena. He waved to her and as she started to climb the ladder to leave the water, he called. "Don't come out. I don't want to spoil your swim, but I thought it was you disappearing in this direction. I only wanted to ask you to join me for breakfast before the meeting starts."

"Give me half an hour," Ruth said, and waving her hand she

re-entered the water and started to swim the length of the pool. She liked Gregory Rollins very much. He had been very helpful to her in her career and she valued his friendship, but since the death of his wife two years ago, she sometimes wondered if he wanted more than friendship. His whole attitude to her had changed, but so subtly that sometimes she wondered if it was her imagination.

Ruth wasn't sure why she'd been asked to attend this meeting. It was usual for a member of the Government of the British Islands and the Governor General to attend, but she wasn't that high up in government circles to warrant her attendance. She had a gut feeling that the main reason for her invitation was that Gregory intended to combine business and pleasure, and ask her to marry him. She stopped swimming, and turning on to her back floated lazily. She had to stop him asking her, for she knew her answer would be in the negative. She didn't want to hurt him, or spoil his remaining time as Governor General, although he had hinted that he might be prepared to stay on after independence. She had a feeling, however, that whether he stayed or not would depend on her.

In her chalet, she swiftly showered and dried her hair, noticing ruefully that the sprinkling of grey hairs was growing each month. "To dye or not to dye," she thought as she brushed the tangled mass of curls into some semblance of order. She slipped into a fine navy coatdress with long sleeves. Even in this hot climate, it was expected that you should wear something formal to meetings, and tights and shoes, not sandals, was the correct order of dress. She fervently hoped that the room would be air-conditioned.

Gregory was already in the dining hall when she arrived. Most of the tables were still empty so they would be able to talk in private. His craggy features lit up as he saw her and Ruth forced a smile as she hurried forward. "I'm sorry if I've kept you waiting."

He got up and held a chair out for her. "I was too eager for your company," he said. "It's three months since we met and I've missed you."

"Any sign of Nadia?" Ruth enquired.

"I spoke to her a few moments ago. She had an early breakfast in her room and she's going to the airport to meet her father and Vonryn. She told me to tell you that she'd see you at the meeting," Gregory replied.

They both ordered a full English breakfast just in case the meeting dragged on. "Did you enjoy your stay in the UK?" Gregory enquired.

"Very nice." Ruth said, taking a sip of the freshly squeezed orange juice. Then a thought struck. "I had a great time in Bath," she exaggerated. "I stayed with Nadia you know. It's amazing how many exiles are over in the UK and so many situated in that area."

Ruth hated lying, but there again it wasn't really lying, she was bending the truth a little.

As they continued eating, she regaled him with tales of her holiday, letting the name of Peter Latimer keep cropping up. Everywhere she went it seemed Peter Latimer had been in attendance. She prayed that Gregory wouldn't meet Peter when he returned home and find out that he was a happily married man with three children, and that on 90% of the outings Ruth had mentioned, Peter's wife had been there as well.

"I've talked too much about my holiday Gregory," Ruth said, thinking that perhaps she had overdone the topic of Peter. "One thing that puzzles me about this meeting though is why did you suggest I attend? Surely there were more prominent members of the government who should have been invited."

Gregory looked at her, his grey eyes revealing a sadness that his calm features didn't betray. Oh God, had he nearly made a fool of himself. All that talk of that man in England. What could he say, he'd only asked her along in order that they could spend some time together in a romantic setting so that he could propose marriage. His years of diplomatic training came to his aid. "I thought it would be of interest for you to attend a meeting of the Islands' Council. Also I remembered you saying that you'd never visited Christenbech and I thought I could show you around before I leave for home. I hope you're not offended." He smiled warily at her.

Ruth poured a second cup of coffee for them both and replied reassuringly. "Of course I'm not offended. We've been friends too long for that to happen." She emphasised the word friends slightly. "You sound as if you've decided not to stay until independence."

"That's right. I've been dithering for quite some time, but I've finally decided." He paused as if considering what words to use. "If things had been different, I might have stayed on until the end, if you see what I mean..." He broke off abruptly wondering if he'd said too much and praying that she wouldn't ask what things.

Ruth felt guilty. She knew all too well what he meant. She'd been right after all. He had intended to ask her to marry him and if she'd accepted they could have made their home here. She hadn't encouraged him to think of her other than as a friend - or had she? One of them had misinterpreted the signals the other had given.

"Who will be Governor General in your place, or is it too soon to say?" She enquired.

"There is someone in mind. It was only mentioned last week and then not openly in Parliament, as the person concerned hasn't been approached as yet, and of course I haven't officially resigned, although I have been asked to let Parliament know my decision as soon as possible. I'll telephone the Prime Minister after the meeting today to tell him of my plans, and I'll also announce my resignation today to the Islands' Council. That is merely a gesture of politeness, as it doesn't really concern them, but I do want their agreement as to the next Governor General. It could be a controversial issue, I'm not sure. With that hurdle out of the way, we can then move on to the most important part of the meeting, the decision on who will be the next Vaga and the continuing peace in the Islands after independence."

Ruth looked alarmed. "What do you mean the continuing peace? Why should things be any different?"

Gregory smiled. "For all your years practising law and then in politics, you're still very naive in some ways. You don't think that Hallam Draymer and Drystan Pendenny are going to sit back and let Lorentia and Sarena enjoy their independence. In their eyes those islands are an integral part of the Tomayon group. There is also St. Helena to be considered. It's only a small island, but now that the male line of the Laridon family has come to an end, the island would revert back to the British on his death. Stephen Laridon isn't that old and appears to be in perfect health. By the time he dies the islands of Lorentia and Sarena will be independent, and as Stephen's daughter, Nadia, is engaged to Vonryn Santella, a distant relative of Hallam Draymer, he will in all probability claim the island. The British Government would be quite happy to see the unification of all the islands under one Parliament and one Head of State, but the people living on Lorentia and Sarena need to be considered. Do they want to be part of the Tomayon group, or would they rather stay separate from the other islands? As I see it, the real problem is who will be Vaga after Hallam Draymer dies. We need a strong leader who will unite all the islands, but without the agreement of Hallam Draymer and Drystan Pendenny on this matter, there could be trouble in store. Drystan Pendenny argues that because Hallam's only son is dead, his son should be next in line and not some distant relative of the Vaga. The answer would be for both those two old, stubborn men to come to a compromise and appoint a successor, one who would be acceptable to them and to all the islands.

"I know very little about them," Ruth admitted. "But I do recollect that I read somewhere that this feud between the Draymers and Pendennys has been simmering on and off for about four hundred years."

"True, but it didn't really matter until independence became imminent. You see there is now something worthwhile to fight for. If Morgan Draymer and Ranulf Pendenny hadn't fallen out all those centuries ago, I think Morgan Draymer could have driven the English from the other islands. The only good thing is that they hated us more than they hated each other. You can virtually say we've kept the peace between them all this time. True we've had to deal with a few incidents, but nothing too serious. Now with us leaving, who knows? I doubt if their descendants have learnt any sense. He looked down at his watch. "If you've finished Ruth, I think we had better leave for the meeting."

Ruth accompanied him out of the restaurant praying that her beloved islands wouldn't resort to civil war. She had thought of independence as something to be welcomed, but now she wasn't too sure.

Until the arrival of the English, Christenbech had been the capital of all the islands. After the capture of the islands of Lorentia and Sarena, the English decided to build a new capital and they looked around for a suitable site. There was a natural harbour on the east coast of Lorentia half way along the Celador Straits and they started building it there, naming it St. Elizabeth in honour of their Queen and also of St. Elizabeth whose saints day it had been when they captured the two islands.

~*~

The taxi from the hotel dropped Ruth and Gregory outside the large stone arch of the old walled city. In front of it there was a large fountain where several jets of water were propelled into the air to varying heights.

"In the dark," Gregory said, "coloured lights beneath the water are switched on and the jets change colour." The stone arch was impressive, built out of different coloured stones, and carved with figures of animals, both real and imaginary. The city was built on a promontory that descended steeply towards the sea and the streets, some of which were stepped, were laid out on a grid system interspersed with tree-lined squares. Free of vehicles it was a peaceful place to wander. As they strolled along, Ruth looked around her with interest.

"It's like stepping back into another time, if you pardon the pun," Ruth said laughingly. "It's so tranquil. I'm so glad that the narrowness of the streets and the steps make it impossible for cars to enter."

As they were early, they were able to stroll leisurely through the quiet streets. Most of the shops were still shut, though a few shopkeepers were pulling up shutters and preparing for a new day. Ruth would have liked to linger and inspect some of them, especially the one that displayed the best of island jewellery, including a wide range of the precious stone envis that could only be found on Envetta. Surrounded by an Aladdin's cave of precious and semi precious stones set in exquisite designs of gold and silver was a large photograph of the rarest envis stone. It was as though someone had plucked a rainbow from the sky and imprisoned it.

"I'd love to see the real thing," she murmured.

"There's one in the museum here in Christenbech and the Vaga's family have a few of the rare stones made up into jewellery."

Gregory looked at his watch. "We'd better be going Ruth. You'll be able to have a good look around after the meeting."

Reluctantly she dragged herself from the dazzling array of jewellery, making a mental note of the name of the shop. Maybe, she thought, after the meeting she would have time to treat herself to a pair of earrings.

Ruth followed Gregory through an alleyway and found herself in another tree-lined square, dominated on her right side by a huge church. The twenty or more steps that led to its massive wooden doors were covered in red carpet.

"It seems as though there is going to be a wedding," Gregory remarked. "This is the Cathedral of St. Matthew. If you have time afterwards, you really ought to take a look inside. The stone carvings of the Stations of the Cross are wonderful and the colours in the stained glass window behind the altar showing the Nativity are splendid." He pointed to another building. "That is the new Great Hall, or as you would call it Parliament."

Ruth turned to look at the Great Hall, which was built around two sides of the square. It was an impressive, though not a large building, again built out of local stone with square crenellated turrets at each corner. The old Great Hall was situated to the front of them facing the sea, but Ruth felt disappointed. After the highly decorated facades of the Cathedral and Parliament Building, the old Hall was a plain stone building set in a small piece of land surrounded on three sides by a high wall with ugly looking iron spikes on the top and on the fourth side the land shelved steeply away to the sea.

"As you notice," Gregory said, "the Great Hall is a misnomer. The 'great' really stood for its importance many centuries ago, and not its size. All momentous decisions were at one time made here."

Although small in size and insignificant in appearance, it was obviously well guarded as, at the main gates, fierce looking guards, armed with machine guns, scrutinised their passes very carefully.

Eventually they were allowed through into the paved courtyard. They entered the hall through two massive wooden doors, into one large room built on two levels. The upper level being a balcony on three sides, with a central wooden staircase descending into the downstairs area. On the wood panelled walls of the balcony were hung oil paintings, depicting various events in the islands' history. Gregory stopped in front of one showing a woman lying on a bed, obviously having given birth to twins as two wooden cribs stood nearby. A fierce looking individual hovered near the babies, holding a knife poised ready to strike at one of them, but a priest stood in between, holding aloft a large primitive wooden cross. "The cause of the feud," Gregory said. "If Christianity had arrived on the islands even a day after the birth of these twin daughters, we wouldn't need a meeting today."

Ruth stepped back and studied the painting. It was well done, and the artist had captured for all time the emotions on the faces of the long dead characters. "It wasn't only here that twins were considered unlucky," she observed. "I didn't realise though that it was part of our culture. Such a shame that healthy babies had to die."

"The Tomayons weren't superstitious about twins," Gregory corrected her. "It was only if they were born to the Vaga. There could only be one Vaga, and never a woman, no sex equality in those days I'm afraid. If the Vaga had no son, but only a daughter, then whoever married her became the next ruler, so to have twin daughters only, was asking for trouble, and that's what happened. The priest saved the child, but on the condition that she never married and had children. With ambitious men around, it was the perfect recipe for disaster."

"But surely the first-born had the most rights?" Ruth questioned.

Gregory laughed. "With identical twins in primitive times, to remember which was the first born was impossible. The mother said she knew, but of course when both girls eventually married, Ranulf Pendenny said his wife was the first-born. Then to make matters more complicated, the other girl married Morgan Draymer, a foreigner, so Ranulf argued that even if his wife wasn't the first-born, no foreigner should be Vaga. To determine his successor, the Vaga decided that the two men should go to Envetta, and the first one to return with the rare envis stone would be proclaimed as such. Morgan Draymer, the hated foreigner, must have found such a stone because he became Vaga. Ranulf Pendenny who returned from Envetta a defeated and broken man, was given the title Larn of Innisver, but in return he had to swear allegiance to Morgan Draymer. There are numerous records of other happenings at that time, but there is nothing about their journey to Envetta. I'm sure some skullduggery took place on Morgan Draymer's part, though I expect Ranulf Pendenny was no angel."

Ruth turned from the painting and started to descend the staircase. Halfway down her attention was drawn to the massive stained glass window that dominated nearly the whole of one wall. It depicted a map of the islands, each island being shown in different colours and the sea in a brilliant turquoise. The sun shone through this window, throwing a myriad of colours that danced across the floor. A large mahogany, oval table, surrounded by ornately carved chairs, were the only pieces of furniture in the hall. The severity of the room was relieved by more oil paintings and the beautiful stained glass window. On the table in front of each chair were name cards and notepads and pens. Jugs of iced water and glasses were placed on silver trays at various points on the table.

Nadia and her father, Stephen Laridon, were the next to arrive. Nadia looked rather depressed and after introducing Ruth to her father, Nadia beckoned her to one side.

"Where's Vonryn?" Ruth asked. "I was hoping to meet him

today."

"I haven't seen him yet Ruth. It's such a let down, especially after all the time we've spent apart. Oh, he phoned me first thing this morning, just as I was about to leave for the airport to meet the plane. He told me that he wouldn't be attending the meeting. He said he wasn't allowed, as it concerns him. Unbeknown to me he'd cancelled the arrangement to stay on St. Helena with my father. Do you know what's going on?"

Ruth shook her head and smiled at the younger girl, who looked as if she carried all the cares of the world on her shoulders. "I probably know even less than you. I don't even think I should be here." She paused, as she didn't want to mention her thoughts about Gregory, it wasn't the time or the place. She put her arm around Nadia's shoulders. "Cheer up. Aren't you and Vonryn travelling back to England soon?"

Nadia's smile was radiant as she thought of her lover. "Yes, you're right. I must cheer up. We're spending a couple of weeks at home and then back to the UK for a short visit to attend Mr and Mrs Vandrell's silver wedding party. I became quite friendly with Michael and his family when I lived in Bath. I hope this meeting doesn't drag on too long. Vonryn told me that he'll arrive in time for dinner tonight, and I thought I'd spend the afternoon in the beauty parlour."

What it was to be young and so much in love, thought Ruth as she took her seat, which was at the far end of the oval table.

Drystan Pendenny and two of his sons arrived next. Both sons were tall and looked very much alike in features, but one was fair skinned with blonde hair, liberally sprinkled with grey, and the other dark skinned with black wavy hair. Shortly thereafter the Vaga, Hallam Draymer arrived. He stood at the top of the staircase for a few seconds looking at the people waiting below. As he descended, Ruth was struck at the likeness between Hallam Draymer and Drystan Pendenny. Both men were in their early seventies with the same acquiline features and wavy iron-grey hair. They could easily have passed for brothers. The only difference was the eyes. Those of Drystan Pendenny were dark brown, almost black, but Hallam Draymer's were a piercing blue.

It had been decided beforehand that Gregory, as a neutral observer, should be in the chair. Ruth stopped her mind from wandering and listened. Gregory was introducing her and saying that she was there to observe the meeting for the British Islands' Parliament. She smiled hesitantly at the people surrounding the table. One of Pendenny's sons, Justin, the dark haired one, smiled back at her and gave a slight wink. Oh my God, she thought. It was obvious that he thought she was there just to spend the weekend with Gregory and for no other purpose. She wondered if Gregory had taken other women with him to meetings and if he had a reputation for this sort of thing. She dismissed it from her mind instantly. Gregory wasn't the type. It was Justin putting two and two together and making five.

"One of your sons isn't here Larn," Gregory addressed Drystan Pendenny.

Drystan nodded. "He sends his apologies and hopes to arrive before the end of the meeting. If he doesn't arrive, my son Justin holds his proxy."

"I'm sorry Sir," Gregory replied, "but there can be no proxy vote today." Gregory glanced at the Vaga, who was nodding his head in agreement.

"The Agenda is very short," Gregory continued quickly before Drystan had time to argue this point. "After this meeting, I shall be informing Her Majesty's Government by telephone and thereafter in writing that I am resigning my post as Governor General." Gregory glanced at Ruth, who tried to avoid looking at him. "I had hoped to continue until independence, but personal circumstances have decreed otherwise. Just before the meeting started, I told the Larn of Pendenny of my decision and told him of the suggestion that his son-in-law, Richard Vandrell, be approached to take the position. My own personal feeling is that Richard would be an excellent choice. I've known him for many years, not as a close friend, but enough to know that he is a man who takes his responsibilities seriously. I know the British Government would have no objection, even though he has no experience. He is, after all, the son of one of the earlier Governor Generals. Normally a Governor General would be appointed by the British Government without your consultation, but in this case it was felt that you should be asked. The decision rests entirely with you, as to whether you accept Richard unequivocally or would prefer someone else appointed."

There was silence in the room and it was obvious that no one else's name was likely to be put forward.

"Can we take a vote on this?" Gregory said. "If you agree, would you kindly raise your hands."

Ruth looked around the table. All hands were raised, even the Vaga's, which was surprising as she didn't think he'd want the son-in-law of his old enemy for Governor General.

Gregory poured himself a glass of iced water. He noted the agreement of everyone present that Richard Vandrell should be approached and then looked across at the Vaga.

"The next and final item on the agenda is to decide on the successor to you Sir. I know Britain doesn't have any rights in this matter, but the future peace and prosperity of all the islands hangs on the right decision. From what I have been told verbally, there are only two names put forward." Gregory looked at the Vaga and smiled. "I think it only correct that you should be the first person to speak on this matter."

The Vaga rose to his feet and, not taking his eyes of Drystan Pendenny's face, started to speak.

"I have come to this meeting against my better judgment. The appointment of Richard Vandrell as Governor General could have been made without such a meeting, and as for the other item on the agenda, my decision..." He paused, "I repeat, my decision has been made as to my successor when I die. Neither the British Government nor the Larn of Pendenny has any say in the matter. I have decided that the next Vaga is to be Vonryn Santella, the only son of my second cousin Vincent Santella. If my son, Morgan, had lived and been allowed to marry the woman he loved, your daughter Drystan Pendenny, there would have been no problem. To this day, I'm not sure in my own mind that his death was an accident."

Drystan Pendenny rose rapidly to his feet. In his anger he knocked his chair, which toppled over backwards. The two old adversaries glared at one another.

"Are you accusing me of murdering your son? I have never made any secret of the fact that I believe myself and my descendants to be the true rulers of these islands and myself the Vaga, but resort to murder, never." He took a deep breath trying to calm himself, and when he started to speak again, his voice and manner were more controlled.

"However, I will not today dispute who is the true Vaga. If Hallam Draymer would care to read his history books, he should know that in the event of the Draymer line not producing a direct male heir, then the succession passes to the Pendenny line. As you all know, I have three sons, one from my first marriage and two from my second, but as all of them has declined the honour, I am nominating my grandson Philip, and because of this neither he nor Vonryn are attending this meeting."

Hallam Draymer smiled scornfully. "Your three sons. How you enjoy throwing that in my face. He turned to Gregory. "You and Miss Graham are impartial observers of this meeting, and I want you both to note that, against my better judgment, I will accept the name of Philip Pendenny as a contender to the succession, but with reservations." He stopped speaking and looked at Justin. "Justin, would you kindly pick up your father's chair so that we may continue with this discussion."

Drystan Pendenny regained his seat, his face white with suppressed anger and listened as Hallam Draymer continued.

"Whilst I accept Philip Pendenny as a contender to the succession, I feel it would not be in the best interests of our country for him to be the next Vaga. I have nothing against the young man personally, apart from the fact that he prefers to spend most of the year in England with his mother's family. That is his right if he so wishes, but can you honestly swear Drystan that you haven't put pressure to bear on this young man. I can see by the look on his father's face that you have."

Ruth cast a glance at James Pendenny. His face was an open book and it was obvious that Hallam Draymer had spoken the truth.

"Both James and Philip know their duty." Drystan spluttered. "My daughter-in-law's father hasn't been well lately, so reluctantly they have to be out of the country for a good part of the year."

Hallam Draymer raised one eyebrow. "If what you say is true about Marjorie's father, then I'm sorry, but their frequent absences have been going on for years, not just lately. You know very well that they're not reluctant to visit Britain. They can't wait to leave here. They're completely Anglicized and you know it. I doubt if they even speak our language fluently. If Ilona and Morgan had married, the blood of both our families would have been joined and the whole country could have united behind a child of that union, but no, you were determined that the only son of your first marriage, to another English woman, should be your heir and also Vaga. Now he in his turn has married into an English family and you want to put your grandson in his place.

Drystan Pendenny inclined his head. "That is my wish," he said.

Hallam Draymer turned to Gregory. "I see no point in continuing this meeting or taking a vote for two reasons, firstly although it is correct that my only son is dead, nowhere is it mentioned that the male heir should be my son or grandson, only that he should be of my blood to the seventh degree, and Vonryn Santella qualifies in all respects, Secondly even if a vote were taken, it would be equally divided between Vonryn and Philip. Naturally myself, Nadia and her father would vote for Vonryn and Drystan and his two sons who are here at the meeting, would vote for Philip. As stated earlier, there is to be no proxy vote."

Gregory got to his feet. "I feel I should ask you if what the Vaga says is correct and that you would all vote the way he predicts."

Everyone nodded their heads in assent, but Ruth noticed that Justin was the last to agree. It was as though he was waiting for something to happen.

"I don't feel there is any point in continuing. We have obviously reached a stalemate," Gregory continued. "However, before closing this meeting, I just want to point out that I had hoped we could come to a decision this morning as to the succession. Independence is coming, and although the Vaga has no real political influence anymore, he is still a powerful figurehead. If we'd been able to appoint a successor, it would have given the people time to get to know him before he in turn became Vaga. I only hope that today's meeting won't plunge the country into separate factions that might result in bloodshed."

Gregory stopped speaking for a moment to give time for his words to be absorbed and hoping that someone would give way.

"Very well, nothing remains therefore but for me to declare this meeting..."

"Wait one moment," a man's voice echoed from the balcony. Ruth had her back to the balcony, but there was no need for her to turn to see the man's face. How many times in her dreams had she heard this voice, only to awaken and shed a few tears for what might have been? It seemed as though Drystan Pendenny's voice came from a long way off as he greeted his other son, Luke Pendenny. She heard him coming down the stairs and steeled herself to show no emotion as their eyes met after all this time. He looked startled when he saw Ruth, but a shadow of a smile flitted across his face. He was still the same Luke, she thought. He looked older and greyer, but then didn't they all. Luke stood behind his father's chair and looked around the table acknowledging everyone's presence with a slight nod of the head. "I must apologise for being late. It seems from what I just overheard, that I have the casting vote and as the meeting isn't closed, I should like to use it. Father, will you accept my vote?"

Drystan didn't turn around to look at his son, he was too busy leaning forward and looking at Hallam Draymer. "Yes Luke," he said. "I will abide by your decision if Hallam also agrees to abide by it." Drystan Pendenny leant back, a satisfied smile on his face.

Hallam Draymer turned to Gregory. "Although Luke is Drystan's son, I feel that as a priest he will vote for the man best suited for the task, so yes, I will abide by what he says."

Everyone glanced at Luke in anticipation.

"Well, ladies and gentlemen, I cast my vote for Vonryn Santella."

Ruth looked around the table at the faces of the other people present. Drystan Pendenny's face had lost the earlier smile and he seemed stunned at the treachery of his own son.

Justin turned to his father. "I'm sorry father, but I agree with Luke. Gregory, I want to change my vote. I too am voting for Vonryn. I should have voted that way sooner, but I didn't have the moral fibre to do it."

Drystan Pendenny shut his eyes swaying slightly in his chair. James hurried over to support his father, and Drystan clutched his oldest son's hand in a tight grip.

"You are the only son I have left now. As far as I am concerned the others might as well be dead. They have always been jealous of you James."

"You know that's not true," James tried to comfort his father. "I agree with them that Philip isn't best suited to be Vaga. He only let you put his name forward because you insisted.

Ruth tried to read the expression on Hallam Draymer's face, but it was a closed mask.

Gregory quickly got all the parties to sign three copies of the document and initial the insertion of Vonryn Santella's name as the Vaga's successor."

No one uttered a word, and as soon as all signatures had been inscribed and witnessed by Gregory and Ruth as independent witnesses, Luke Pendenny turned swiftly and walked from the room through a door set in the corner, one that Ruth hadn't previously noticed. The noise of his footsteps echoed through the silent room.

Ruth sat there. She was as stunned as Drystan Pendenny, but for a different reason. The priest she had known and loved was the son of the second most powerful man in the islands. To the end of her life she would never remember if Gregory closed the meeting formally, but knowing him, he probably had. She remembered him saying something to the effect that he would arrange for delivery of the signed documents to the respective parliaments.

When she started to recover from the shock she'd received, she found that she was the only one remaining seated at the table. She could see the back of the Vaga leaving through the side door, and the remainder were huddled together talking. Her thoughts were in turmoil. She couldn't let Luke go out of her life again. She would settle for friendship if that was all he could offer. Suddenly galvanised into action, she rushed out through the side door and saw the Vaga and Luke, now surrounded by armed guards, leaving together in a powerboat. As the boat sped out to sea the wind ruffled his hair, still thick, but now liberally sprinkled with grey. Turning to face the wind, he saw her standing there and raised a hand in farewell. He called out something, but the noise of the boat's engine and the wind carried his voice away. Ruth felt someone tap her on the shoulder. It was Nadia. "I saw you come out here and sensed something was wrong."

Ruth was distraught. "I must follow him Nadia. Where can I hire a boat? They seem to be heading for that small island out in the bay." There was an urgency in Ruth's voice that made Nadia look at her older friend more closely. "Father Luke!" She shook her head in disbelief. "It can't be. Are Father Luke and Luke Pendenny one and the same person?"

Ruth nodded.

Nadia looked bewildered. "You must have known that Luke Pendenny was a priest."

"I probably did, but how would I connect Father Luke living and working in a small fishing village with Luke Pendenny. If I ever knew he was a priest, I would have thought that, as the son of Drystan Pendenny, he would be in a large town in charge of a Cathedral or at least a very large church."

Ruth clutched her friend's arm in despair. "Please help me Nadia. I must follow him. I must know the truth after all these years. Help me get a boat."

"If you waited until low tide you could walk out there over the causeway, but you can't follow him. That small island is Zerrebar, the home of the Vaga. No one lands except by invitation. The best that could happen if you tried to land, is that you would be arrested, and the worst scenario is that you could be shot."

"Why didn't you tell me Nadia? I thought we were friends."

Nadia touched Ruth's arm comfortingly. "You're not thinking clearly. You only told me about Luke last night, and as you yourself said, how could anyone connect a priest from a small fishing village with the son of Drystan Pendenny. I'm as surprised as you. After all these years, are you positive?"

"Of course I am. I just don't understand. It doesn't make sense."

"No it doesn't," Nadia agreed, "but it's pointless staying here. Come on Ruth let's go back to the hotel."

Ruth watched the boat as it sped away from her. She looked longingly at the secret forbidden island that shimmered in a heat haze as the sun climbed relentlessly higher in a clear blue sky.

~*~

Gregory and Stephen Laridon had further business to discuss over a working lunch, so it was decided that Ruth and Nadia should journey back to the hotel together and all meet up later for dinner, where at long last Ruth would meet Vonryn.

Ruth was silent throughout the short journey back to the hotel, all thoughts of looking around Christenbech and shopping for jewellery forgotten. Nadia also refrained from speaking, firstly out of sympathy for Ruth, and secondly she was still reeling from the shock she had received that Vonryn was to be the next Vaga. She wondered if he had known what was on the agenda, or if he was as much in the dark as she had been.

Nadia was about to pay off the taxi driver, when Ruth stopped her. She spoke to the driver. "I'm leaving in about ten minutes. Would you mind waiting?"

"No lady," he replied. "It's fine by me, so long as you remember the meter's ticking. Where do you want to go, the airport or the harbour?"

"The airport." Ruth answered. Ruth almost dragged the protesting Nadia to her chalet.

"I intended leaving tomorrow anyway," she said as she flung her few overnight things in her bag. "Luckily I had the bulk of my clothes delivered straight to my home."

"What if you can't get a flight," Nadia protested.

"I'll stay in the airport hotel then." Ruth was adamant that she was leaving.

"But that doesn't make sense. Let me ring the airport first." Nadia dialled the number hoping that all the flights out that day had left, or if they hadn't, that there wouldn't be a seat available."

Nadia turned to Ruth. "There's a flight leaving in an hour and half. Are you sure about this?"

Ruth nodded and Nadia, knowing when she was beaten, made the booking.

"You won't meet Vonryn, and what will Gregory say?" Nadia remarked as they walked to the waiting taxi.

"I'm really sorry I won't meet Vonryn, but there'll be plenty of opportunities when you return from England. We'll meet up one day I'm sure and I'll definitely be there for your wedding. As for Gregory…" She paused thoughtfully. "I'll see him within the next few days and apologise. He'll understand, and to be honest Nadia, if he doesn't, I couldn't care less." She handed Nadia a cheque. "I wrote this out whilst you were booking the flight. I've made it out to you. After I've gone, will you pay my bill? It should be more than enough to cover it. If it isn't you know I'll pay you back."

Nadia looked at the amount of the cheque. "I'm sure that's too much. Look I'll post you the difference as soon as I can. I thought the Government would be footing the hotel bill anyway."

"They were supposed to, but I prefer it this way." Ruth kissed her friend. "Telephone me when you get back from England and I promise we'll try and arrange to meet for dinner; the elusive Vonryn as well."

Nadia felt her eyes starting to fill with tears. She always felt emotional at any parting. This is ridiculous she thought as she wiped the tears away. They would be meeting again in a few short weeks. She waved to Ruth until the taxi disappeared out of sight.

Ruth made it to the check-in desk just in time. She scarcely noticed her fellow passengers; her thoughts were in such turmoil. On arrival home, she felt mentally and physically exhausted.

~*~

Home was a low rectangular shaped dormer bungalow, perched at the top of a hillside, with commanding views of the sea and main harbour of St. Elizabeth. A small self-contained flat for Maria, her housekeeper, was tucked away at the side of the bungalow.

During her first evening home, the telephone rang at half hourly intervals. Acknowledging herself to be a moral coward, she ignored its persistent ringing, letting the answering machine take over. All the calls were from Gregory, who sounded none too pleased at her defection. After a good nights sleep and a morning spent lazing on the patio and being spoilt by Maria, she felt calmer. Over a light lunch of salad and fresh fruit, she came to a few decisions, one of which would be to telephone Gregory that evening and apologise. In the meantime, she spent a while going through any mail her secretary hadn't been able to deal with during her long absence. There were the usual run of letters, complaining about mundane matters, but much of the correspondence came from people worried about imminent independence and the possibility of joining with the other Tomayon islands. These were mainly from ex pats who had settled in the islands because of the climate, but who liked to think they were still on British soil. After yesterday's conversation with Gregory and the subsequent meeting, she couldn't truthfully allay their fears at the moment, and she put those letters to one side for the time being. The islands had been peaceful for such a long time that the thought of an outbreak of even limited military action between rivals couldn't bear thinking about. What long buried resentments and rivalries would awaken after the British left.

"Surely no one in their right minds would want to start anything," she mused aloud.

Putting such depressing thoughts out of her head, she dealt with some of the other correspondence, dictating suitable replies into a tape recorder for her secretary to transcribe the next morning.

The day was becoming ever more hot and sultry, so putting the tape recorder to one side, she poured herself a cool drink and went out on to the patio again, settling herself on a lounger by the side of a small oval swimming pool. A retractable canvas awning was attached to the house, giving welcome shade in that area. The sea was as calm as a millpond, with only slight ripples of white foam coming from skiers, as boats pulled them effortlessly through the blue water. She was feeling pleasantly drowsy when she heard the doorbell. Maria was out, so after wondering whether to let whoever it was think she was also out, thought better of it and dragged herself reluctantly off the lounger and went to see who was there. It was Gregory, but not the poised, well-groomed man she knew. His appearance was dishevelled and he desperately needed a shave. Without a word he pushed past her into the hall and then into the lounge. He thrust a letter in her face waving it about. She had never seen him lose control before, but strangely she didn't feel threatened, only curious.

"This was left for you at the hotel reception in Christenbech." It was obvious that the envelope had been opened. It was Ruth's turn to be angry.

"What right do you have to open my mail?" she demanded.

"Every right," he shouted. "The envelope bears the Draymer crest. I wanted to know why a Lorentian MP was in correspondence with the Vaga, and when I read it, I knew I had to face you with it and find out the truth."

"You've actually read it?" She interrupted. "How dare you!"

"Yes, I read it, and if I hadn't a great affection for you I wouldn't be here now demanding an explanation. You would be answering questions to the police."

Ruth sat down on the couch. She felt utterly bewildered.

"I think you'd better give me the letter Gregory. It's not like you, flinging wild accusations about. I honestly don't understand what this means."

She took the letter from him. It was very short, only a few lines and it wasn't from Hallam Draymer, but was written in the familiar handwriting of Luke Pendenny.

She looked up at Gregory, a smile hovering around her lips.

"This is in Tomayon. Who translated it for you?"

"No one. I've picked up a smattering of the language during my time in the islands and looked in a dictionary for the rest."

Ruth laughed out loud at the expression on Gregory's face, which grew more thunderous by the minute.

"What do you think it says?" She asked

"The letter's from Luke Pendenny saying he was sorry he'd lied to you and asking you to meet him in the Cathedral that evening so he could explain what he felt was a betrayal on his part. There could only be one explanation, you've been conspiring with him behind our Government's back, to have Philip Pendenny as the next Vaga and take over the British Islands after independence, and then Luke turned up and voted for Vonryn instead. What did they promise you, that you would be Prime Minister of the new united Tomayan islands?"

"Don't be so ridiculous," Ruth snapped. "It doesn't make the slightest bit of difference to me who the next Vaga will be. You're not thinking clearly. I was only at the meeting because of you remember." She put out a hand and touched him tentatively on the arm. "I'm sorry, but you must admit the situation is farcical. You've blown everything out of proportion."

Suddenly Gregory had her in his arms and was kissing her passionately. She tried to free herself from his embrace, but his two hands were on her shoulders and she couldn't move.

"I'd do anything for you Ruth, even withholding this letter. We can burn it now and forget it ever arrived. It's too late for you to meet Luke so no harm has been done."

"Yes, it is too late," she said sadly, finally managing to extricate herself from him. She knew now that she'd been right. She'd felt nothing from his kisses and the thought of anything more intimate repulsed her. Why had she run away from Christenbech? If she'd stayed she could have met Luke and discovered the truth. Did she still love him? She didn't know, but she would have liked the chance to find out. Luke probably thought that as she hadn't turned up she didn't want to see him again.

"Come on Gregory," she coaxed. "Let's go out on the patio and have a cool drink."

She fetched some iced peach tea from the refrigerator and poured them both a drink.

"You know you should never try to translate from one language to another when your knowledge of that language is only small. It never works."

Gregory sipped the iced tea and after promising Ruth that anything she told him would remain in strictest confidence, he listened carefully as she told him the story of her youth in Leil.

After hearing her tale, he looked shamefaced and admitted that it was his love for her that had made him behave stupidly. He apologised profusely for doubting her integrity, and even knowing it was a lost cause, he proposed marriage.

She turned him down as gently as she could.

"What happens now?" He asked "Will you contact him, tell him that you received his message too late?"

Ruth shrugged her shoulders.

"I don't know. It may be better to let the past stay where it belongs."

Gregory left shortly afterwards, refusing an invitation to dinner. When he'd gone, Ruth didn't know whether to laugh or cry. She didn't want Gregory for a lover, but she would miss their friendship. Oh they'd agreed to remain friends, but Gregory was a proud man, and she doubted if they'd ever meet again once he left the islands.

Suddenly she felt very lonely, and although the sun still beat down as relentlessly as before, she shivered. Everything was changing. There were questions that needed answers, and emotions, which she'd thought long dead, had resurfaced. Perhaps tomorrow, or next week, or next month, she'd go searching for answers.

Chapter 4

June

Dear Mum and Dad,

This letter is being written on the train, so if my handwriting is wobbly you'll know the reason why. We had a lovely weekend together with all the family. The only trouble was, with so many people to see and things to do, we didn't have time to talk as mother and daughter. I was sorry about that. At least we had that other weekend together when you came to Bath.

There aren't many people travelling today, it's very quiet. Michael and I have both got window seats. He bought a book on Cardiff station and he's completely engrossed in it. There's a table in between so I don't have to balance the notepad on my lap. Michael said to thank you for your hospitality and to say that he enjoyed himself very much. He thought everyone was very friendly and made him feel really welcome.

He thought the Welsh valleys were lovely. He had the general impression that most people have of them, of being full of black slag heaps. He was pleasantly surprised to see how green and wooded the valleys are. Most people only look at the narrow streets of the old mining villages, with their rows of stone terraced houses, not realising that a few minutes walk away are the mountains. Once above the valleys you can feel you're miles out in the country and yet look down on the same terraced streets, with their red and green concrete tiled roofs. We were very lucky that the sun shone, everything seems nicer than when it drizzles and a grey mist hangs over the valley.

At last you saw my engagement ring. The jeweller took longer making it than we thought he would. As I told you Michael and I went up to London to the Bank where Michael's mother keeps some of her jewellery that she never wears, and also there is a small collection of uncut stones. Michael didn't know anything at all about these until he told his parents that we were getting engaged, and Mr Vandrell told us to go up to London to chose a stone, and he recommended a jeweller to us. It seems strange keeping things up in London, but Michael said his parents have moved around so much that it seemed the most sensible thing to do.

Whilst we were there, I had a look at Mrs. Vandrell's jewellery. There was one ring that I loved. Michael didn't know what type of stone it was. It had an old-fashioned heavy gold setting, and the stone glowed with all the colours of the rainbow. It wasn't a soft stone like an opal. When we described it to the jeweller who made my engagement ring, he got quite excited and said it was an Envis stone, and the colour we described was very rare, and only to be found in the Tomayon islands, which of course ties in with Michael's mother's family background. The jeweller had only seen photographs of such a stone and Michael suggested that he write to Mr Vandrell for permission to go and see the real thing. Michael and I then wondered if it was the type of gem that the first Morgan Draymer and Ranulf Pendenny had to bring back for the Vaga. It's strange if it is, because I'm sure Michael's father said only members of the Draymer family could own one.

In your last letter you said you couldn't remember the name of the stone in my engagement ring. It's one of the Envis range of semi precious stones, similar in colour to the rare water melon tourmaline from Brazil, except of course it isn't one and there are differences. Everyone who has seen it is fascinated with it because as the name suggests it looks like a watermelon with the green outer edge and a transparent white zone surrounding the pink interior. I could have had a much more expensive stone, Michael said to take my pick, but I liked this one.

The nearer it gets to meeting Michael's mother, the more nervous I get. I've still not met her. As you know, I've been very lonely in my flat now that Nadia has left and Michael seems to spend most of his time travelling between Bath, the Isle of Wight and London. He could go into the law firm here in Bath where his father was, or he's been offered a job in London, but he can't, or won't, make up his mind. We nearly had our first quarrel over that, but we soon made it up. He says he doesn't want to rush into anything. That is the only problem with having plenty of money, ha, ha, if you're poor you take the first job you're offered, you can't afford to sit around and wait.

As I was saying, I've been lonely in the flat so I started going to the Exiles Club on my own. I know I'm not an exile, but I'd got to know quite a few people there and it was good to get out for an evening to have some company.

When we did get five minutes to ourselves over the weekend, you asked me if there was something worrying me, but then someone came into the room and it was impossible to find another moment to talk to you. I went to the club one Wednesday evening. It was a fairly quiet night, so I decided to leave early. I thought I'd better go to the loo before ringing for a taxi to take me home. The ladies cloakroom is 'L' shaped and there are exits at each end. Two girls I knew slightly were seated at the mirrors repairing their makeup. The mirror is around the corner from the toilets near one of the exits. I'd seen them earlier on in the club and they didn't have any boyfriends with them, so when I saw them in the ladies, I thought I'd go and say hello and perhaps I could join them for an hour or so. I really didn't want to go home to an empty flat. I was feeling pretty low. I'd turned the corner obviously, otherwise I wouldn't have seen them, but they hadn't seen me.

I was just going to call out to them, when I heard one of them mention Michael's name. She was talking about his mother really and not Michael. She was saying that Mrs Vandrell always managed to break up every relationship Michael had with a girl. I couldn't believe it, because although Michael is very fond of his mother, he doesn't give the impression of being a mother's boy. I couldn't go up to them after hearing that, they might have realised I'd overheard them, but perhaps I should have confronted them there and then and got to the bottom of it. Anyway I didn't. I quietly left by the other door and went straight home. I tried to put it out of my mind, but I can't. I broached the subject to Michael on the train coming down to you in a sort of roundabout way. I didn't want to tell him everything I'd overheard. I did mention that I was very nervous about meeting his mother and did he think she'd mind about our engagement. He just laughed and said there was nothing to be worried about, and that we'd get on famously. At that moment, he reminded me of Dad. You know what I mean. When Dad tells you it will never happen, you know jolly well it will. Sorry Dad, but it's true. Anyway we'll soon find out if it's correct what the girls said. I've made up my mind that she's going to have a fight on her hands if she tries to come between us.

I've just noticed that we're coming into Bath station, and Michael has put his book down to go and look out of the window to see if he can see his father. Mr Vandrell said he might join us on the train today. I know he had some business to attend to in Bath and it depended on how long it took. Even if Mr Vandrell doesn't catch the train, I'm going to insist Michael puts his book down and talks to me for a while. I'll finish this letter to you later on tonight or tomorrow morning. I'll have met my future mother-in-law by then, so will let you know what I think.....

Chapter 5

Richard Vandrell walked slowly along the banks of the River Avon. It was a glorious summer's day; no cloud marred the azure perfection of the sky. Now in his fifty-fourth year, he was still a good-looking man. He carried no excess weight and time had dealt gently with him. He still had a full head of hair, and although much of it was grey, it only served to make him look distinguished.

There was an hour to kill before meeting his brother-in-law, so he spent the time wandering around the streets of Bath, mingling with the tourists. He loved the city with its Georgian houses and hadn't wanted to move away. As usual after a few years his wife, Ilona, had become restless. He'd lost count of the number of moves they'd made during their marriage. Bath was the longest they'd ever stayed in one place.

He saw a throng of people and stopped to watch a man, dressed all in black miming to music. The movements were in slow motion and told a tale of love and hate, culminating in the man's death. The tourists applauded at the end and dropped coins in a hat on the floor. The man had been able to reach out silently and touch the audience with the passion and pathos of his story. Placing a coin in the hat, Richard decided to make his way back to the riverbank.

He sat down on a bench and waited for his brother-in-law. Shutting his eyes, he let the warmth of the sun relax his mind and body. In this calm state, he thought of the crumpled letter in his pocket, the contents of which would bring him to a crossroads. For too many years he had allowed himself to drift with the tide, not having money problems and being moderately happy working as a solicitor in whichever town he happened to find himself, he had let the years slip carelessly through his fingers. Why had he let Ilona talk him into moving to the Isle of Wight? It wasn't that he didn't like it there, it was a lovely island, but his heart was in the Tomayon Islands, the one place that Ilona refused to live. He often wondered how she could keep her bitterness alive for so many years.

He opened his eyes and saw his brother-in-law approaching and waved. It was the first time they'd met in five years. Justin was very tanned and his handsome face was as Richard remembered, although very lined through too much exposure to the sun. Richard noticed that Justin's green eyes still twinkled with a hint of youthful mischievousness.

Did you receive the letter?" Justin asked as he sat down beside his brother-in-law.

Richard nodded, reaching into his pocket and pulling out the crumpled envelope. "As you can see, it has been very well read." Ever since receiving the letter a week ago, the contents still amazed him.

"Do you want to be the last Governor General of the British Tomayon islands?"

For a moment Richard didn't answer. His thoughts went back to the time when his father had been Governor General; of his teenage years spent in the semi-tropical island of Lorentia; of meeting and eventually marrying Justin's sister, Ilona.

"Why me?" He looked at Justin enquiringly. "Oh I know my father was Governor General, but I'm only a retired solicitor, who has practised in about every county in England, and of course I'm married to the daughter of Drystan Pendenny." His voice was bitter.

Justin patted Richard's arm. "I know what you've been through. Was my sister worth it?" He paused. "Don't answer that."

Impulsively Justin jumped up. "Come on, my car is over there. I know a marvellous place where we can have lunch and we can discuss matters in comfort."

Richard smiled; Justin definitely hadn't changed. All Justin asked for was a quiet life with no demands on him and plenty of money and the time to enjoy himself. Richard watched as his brother-in-law expertly manoeuvred his car through Bath and soon they were settled in the restaurant of a hotel on the outskirts of the city. On the way there they spoke of inconsequential matters.

The restaurant wasn't crowded and a waiter escorted them to a table for two near a large picture window overlooking the River Avon. They both declined soup and opted for fruit juice, followed by tiny new potatoes, fresh peas and home cooked ham and chicken pie, the pastry of which melted in their mouths. It was only after they'd finished their rhubarb tart and cream and were relaxing over a pot of coffee that Richard said. "Well Justin, I'll ask again, why me?"

"Simple dear fellow. You are the best man for the job. Everyone thought that Gregory Rollins would stay on, but he suddenly announced his resignation at the Council Meeting. He'd spoken to father about this just before the meeting started and it was agreed that your name should be put forward. Hallam Draymer agreed as did all the others, so if you want the job, it's yours."

"What about the British Government, surely they have some say in the matter?"

Justin raised his glass. "To the new and last Governor General; Richard Vandrell."

He put his glass down on the table.

"Seriously though Richard, independence is being given to the British Tomayon Islands very shortly, so no one from Britain wants the appointment. Who would want to uproot himself and his whole family for a few months? Therefore the British Government is quite happy to go along with you. You've no skeletons in your cupboard. Oh yes, you've been thoroughly checked out make no mistake about that, and as you said you're married to my sister. That obviously was another point in your favour. Be honest, how many people in the British Isles have a clue where the Tomayon Islands are, let alone care who the last Governor General will be."

He paused. "Well, what do you say? Was my toast premature?"

Richard stared out of the window at the well-tended lawns

that sloped gently down to the riverbank. A chance to see his beloved Tomayon Islands again. To go home, for that was how he felt. From the day he'd arrived with his father at Government House, he'd known that the islands were where he wanted to spend his life. Richard should have returned to University in England after the summer recess, but he'd persuaded his reluctant father that it would look good if the Governor General's son were to attend a Tomayon University, and it was at Carlia University that he'd first met Justin. In the holidays, he'd been content to tag along in the shade of the Pendenny brothers, and worship from afar their sister, Ilona. James, the eldest son of Drystan Pendenny by his first wife, who'd been English, was completely different in colouring and outlook from his two half brothers and half sister. As Richard's heart was in the islands, so James longed for the green and gentle countryside of England. Richard had loved Ilona from the first moment he'd laid eyes on her. After twenty-five years of marriage, she was still beautiful. There was no grey in the dark red hair that she wore in a severe bun, and only occasionally now let hang loose to her shoulders. Her green eyes, so similar to Justin's held no sparkle. After Morgan Draymer had died, she'd finally learnt to laugh and smile again, but the smile never reached her eyes. She'd had no eyes for anyone but Morgan when he was alive, and on his death, she couldn't, or wouldn't, let go. Once the Pendenny brothers and he left University there was no reason for their paths to cross very often, and they saw less of one another, although he heard all the gossip from his sister, Leah. Luke had taken himself off to, as Justin phrased it, some Godforsaken fishing village to convert the ungodly, and Justin was desperately trying to avoid getting any sort of paid employment, although Drystan had finally threatened to cut off his allowance. Justin at that time was courting Leah and numerous others, which didn't make for an easy life, but Justin revelled in the deceptions, uncaring of the hearts he was breaking along the way. Richard sometimes envied Justin's free and easy approach to life, as he sweated every day doing articles in a solicitor's office. Richard's father's term of office as Governor General was coming to an end, but both he and Leah wanted to remain in the islands. Leah was hoping to marry Justin and Richard wanted to stay near Ilona and spend the rest of his life in the islands. It was ironical he thought, if he hadn't married Ilona Pendenny, he could have stayed on the islands and not spent the best part of his life never putting down roots anywhere.

Richard's father eventually returned to Britain and Richard and Leah rented a flat in St. Elizabeth. Justin often came around and it was in their flat that they'd all met Morgan Draymer. It was obvious during that summer that Morgan and Ilona were in love and Richard, with a generosity of spirit he didn't really feel, had given them his silent blessing. What a marriage that would have been. Morgan Draymer, the only son of the Vaga, and the daughter of the Larn of Innisver. As a newcomer to the islands and living in St. Elizabeth the capital of the island of Lorentia, he had little knowledge of the islands' history, so when Ilona and Morgan confided in him that they'd fallen in love, he couldn't see any difficulties, until they told him the story of the ancient feud. Even then he thought that both fathers would surely relent when he saw how much in love the pair were. He came out of his reverie to find Justin staring at him.

"I don't want to rush you, but the island's council and the British Government need to know within the next forty-eight hours. I could see you were miles away. Were they happy memories?"

Richard smiled ruefully. "Some were. I'd better not start saying do you remember, or we'll be here for ever, getting more depressed the more we recollect. We did have some happy times though. Where did the years disappear to Justin? You married my sister and I married yours, brothers-in-law twice over. Have you been happy?"

"What's happy? You can't spend your life in a state of euphoria, so I suppose if you're not suicidal, that could be called happy. I try not to question things too much, just take each day as it comes." Justin replied.

"Yes, you would. You have the right attitude, but be honest would you have married Leah if she hadn't blackmailed you into it? I could never believe how my own sister could be such a vindictive person. I know she was besotted with you, as I was with Ilona, but I've never been able to forgive the way she used Ilona's secret and heartbreak for her own ends."

"It's strange, Richard, I think I would have married Leah eventually, once I'd got the wildness out of my system. Underneath that inferiority complex and unnatural jealousy of Ilona, Leah could be kind hearted. She never seemed to realise that she was beautiful too, but in a different way. Of course, once she threatened to expose Ilona's secret to my father, she killed any vestige of love I once had for her. Still that's all in the past and we jog along. together somehow."

Richard glanced down at his watch. "Damn, I've missed the train to Portsmouth, but it doesn't really matter, I only said I might be on it. I'll check into a hotel in town for the night. I've got some overnight things in my briefcase."

"There's no need to check into a hotel. Leah and I are staying with James and Marjorie, which isn't far from here. Philip is away at the moment, so I know there's a spare bedroom. Anyway there's mountains of room in her father's house. I'll go and give them a ring and find out."

Justin wasn't away long. He confirmed that James and Marjorie would love to see Richard again and that there would be no problem about his staying overnight.

"Do you want to telephone Ilona from here to tell her where you're staying?"

Richard shook his head. "I'll phone later this evening. I doubt if she'll be in at this time and I did warn her that if I wasn't on the same train as Michael and his fiancée I wouldn't be home until tomorrow."

~*~

Marjorie's father owned a large country estate and on their frequent stays in England, Marjorie and James lived in the Dower House. It was both James and Marjorie's wish to make this their permanent home, and now that a decision had finally been made

49

as to the Vaga's successor, this dream could become a reality. At the moment, the greater the distance between themselves and Drystan Pendenny the better. This was the first time Richard had visited James and Marjorie. Although they had lived in close proximity for the last few years, their meetings had always been in town. He looked around him with interest. The Dower House was an attractive stone-built three-storey building set back slightly from the narrow country road. The adjacent large iron gates opened onto a tarmacadamed driveway that meandered through grasslands, where a herd of Jersey cows grazed peacefully. In the distance, he could see the graceful lines of the big house whose stones over the centuries had mellowed and blended perfectly into the landscape. As Justin parked the car, Marjorie and James came to the door and greeted Richard warmly.

"Are you sure it's all right for me to descend on you without warning?" Richard asked, kissing Marjorie on the cheek.

Marjorie's smile lit up her horsey features that radiated genuine warmth for her brother-in-law. "Don't be silly. We like visitors, and anyway, you're not a proper visitor, you're family. As Justin told you, Philip is away at the moment with his grandfather, heaven help him, so you can have his room. I'll show you up and then perhaps you'd like a cup of tea, or something stronger. James will put the kettle on, because whatever you choose, I'm dying for a cuppa."

Philip's room was on the top floor, but when they reached the first landing, Richard paused and looked out through a large window at the green English countryside.

"James belongs here and so does Philip." He hadn't realised he'd voiced his thoughts aloud.

"Yes, they both do." Marjorie agreed and came to stand by him. "You don't though Richard. Even though you were born here, your heart is in the islands, and now you can go back if you wish."

She patted his arm comfortingly. "James and Philip love it here. Oh they like to go back to the islands to see my parents-in-law and to soak up some hot sun, but they're always glad to return and that is why I'm glad that the successor to the Vaga has been named and it wasn't Philip."

"Justin didn't say anything about that over lunch. Who has been named?"

"Vonryn Santella, a distant cousin of Hallam Draymer. I've never met him, but I understand from Justin that he is coming to your silver wedding party with his fiancée Nadia Laridon."

"Yes, Ilona and I know Nadia. I think Ilona mentioned that when she accepted the invitation she asked could she bring her fiancé. Naturally we said yes."

"I think you'd better keep Drystan and him apart then. Drystan was out voted at the meeting. He wanted Philip for Vaga. You'd better ask Justin or James about the meeting."

"That's all we want is bad feeling at the party. To be honest Marjorie, I've left most of the organising of it to Ilona, but I don't feel too guilty, because I've had to wind up things here in Bath and arrange the lease on the house in the Isle of Wight."

Marjorie looked at him searchingly. There seemed to be problems in that marriage, but she wasn't one to pry.

"What is Philip doing now?" Richard asked.

"He works with computers. He's quite good at it, or so I'm told. I can switch on the one we have in the estate office at the big house, and I know how to get certain information from it, but that's about all. Of course eventually Philip will take over the running of the estate, but hopefully that will be a long time in the future." She paused for a second. "I didn't influence James or Philip to live in England you know." Her blue eyes looked directly into his.

Richard looked puzzled. "I don't understand what you're saying. I know you wouldn't do that."

She shrugged her shoulders. "It doesn't matter. It was only something Drystan said to me after the meeting. He was angry that both Luke and Justin voted against him. He disowned them, but of course he'll soon change his mind and start interfering in their lives again. We were naturally staying with him and we knew his heart was set on either James or Philip being Vaga. Once James said he had no intention of standing and Philip only did it because Drystan put pressure to bear, the atmosphere was very strained. If it hadn't been for James' stepmother, I think we would have been tempted to move out before the meeting and stay in a hotel. James is very fond of his stepmother. She always treated him as if he were her own. She begged us to stay and we agreed, especially once we cooled down and realised what the press would make of us moving out. Hallam Draymer would have made sure they found out. However, after the meeting the tension was unbearable, so James and I left the next morning, but for some reason Philip decided to stay."

"Don't take any notice Marjorie. My father-in-law and Hallam Draymer both enjoy this stupid feud. They are both stubborn old men who like to get their own way, and as I said a few seconds earlier, James and Philip belong here. I didn't realise such a lot went on at that meeting. Justin told me that I'd been proposed as Governor General but didn't tell me any more. I wish I'd been there."

Marjorie started to ascend the next flight of stairs, but suddenly stopped and turned to Richard. "Yes, you're right, the meetings over, everything is settled and we can get on with our own lives and if Drystan doesn't like it, that's his problem. Vonryn will be the next Vaga, and you'll be the next and last Governor General, or will you?"

Richard smiled. "I'm seriously considering it and I'll give my answer informally to Justin tomorrow and follow it up with an official letter."

"Aren't you going to consult Ilona?" Marjorie asked.

Richard shook his head. "This is my decision Marjorie. Ilona can come with me if I decide to accept, or she can stay on the Isle of Wight."

'I was right,' Marjorie thought sadly. 'There is trouble in that marriage. The worm has finally turned. I wonder if Ilona realises or even cares.'

They continued up the next flight of stairs in silence and Marjorie showed him into a light airy room that, apart from a bathroom, covered the whole of the top floor. "This is Philip's pad when he's at home."

It was a pleasant sparsely furnished masculine room. One wall was taken over completely with shelves, containing a television and CD system and a wide range of books, videos and CDs. Tucked away in one corner was an old computer that had obviously been well used. All the walls and ceiling were painted white, but Richard blanched slightly at the carpet, which had a black background with geometrical designs woven into it in the most garish of colours.

Marjorie grinned. "I gave Philip his head as to the decor and furnishing. He lost interest after the carpet, so I dealt with the rest."

Richard looked at the abstract prints on the wall. "I can't say I like or understand modern art, but they do go with this room."

"Yes, I thought that. As you can see there aren't any curtains. I couldn't find any material that would go with this ghastly carpet, so I opted for plain white blinds."

Marjorie walked to the pair of louvered doors at the far end of the room.

"This one is a walk-in wardrobe, and the door nearest the window is the bathroom," she said.

She turned to Richard, a worried expression on her face. "I hope Drystan isn't taking his temper out on Philip, but it was his decision to stay. I feel sorry for him you know."

For a second Richard looked bewildered as he worked out whether it was Drystan or Philip she felt sorry for, and then astonished. "I presume you're talking about Drystan and not Philip."

"Of course I mean Drystan. Oh I know he's opinionated and brow beats people, but I do try to understand what motivates him. He and Hallam have had this lifelong dream of independence and when Morgan Draymer died, Drystan had visions of his dream coming true with his son James as Vaga over all the islands. It is just unfortunate that James didn't want to realise his father's dream. Philip was happy to go along with his grandfather when it was still a dream, but this meeting was too close to reality, but he didn't have the courage to face his grandfather with the truth. He was relieved when first Luke and then Justin voted against him. It must have been a bitter pill for such a man to swallow."

Richard was thoughtful. "I never looked at it like that before. Thank goodness he didn't think of putting Michael's name forward."

Marjorie shivered. "I don't think you should say things like that even in jest. I've got a feeling we haven't heard the last of this matter yet."

Richard opened his briefcase, laid his pyjamas on the bed and took out an electric razor and toothbrush and toothpaste.

Marjorie pointed laughingly in the direction of the bathroom. "You believe in travelling light."

He grinned at her. "Like all good ex-boy scouts, I believe in being prepared. Change of shirt, underclothes, pyjamas, socks, toothbrush and paste and rechargeable electric razor, that's all you need. I call this my emergency kit in case I can't make it back home. Now how about that cup of tea you promised me. It sounds most welcome."

James had made the tea and was gingerly carrying an overloaded tray into the drawing room as Marjorie and Richard descended the stairs. Marjorie winced, praying that James wouldn't drop the lot. It was a pleasant room, comfortably furnished with deep, chintz covered, armchairs and a sofa that one could sink into. Richard noticed the expensive furniture and statues, but for all the trappings of wealth, this was a room that had a well lived in appearance. French windows opened out on to a terrace that stretched across the back of the house. Justin lolled untidily on a deck chair, his eyes closed. Leah, Justin's wife and Richard's sister, was seated by the rustic wooden table, as far apart from her husband as possible.

Richard hadn't seen his sister for almost five years. She was as usual immaculately dressed, her smooth dark hair swept up in a classic French pleat.

"On the move again I hear, brother dear," Leah sneered. "Why don't you put your foot down with that bitch of a wife of yours?"

"Leah!" Justin jumped up out of the deck chair and it seemed for a moment as if he would hit her, but Richard motioned him back.

"It's nice to see you again Leah. How long is it since I last had the pleasure?"

Leah didn't answer, but vigorously started stirring the tea which James had handed her. The five of them sat in uncomfortable silence sipping their teas as if their lives depended on it.

Marjorie was the first to escape, murmuring something about preparing dinner, which none of the others believed, as it was much too early.

In desperation James poured them all a stiff drink, although Richard wondered if that was a wise move. His beloved sister could always be counted upon to cause trouble. He studied his sister surreptitiously. What had happened to turn a young, not unpleasant girl, into this bitter middle-aged woman? 'What a mess we've made of our lives,' he thought sadly. At least James and Marjorie are all right so long as Drystan leaves them alone to live their lives as they wish.

"Did you tell Richard about the meeting?" James asked Justin.

"Not fully."

"It's all right," Richard interrupted, "Marjorie brought me up to date with most of the salient points. I understand Luke managed to drag himself away from that backwater fishing village to vote. I still don't understand though why you or Luke weren't nominated."

Leah snorted derisively. "If I'd had my way Justin would have put his name forward. He knew James and Philip weren't interested and Luke - well Luke is happy just being himself, but no Justin didn't want the position either, and then to cap it all Luke voted for this unknown; this Vonryn Santella."

"He's not exactly an unknown. The Vaga has always taken a special interest in him. Anyway, I've no ambition Leah. You knew that when you married me. I like a quiet life." He turned to Richard. "It was touch and go whether Luke would make it. I was on pins as his vote was crucial. I could have voted against Philip, but apart from the fact that I'm a coward, Luke and I had agreed what line to take, as it was obvious that either he or I would have the casting vote. We thought that he being a priest would make it look as though the Church were behind the decision."

"What about Michael?" Leah asked unexpectedly.

Richard looked surprised. "Strange you should say that. Marjorie made a similar remark whilst we were upstairs."

"His name was never mentioned, although in law he would have as much right as Philip," James said thoughtfully. He looked at his watch and stood up. "If you'll excuse me I've got to go up to the big house to see my father. Help yourself to any drinks you want."

An uncomfortable silence descended after James had left. Justin poured them all second drinks and Richard wished he had caught the Portsmouth train and gone home.

"If Ilona and Morgan's son had lived, there wouldn't have been any problem," Leah said abruptly.

Justin sighed. "What possessed you to bring that up? You know how few of us there are who know what happened the year Morgan died. We agreed never to mention it again."

"Why not? There was no shame in it. They were married for God's sake, your brother Luke saw to that. The son and daughter of the two most powerful families being married secretly in a tiny village church. How you managed to keep it from Drystan and his army of secret police, I'll never know." She laughed scornfully and Richard wondered if she'd been drinking before he arrived.

"Ilona isn't convinced it was kept from him, although he has never said anything," Richard replied. "Anyway Leah, what does it matter. It all happened a long time ago."

"Yes," Leah said. "Many years ago, and look how one man's death changed our lives. You married Ilona. She wouldn't have looked at you twice, Richard, if Morgan had lived. It would have been interesting to see how long he would have stayed faithful to her if he had lived. He was heavily involved with Barbara someone or other before he met Ilona." Her brow furrowed as she tried to remember Barbara's surname. "I remember, she was Barbara Nadell and she married Vincent Santella. I'd forgotten that. Do you think that Barbara was pregnant with Morgan's child when he met Ilona? Or maybe he kept on seeing Barbara as well. Perhaps that Vonryn is Hallam's grandson and not some distant relative."

Justin looked exasperated. "For heaven's sake Leah, you do talk nonsense sometimes. We all know that Morgan was engaged to Barbara before he met Ilona, and, to put it crudely, dumped her for Ilona. I'm sure he wouldn't have gone back to having an affair with Barbara straight after he'd married my sister."

"Perhaps Hallam Draymer pushed him into marrying Ilona. Just because your father didn't want the marriage, doesn't mean to say that Hallam didn't want it for political reasons."

"I don't believe that. My sister and Morgan were very much in love."

"Yes," Richard said quietly almost to himself. "They were very much in love. I've always been second best. I know she married me on the rebound."

"It's a good job that the baby didn't live. If it had, she couldn't have kept it." Leah said.

"I've never understood why not." Richard argued. "Even with Morgan dead Hallam would have protected Ilona and the baby and eventually Drystan would have accepted the situation, or I'd have given the baby my name and brought him up as my own. I could have pretended that it was me Ilona married and not Morgan. I'm sure that Justin and Luke could have produced the necessary paperwork to prove it."

"We'd have tried, but whether it would have passed father's scrutiny we'll never know." Justin said. "However, Hallam Draymer would never have let you or my father take his grandson. What Leah says is right."

"If my beloved father-in-law had got his hands on the baby, heaven knows what would have happened to him." Leah interrupted.

"You go too far Leah, my father would never have hurt the baby. The worst thing he would have done would be to get the baby adopted. A couple desperately wanting a baby wouldn't have asked too many questions and of course, my father would have stayed well in the background. You never did understand Richard, but my father's one aim in life, after Morgan died, was that James should be Vaga."

"If we'd had a son…" Leah's face softened, revealing a well-hidden side to her nature. "Your father might have considered him. It's strange," she mused further. "Luke never married, and he could have. Priests don't have to be celibate. I remember some gossip you told me once Justin about a young orphan girl that he was in love with. He could have got married and had children, and another strange thing is that we haven't any children either. There was nothing wrong with me, I know that because I had tests." She smiled at the expression on Justin's face. "Oh I never bothered to tell you, there didn't seem much point. In the beginning I kept the tests secret because I didn't want you to be disappointed in me, but of course when I found out that there wasn't any reason why I shouldn't conceive, I knew it had to be you. I loved you so much then that I thought if I told you it might make you feel less of a man, so I kept it to myself all these years."

"That was nice of you," Richard felt a warmth of feeling for his sister that he hadn't experienced since their childhood.

"You're too nice for your own good Richard," Leah remarked sarcastically. "Many years later, I overheard some gossip about one of Justin's many mistresses and how much he'd paid for an abortion for her. There was nothing wrong with him. He didn't want to have a child with me. It was as though both Justin and Luke made a conscious decision not to have children, but although I've thought about it, I still can't find a reason." She broke off speaking and looked hard at her husband. "I'm right aren't I Justin?"

Richard looked at the expression on Justin's face and groaned inwardly. He didn't like what he saw and he knew for sure that he wasn't going to like what Justin was about to say, but he felt glued to the spot, unable to move.

"That's right Leah." There was an ugly expression on Justin's normally placid features. "From the day you blackmailed me into marrying you, I made a vow that I'd never give you the children I knew you wanted. Any love I ever had for you, you killed stone dead. You changed from the girl I thought I knew and wanted to marry and became some irrational jealous monster. My sister never did anything to hurt you. She was and is beautiful, but couldn't you see, you were beautiful in your own way."

Leah's face crumpled and for a moment Richard thought she was going to cry. In a matter of seconds an inscrutable mask descended over her features and there was nothing to show the turmoil of her thoughts as she digested the news that Justin had intended to marry her.

"You got what you wanted, but I made sure you'd pay for it," Justin continued. "You weren't born on the islands so wouldn't have known about the Kralo plant that was used as a male contraceptive. It isn't 100% effective, as was proved by the abortion I had to pay for, but do you remember the time when I had my appendix out and you were so worried about me, being so sweet and bringing me all my favourite books and chocolates, well I thought I might as well kill two birds with one stone and I had a vasectomy at the same time."

Leah's mask dropped and her face contorted with anger. Slowly she picked up the jug of water on the table and tipped it over Justin's head. It trickled down his laughing face as Richard watched on in horror.

"I'll never forgive you and I'll get even with the lot of you if it's the last thing I ever do," Leah shouted as Justin laughed even louder.

Richard got up quickly taking the water jug away from Leah, as he had visions of her hitting Justin with it now that it was empty. "I don't want to hear any more of this. It's between the two of you, but Leah please, don't go stirring up trouble. Life is too short. What's done is done. If you can't stand the sight of one another then separate. I know I'm a fine one to give matrimonial advice, but for God's sake talk to one another and try and calm down by this evening. I'm sure Marjorie won't want a repeat performance at dinner tonight."

He walked away around the corner of the house and took the jug into the back hallway, putting it down on a table there. The sound of Justin's horrible laughter still rang in his ears. What would Leah do? She was capable of anything, and after what he had heard, could he blame her? Without realising it, he had left the Dower House and had walked almost to the big house. James was just bidding his father goodbye, but on seeing Richard, James' father greeted him warmly and invited him in for a drink. It was obvious by the look on Richard's face that something was wrong.

"Justin and Leah quarrelling again?" James asked in a matter of fact way once he and Richard were settled in two leather armchairs in the library. Richard nodded. "Yes, it was a particularly nasty scene that I shouldn't have witnessed. I'd heard rumours that things weren't going all that well with them, but I didn't realise it was this bad. Why on earth don't they get a divorce?"

James shrugged his shoulders. "Who knows what holds married couples together. In some cases it's the children, in others it's a fear of being alone. Don't worry Richard we'll linger up here with my father and drink his excellent brandy, Marjorie won't mind. She told me to disappear, but I felt guilty leaving you alone with them, that's why I was coming back sooner than expected. Don't forget we've seen a lot of them over the years and we're used to their rows. Marjorie will leave them to it and stay in the kitchen out of their way. We'll meander down just in time for dinner." James rubbed his hands together, "Ah here comes father with that heavenly brandy I mentioned."

Richard smiled as James' father poured them each a glass of brandy. "I'll drink to what you just said James," They lifted their glasses and clinked them together, whilst James' father looked on in bewilderment wondering what the toast was.

Richard sipped his brandy slowly. Through the large windows the vista of the peaceful English countryside calmed him, but he still couldn't help wondering what mischief Leah would get up to.

Chapter 6

June

Dear Mum and Dad,

Michael's father wasn't waiting for the train at Bath. He only said he might catch it. Our train was on time in Portsmouth and we took the ferry from Gosport to Ryde on the Isle of Wight. The sun was still shining when we arrived and my first impression of the island was a good one.

The house Michael's parents have is on the south side of the island, but far enough away from the crumbling coastline, so there is no danger of it falling into the sea, at least for the foreseeable future. Michael says that they've only rented it for the summer. His parents are like gypsies, at the most they only stay a few years in one place, and now that Mr Vandrell has retired, he hasn't got the excuse of his business to keep him in one place for very long.

I've finally met his mother. I really don't know what to make or say about her. She is still a very attractive woman, with a slim figure, good complexion and she has red hair like mine, but hers is much darker. (I doubt if it is natural now at her age). She was very polite to me, in fact the perfect hostess, but there was no warmth there if you know what I mean. I felt she was just going through the motions; perhaps it's my imagination. If I hadn't heard those girls talking, this image of her might not have entered my head and is probably clouding my judgment. I'm looking for problems, where hopefully none exist.

It's a very big house. I think there are ten bedrooms and don't know how many bathrooms. There is a beautiful wisteria climbing up the front of the stonework which reaches my bedroom window on the second floor. If you're American that's the third floor. My room is very comfortable, not very big but pleasantly furnished with my own portable TV and video, one of those that you can play things on, but not record. I haven't got an en suite bathroom, but there is a small hand washbasin in the corner. From the fairly small dormer window there is a beautiful view of farmlands stretching to the coastline.

Michael took me for a quick tour of the island this morning. Saw the most popular sights such as the Needles and the outside of Osborne House. I loved Shanklin village. I remember you telling me about it being lit up in the summer evenings when most of the shops stay open. We didn't really stop to explore anywhere, only to have a quick cup of coffee in Shanklin.

The silver wedding party is next Saturday. They are having a marquee in the garden. Obviously, it is a huge garden. Can you imagine a marquee in ours? Mrs Vandrell has caterers coming in to do the whole thing, so I won't have to help out making sandwiches and sausage rolls etc. Only joking, it's going to be a bit more upmarket than a do down the local club. I hope I'm not beginning to sound like a snob. I still find everything a bit strange, and am scared I won't fit in, but Michael says just to be myself and everyone will love me. I don't know about that, but I do know which knives and forks to use, but as it is going to be a buffet meal, it will be quite informal. It won't be a terribly big affair, mainly family and friends. As I said they've moved around the country so much that what friends they have made will have to travel and stay overnight. This is a big house but not that big so arrangements have been made for some guests to stay in a nearby hotel. I should imagine that only close family will be staying here. Michael's grandparents are definitely coming and he is thrilled at the thought of meeting them at last. We haven't decided what to buy his parents yet. What do you give people who have everything? Michael and I are going shopping tomorrow. I thought of individual presents, such as earrings for Mrs Vandrell and cuff links for Mr

Vandrell, but we'll see.

The house is set back a little way from the road, with two gates and a semi circular drive. It would be ideal for you Mum, no more struggling to reverse the car in or out. You could drive in one way, park the car, and then next morning drive out the other way. I'm not knocking your driving, you're a very good driver but I know you hate reversing. It's quite a pleasant looking house, made out of stone, with that big wisteria I mentioned growing up the front wall. Each side of the oak front door there are large square bays to both the ground and first floors, and on the second floor there are three small dormer windows.

Nadia and her fiancé are arriving on Thursday evening. It will be lovely to see her again. I think she will be in the bedroom next door to mine, so we can have a good gossip. It's time for lunch now so I'll finish this letter off afterwards. Michael is going to shift some junk from a bedroom up in to the attic space, as Mrs Vandrell miscounted. Philip, Michael's cousin, will be coming; at least they presume he's coming. I'm being flung into the lion's den with all these relatives descending en masse. After Michael has cleared the junk he and his mother are going to the ferry to pick up Mr Vandrell. I said I wouldn't go, but would have a quiet afternoon, finishing this letter and reading or watching a video. I noticed that someone has kindly put a selection of videos and books here for me.

We only had a light lunch, as we'll have a cooked meal tonight. It was just salad and tinned salmon and fresh fruit to follow. I wasn't very hungry. I think it's nerves, as usually I'm always starving. The house is very quiet at the moment. Michael popped his head around the door to see if I've changed my mind about going to collect his father, but I said I'd rather leave it and meet him at dinner that evening. I saw him drive off a few minutes ago. He's gone early as he wanted to do some errands for his mother, as she also changed her mind about going. I think she must be having a lie down as I can't hear her moving around....

….It's no good Mum, I can't keep on writing about how lovely things are. They aren't. We did have a lovely lunch as I said, and it was only after Michael left that things went wrong. I decided to watch a video and just picked the top one off the pile. It was horrible. The video itself was short, about ten minutes, but it was all about us. It showed our house, the places where Dad and Tom work, the school I went to and a list of all the jobs I've had. There were photostat copies of Birth and Marriage Certificates on the screen. It was a terrible invasion of privacy. I don't know what to do. I feel like packing my bags and walking out now without even seeing Michael again. How could his mother do something as horrible as this? She must have hired a private detective to look into the family's past. I'm pretty certain we don't have any dark secrets, but I feel so exposed. I'm not sure if the video was put here by mistake, or whether someone wanted me to see it.

I noticed a post box down the road and I'm going to pop out and post this letter to you. Michael gave me his key so I can let myself back in, but how I'm going to face Mrs Vandrell I haven't a clue. I think I'll have to ask her for an explanation, but I'm too angry at the moment. When I speak to her I don't want to lose my temper.

Try not to worry about me. I know that will be virtually impossible after what I've written, but I'll ring you to let you know whether or not I decide to leave and return to Bath.

Love,
Kathryn
xxxx

Chapter 7

Ilona sat in the kitchen drinking tea with Mrs Malloy, her daily help. Tea drinking at eleven o'clock seemed to be a ritual with all the dailies she'd employed, and over the years these had been numerous. Through the window she could see the men erecting the marquee for the silver wedding party on the following Saturday. She'd thought that because of their move to the Isle of Wight not many of their friends would accept invitations to attend, but it was surprising the number who had accepted. She was half listening to Mrs Malloy grumbling about her health, the government and her lazy husband, but the other half was thinking backwards further than twenty-five years. It was a luxury that she very rarely afforded herself. Memories were better buried where they belonged in the past, not raked up to bring heartache for things that could never be.

She remembered vividly the day her brother Justin had brought Morgan Draymer home with him. He had thought it great fun to have a Draymer in Innisver Castle, but he had also been cautious enough to make sure that their father, Drystan Pendenny, wouldn't be there. Instantly there'd been a strong physical attraction between them, almost love at first sight, although Ilona had enough of her father's down to earth attitude to question this. At that time Morgan was engaged to Barbara Nadell, but it hadn't stopped them becoming lovers and for six months they'd met clandestinely with the help of Justin and his girl friend Leah Vandrell and her brother Richard. Morgan had broken off his engagement and they'd had wonderful days lazing in the sun and romantic evenings eating dinners in out of the way restaurants and afterwards walked hand in hand along the beach and watched the sun go down in a spectacular blaze of red and gold. It was on such a night that Ilona told Morgan that their passionate and careless lovemaking had resulted in her becoming pregnant and that was when the dream started to crumble.

Spoilt from the day she'd been born, the only girl amongst a family of two older brothers and half brother, she'd expected no resistance from her father, but her mother had warned her not to tell him that she was pregnant. She could remember the scene in the library as if it were yesterday. All the immediate family, apart from her brother Luke, had been present that day. They had waited apprehensively in the library whilst Ria Pendenny told her husband that they wanted to get married. Morgan and she had held hands defiantly and waited for the storm that was about to break around their heads. It hadn't been long in coming. Drystan's roar of anger had echoed down the corridor and Ilona had clasped Morgan's hand even tighter than before.

"Your father put you up to this," he'd bellowed at a bewildered Morgan, who had managed to stay polite under such extreme provocation. Morgan had protested that he loved Ilona and that his engagement to Barbara had been a mistake.

Drystan had scoffed. "Love," he'd sneered, "is for other people. We marry for territory, wealth or power, not necessarily in that order. I know what is in your father's mind. He thinks that, if you marry my daughter, Innisver Island will be joined with Quan Tomay and Envetta once I'm dead, but let me tell you, James is my heir."

Morgan and Ilona had listened to a long tirade in silence. James, Justin and Ilona's mother had all tried to cajole and persuade Drystan, but his mind was made up and when he threatened to call the guards to have Morgan removed physically from Innisver Castle, Ria had gently taken Morgan's arm and told him to leave. She'd personally escorted him out of the house and through the castle grounds.

~*~

Ilona realised that Mrs Malloy had asked her a question and was waiting for a reply.

"I'm sorry Mrs Malloy. I was miles away."

Mrs Malloy grunted. It was obvious that she had no time for daydreamers. "I was only wondering if you'll be wanting my daughter Rosie to help out this week, seeing you've so many people staying here."

"I must apologise," Ilona said. "I should have asked you sooner. Obviously outside caterers are doing the food for the party, but with eleven extra people staying here..." Ilona paused. "I think it's fourteen extra." She started to count on her fingers. "There's my parents, that's two, Marjorie and James; four, Leah and Justin; six, Luke and Michael and his fiancée Kathryn makes nine, and of course, I said I'd put up Nadia and her fiancé, and the three bodyguards in the garage flat, making fourteen. Oh no, I've forgotten Philip. Where can I put him?"

"How about that small box room. Underneath all those boxes, I know there's a single bed. I'll clear it out this morning and make up the bed and if you'll see it's aired that will be your problem solved. I'll put all the boxes on the landing. I don't think there's anything heavy in them and perhaps Mr Michael can take them up to the loft for you when he and his fiancée return from their tour of the island."

"I'm ever so grateful Mrs Malloy. I really don't know what I would have done without you. Tell Rosie I'll be glad of her help, that is if she isn't engaged elsewhere. It's a good job that the freezer is full. At least we won't starve. Can you think of anything else we've forgotten?"

Mrs Malloy gulped the last dregs of her tea noisily and shook her head. She poured herself a second cup of tea and helped herself to another custard cream biscuit, which she dunked in her tea.

"It will be like the old days. There was always something going on, parties nearly every week. My mother used to work up here then, and I'd come and help out."

Ilona wondered how she could tactfully interrupt this soliloquy, which she knew from bitter experience if left unchecked could go on for a long time, when the telephone rang.

Mrs Malloy made to lift her large bulk out of the chair, but Ilona forestalled her.

"You stay and finish your tea Mrs Malloy. I'll answer it."

Ilona was going through the door when Mrs Malloy called her back. "I took some videos up to Mr Michael's fiancé's room like you said. There was a new one in the drawing room, so I took that up as well."

"That's fine. Thank you." Ilona hurried out before the telephone stopped ringing.

It was Richard, as she guessed it would be, telling her which ferry he would be on and explaining that he had spent the night with Marjorie and James. They kept their conversation short, but Ilona felt that there was something he wasn't telling her. She had a feeling also that there was something Mrs Malloy had said that was very important, but for the moment she couldn't think what it was. After putting the receiver down she wandered into the lounge and sat on the sofa. She picked up the current day's paper, but it was no good, without her glasses she could only read the large print. She didn't want to return to the kitchen, as she hoped that Mrs Malloy would take the hint and busy herself with clearing out the box room. After about ten minutes when she heard Mrs Malloy laboriously climbing the stairs, she decided it was safe to venture out and putting the paper down, she returned to the kitchen. She felt at a loose end, and as lunch was to be a light meal it was too early to start any preparations. Ilona looked out of the window at the blue skies and sunlight streaming through the panes of glass and quickly going to the hall, she picked up her handbag. She went up to the first landing called to Mrs Malloy that she was going to the village.

As she strolled leisurely along, her skin warmed from the rays of the sun, she took deep breaths. This was what she needed before the remainder of her guests descended to disturb the peace of the house. Michael and his fiancée had arrived the evening before. Ilona liked the look of Kathryn and her lilting Welsh accent was enchanting. Kathryn was slim with a heart shaped face, framed by shoulder length wavy hair of a delicate light red gold colour. She had a fair skin that would easily burn and blue eyes that looked directly at the person she was talking to. Ilona smiled to herself. Heaven help any children they have. With red hair on both sides of the family, they would probably have a few carrot-topped children, although it could skip a generation. Kathryn had been very quiet over the evening meal the night before, but it wasn't from shyness, of that Ilona was sure. Ilona hadn't been able to gain any strong impression about Kathryn, but she wasn't, however, deceived by the seemingly fragile air of her future daughter-in-law. She had a feeling that beneath the public facade lay a will of iron. It was as though they were two boxers dancing around one another before the first punch landed.

On returning from her walk, Ilona met Mrs Malloy trundling down the drive on her way home.

"I've cleared the box room and laid the table in the dining room," she said.

Ilona thanked her and as she reached the front door, Michael and Kathryn drew up in his car. They were laughing and Kathryn's eyes sparkled as she looked at Michael. For a second Ilona felt a pang of jealousy shoot through her, not because her son now loved another woman, albeit in a completely different way, but jealous of her own lost youth. Lunch was a more relaxed meal than the night before. Ilona apologised that it was only salad, and said she'd be preparing a hot evening meal ready for when Richard arrived home. Kathryn wasn't as quiet as the night before. The morning tour of the island had done her good and the conversation around the table was quite animated. Ilona managed to get Kathryn to open up and tell them about her early life and her job in the travel agents. Michael beamed with pleasure, for it seemed that the two most important women in his life were going to get on. Kathryn helped Ilona clear the table and load the dish washer, and after being told that there was nothing else that needed doing, she said that she would go to her room for a while and finish the letter to her mother that she'd started writing on the train. Michael gave her a key so that she could go out for a walk if she got fed up of staying in her room whilst Ilona and he fetched Richard.

"I don't think I'll come with you after all," Ilona said. "I'm expecting a few phone calls and I want to check again that everything is ready."

Michael laughed and kissed his mother lightly on the cheek.

"Everything is perfect, as well you know."

"Before you go to meet your father Michael, would you clear the junk from the landing outside the box room? Mrs Malloy has stacked the boxes ready. They're not heavy, but I couldn't expect her to carry them up to the attic. I miscounted the number of guests, I'd forgotten that Philip would be coming."

"I'll do that next," Michael said, "and if there is anything you've forgotten, I'll leave a little early and get it for you."

Ilona nodded. "I'm going out to the garden to pick a few roses. Give me a call when you've finished and if I can think of anything, I'll make a list."

Ilona heard Kathryn and Michael talking and laughing as they went upstairs and she smiled. Everything was going to be all right. She liked Kathryn, who from the conversation they'd had over lunch, seemed to have her feet planted firmly on the ground, unlike Michael who tended to be too impulsive at times.

As she left the kitchen, she suddenly recalled what it was that Mrs Malloy had said that was important. She remembered quite clearly now. Mrs Malloy had said she'd taken the video from the drawing room and put it in Kathryn's room.

"Damn and blast the woman," she said under her breath. Ilona knew that she'd only been trying to be helpful, but that video was one that Kathryn mustn't see. Her thoughts raced, how could she retrieve it. It was going to be well nigh impossible, at least for the time being. If only she'd listened properly to Mrs Malloy she would have been able to go upstairs whilst Michael was showing Kathryn the island. Kathryn had said she was going to finish writing a letter to her mother, and it was such a lovely day, surely a young girl wouldn't want to spend it cooped up in a bedroom watching videos. Ilona shrugged her shoulders. It was pointless worrying about something that might never happen. She would keep an eye out in case Kathryn went for a walk and then she could slip upstairs and retrieve it. She couldn't think of a plausible excuse to go upstairs and ask Kathryn for one video.

Ilona picked up the secateurs from a drawer and wandered out into the garden. Mrs Malloy's son-in-law, Bob, came in two days a week to do the garden. It was part of their tenancy that they paid his wages and Ilona knew that it was money well spent. Bob kept the lawns in an immaculate condition, their velvety green smoothness would have delighted the heart of many a lawn green bowler. The borders were free from weeds and the rose trees regularly sprayed for all the diseases and pests that roses were prone to. The kitchen garden was hidden behind a privet hedge and this too was Bob's pride and joy. Mrs Malloy said that there were plenty of fresh vegetables and fruit, either in season or soon to be in season. Ilona took her word for this as her ideas about vegetables and fruit was to see them packaged in a supermarket.

She cut a bunch of roses, cursing to herself as a thorn pierced her skin. She should have put on gardening gloves, she thought. She sniffed appreciatively at the roses. She didn't have a clue what variety they were, but they were so beautiful and their perfume filled the air. There was a lovely crystal vase in the drawing room that would complement their beauty.

As she re-entered the house, she could hear Michael clattering up and down the attic stairs. Why can't he do anything quietly, she wondered. She quickly made a list of items she wanted Michael to get in town before she fetched the vase from the drawing room. They almost collided as she was returning to the kitchen.

"Slow down Michael," she said. "Don't forget everything we break has to be replaced at the end of the tenancy. Here's the shopping list I made out for you."

Michael shook his head in amazement as he read the list.

"Surely we don't need any of this. I've looked in the freezer and the drinks cabinet. We've got enough food and drink to feed an army."

"I know," Ilona replied, "But get it in any case. You're going very early to meet your father, even with my shopping to do, you'll still have a couple of hours hanging around. What are you going to do with yourself?"

Michael tapped his nose. "Keep that out mother," he said mysteriously. "I've got things to do in town."

For a few seconds after Michael had driven off, Ilona wondered whether to go upstairs and chat to Kathryn. It would at least prevent her from watching the videotape. As she started to ascend the staircase, the telephone rang. It was her mother, Ria, and although it was long distance, Ilona settled herself down in the armchair ready for a long chat. Over the years they hadn't seen hardly anything of one another. Ilona felt guilty at times, for the quarrel had been with her father, but Ria had got caught in the crossfire. Michael too had never known his maternal grandparents, but at least they would be meeting for the first time this weekend. She wondered how she would feel if Michael and Kathryn had children she'd never see.

"What time will you be arriving on Thursday?" She asked

Ria's voice was as clear as if she was making a local call. "We may not be coming at all. We're in St. Helena with Stephen Laridon and Nadia," Ria said.

"What on earth are you doing there?"

"It's a long story and as usual it all started because of your father. You know about the meeting in Christenbech to appoint a successor to the Vaga."

"I knew there was a meeting and as Richard has been staying with James, he will probably tell me the full story tonight when he comes home. What has that got to do with you being in St. Helena?"

"James told your father that he didn't want to be Vaga, and although your father put Philip's name forward in the meeting he wasn't appointed as the Vaga's heir. After the meeting Philip told his grandfather that he'd never wanted to be Vaga anyway, and James and Marjorie left for home early. I couldn't blame them, the atmosphere in Innisver Castle was frosty to say the least."

"I can imagine," Ilona said dryly.

72

"Philip stayed on," Ria continued. "I didn't understand why. Things were still unpleasant. I tried to smooth things over, but you know what your father is like once he gets an idea in his head. He kept on and on at Philip to make him change his mind, though what good that would have done, I don't know, since a vote was taken at the meeting and Vonryn Santella was declared Hallam's successor. I thought it strange that Philip didn't once get angry or retaliate when Drystan said really cruel and unkind things to him. I thought at the time it was slightly out of character, because although Philip's a lovely polite young man, I know he has a temper and even he must have a breaking point. Of course, I realise now that he had a plan in mind."

Ria was becoming more and more distressed as she carried on speaking.

"Mother, please get to the point. I can hear that you're upset, and it must be pretty bad for you to say you won't be able to come to the party. I know how much you've wanted to see your grandson."

"To cut a long story short Ilona, Philip has disappeared."

"What do you mean disappeared?"

"Well that wasn't quite the right word. We know where he is. He left a note for us. The maid found it when she went in to tidy his bedroom and found that the bed hadn't been slept in."

Ilona was beginning to get exasperated.

"If you know where he is, he can't have disappeared, so just go and collect him and bring him here with you. I've just this morning prepared a room for him."

"It's not as simple as that. I'm trying to explain dear the best I can."

"Mother," Ilona tried to sound stern. "You're not speaking to father now. You don't pull the wool over my eyes with that little old me routine. It's genuine that you're upset, but you've a logical, calculating mind. I've seen you in action remember."

"You're right Ilona. I must pull myself together. Going to pieces won't help anyone, but when you're just sitting waiting, it's worse than going out and doing something. The gist of the story is that your father had been ramming the old story about the first Morgan Draymer and Ranulf Pendenny down Philip's throat. Remember the tale where both men married twins and then rushed off straight after the wedding ceremony to Envetta to search for an Envis stone. The first man to return with such a gem would be Vaga. Drystan said to Philip one evening that if Philip were a true man, he and Vonryn would do the same thing. Anyway, that is where Philip is now. He's on Envetta somewhere. He went on his own, didn't even take a guide."

Ilona took a deep breath. She knew how dangerous the interior of that island could be.

"How could he be so stupid?"

"He doesn't really know the islands as we do Ilona. It must have seemed like a game to him. He wasn't really brought up here, so he probably thought that Envetta was like the other islands, but as you know it's not. It's a dangerous place."

Ilona's thoughts flew to the six months she'd spent on Envetta when she was pregnant. Hallam Draymer had decided after Morgan's death that Envetta was the best place for her to hide away until her baby was born. He owned two houses on the island, a large one on the summit and a small bungalow hidden away in a small rift valley that nestled between the mountains. Both buildings were locked and shuttered for six months of the year, but it was too dangerous for her to live in the big house, so she'd given birth to her first-born son in the small bungalow. She remembered the narrow fertile coastal plain that soon gave way to densely wooded hills and narrow ravines, through which tumbled turbulent flowing streams making their way to the sea. During the winter, clouds gathered far out to sea and as they came to the mountains, they emptied most of their contents over them. The rainfall over Envetta was well above average for the other islands, and even during the summer months there could be quite a lot of rain. In both seasons, but especially in the winter, well-trodden paths became mudslides and were perilous to negotiate.

"Have you told Marjorie and James?"

"Your father said to leave it until tomorrow."

"What father says is law of course," Ilona said sarcastically.

"Yes dear. Your father is the law in Innisver."

"But not on Envetta mother. It is for Hallam to decide surely."

"For once he agrees with Drystan. It's probably the only thing they've ever agreed on. We discovered Philip's letter early and Vonryn Santella and guides are out searching. It hasn't rained lately so hopefully the paths won't be too difficult to negotiate. If anyone can find him it will be Vonryn. You remember he's Barbara Nadell's son and Nadia's fiancé."

"Yes, I know perfectly well who he is. He and Nadia are supposed to be coming to my party as well as you and father. I'll wait until Richard comes home and if you've no news about Philip, I'm going to tell Marjorie and James myself. They've a right to know."

"Yes you're right. As soon as Richard arrives home phone me here at Stephen's house. The number is 469321. I don't know if the code is the same as Innisver, but you can easily find that out. If Philip isn't found by then, I'll speak to James myself if you don't want to do it. Changing the subject Ilona, what has Richard decided?"

Ilona was puzzled. "Decided?"

"Yes, is he going to accept the post of Governor General to the British Islands, at least until independence?"

Ilona though shocked tried to be evasive without letting her mother know that Richard hadn't even mentioned the matter to her.

"We haven't really had time to discuss it. He stayed overnight with Marjorie and James and I'm not expecting him home until early this evening."

Ria didn't tell her daughter that Richard must have had the letter at least a week and it was obvious that Ilona knew nothing about it.

"Yes, you can discuss it tonight when he comes home." she said. "Changing the subject Ilona, Leah telephoned your father yesterday evening. She managed to track us down in St. Helena. It was rather awkward, but I think we managed to put her off the track of why we were there. We said it was convenient as we would be travelling with Vonryn and Nadia. I don't think she really believed us, as she knows that Drystan can't bear the thought of Vonryn being the next Vaga. We couldn't tell her about Philip, especially as she is staying with James and Marjorie. Leah would delight in giving them bad news."

Ilona agreed with her mother. During their late teens Leah had been her friend and had even stayed with her on Envetta during her pregnancy and subsequent birth. It was obvious even then that Leah had been jealous of her, but for some inexplicable reason this had grown worse over the years. "Do you know what she wanted?"

Ria was unable to enlighten her daughter. "He took the call in another room and unfortunately there wasn't an extension in the room I was in, otherwise I would have eavesdropped."

Ilona smiled to herself. That was typical of Ria. Under normal circumstances she would never listen in to a private conversation, but her mother knew Leah of old.

"That's a shame. Why all of a sudden should Leah telephone father. She's never made any secret of the fact that she can't stand him or the rest of the family. I don't understand why she's become so bitter. The only reason she is halfway polite to him is that he holds the purse strings and without his help she wouldn't enjoy such a comfortable existence. She's up to something, but what?"

"Stirring up trouble for someone, I don't doubt," Ria replied. "Leave it with me. I'll see what I can find out and if she's up to something, I'll see if I can deal with it. Your father need never know."

That was typical of island women of her mother's generation, Ilona thought. Subservient to their men folk at all times, it was a game the women played, a façade that kept the men happy and unsuspecting whilst the women more often than not ruled the roost.

"This phone call must be costing Stephen Laridon a fortune," Ilona said. "I'll ring off now and speak to you again after we've had our evening meal. Hopefully you'll have good news about

Philip by then."

Ilona said goodbye to her mother and sinking back in the armchair she shut her eyes. Her mother had given her so much to think about she didn't know where to start. There was nothing she could do to help find Philip, only pray that he would be found safe and well. Leah, she was sure, was hatching something with Drystan. Ilona felt she could safely leave that problem in her mother's hands. Ria was not the timid consort to the Larn of Innisver that she made herself out to be. Ilona knew from experience that Ria's backbone was pure steel and her quiet doggedness could get at the heart of most mysteries.

The one thing Ilona could deal with herself was her own husband and whether or not he wanted to be Governor General. She had a gut feeling that it was already a fait accompli and that it was she who would have to come to a decision and not Richard. Was their silver wedding to be their swan song? Richard had always been there for her and she admitted to herself that this fact was one she had always taken for granted. She only had the afternoon to think about what to say to him when he came home.

She looked at her watch. It was still too early to put the leg of lamb in the oven. She needed something to make her relax and remembered that *Murder She Wrote* was on television that afternoon. She flicked the remote control and settled down to watch Jessica Fletcher. I wouldn't invite her to my silver wedding, she thought; someone would get murdered. Leah or my father would be the first choice for victim. They'd both made many enemies over the years.

After an agreeable hour during which time Jessica Fletcher had discovered the real murderer, Ilona thought she'd make a pot of tea and take a cup up to Kathryn, but as she switched the television off, she heard the sound of the front door being closed. Looking through the window she saw Kathryn walking down the drive holding a letter.

Kathryn had obviously finished the letter to her mother and was going down the road to the post box, Ilona thought. That would give her ten minutes to get upstairs and retrieve one tape

77

and put another in its place. She picked up the offending video, thankfully a different colour to the other boxes, otherwise she'd have had to go through them all. The lightness of the box confirmed Ilona's worst fears. The tape was already in the machine and Kathryn had already seen it, or intended to watch it on her return. Ilona quickly substituted another video in the VCR but left the different coloured box, on the off chance that Kathryn hadn't yet watched the tape. The box was too distinctive to take and would definitely be missed. Making her way down from the second floor, Ilona pondered where was the best place to hide the tape and decided it would be safest in the farthest recesses of her own wardrobe. She'd have a few words to say to her father about having it sent here instead of to Innisver.

~*~

Kathryn had obviously gone further than the letter box, because dinner was almost ready when she returned and the aroma of roast lamb and rosemary filled the kitchen. Ilona heard the front door being opened and waited to see if Kathryn would come to the kitchen. It was uncharacteristic of her not to offer to help, and Ilona knew then that she'd seen the tape and wanted to stay out of Ilona's way. Kathryn was half way up the first flight of stairs when Ilona came out of the kitchen. There was no good beating about the bush, Ilona thought.

"You've seen the tape haven't you?" she called up after Kathryn. Kathryn turned and Ilona could see that she'd been crying. "Kathryn, please come down to the kitchen and have a cup of tea or a sherry. Anything, but don't go up to your room and mope and think the worst about us; me especially. I can see from your face that you think I am the culprit."

Kathryn reluctantly came back down the stairs, and hanging her jacket in the hall, she took the glass of sherry that Ilona offered her.

"I haven't got time to explain now, too much has happened today. Philip, Michael's cousin, may be lying injured or even dead on Envetta, and there are other problems I have to deal with before today is out. Also, there'll be two hungry men coming home shortly, so I've got to finish cooking dinner. Will you trust me until tomorrow? I'll get Michael and his father out of the way and we can talk. I promise you one thing, I had no hand in the making of that tape."

Kathryn and Ilona stared at one another. Ilona could see from Kathryn's face that she wanted to believe her future mother-in-law.

"Yes, I'll trust you until tomorrow, but I've already told my mother about the tape in the letter I posted this afternoon."

"That's the least of our worries. You can phone her tomorrow to explain about the contents. She probably won't get the letter for two days anyway. I'll be very surprised if it plops through her letter box tomorrow."

The phone could be heard ringing in the drawing room.

"If I owned this house," Ilona said, "I'd definitely have an extension in the kitchen."

"Do you want me to answer it?" Kathryn asked.

"Please. It may be my mother with news about Philip. Kathryn, if the call is from St. Helena talk to Nadia and tell her about the tape. She'll help set your mind at rest until tomorrow."

Whilst Kathryn was on the phone, Michael and Richard arrived. Richard kissed Ilona perfunctorily on the cheek. Ilona looked at him searchingly. This was the man to whom she'd been married for twenty-five years and in all those years he'd always been open in everything he did and said. Now he was keeping something from her and she wondered when he would broach the subject of Governor General. Probably after dinner when they were alone, she supposed.

Kathryn came hurrying in from the drawing room.

"Philip has been found alive and well, a little bruised and battered and suffering slightly from lying out overnight when the temperature dropped but he'll be well enough to join us here on Saturday."

"Thank heaven for that," Ilona said. "One problem solved."

Michael and Richard looked puzzled.

"I'll tell you all about it over dinner," she said.

"Oh, by the way," Kathryn said, "Philip was clutching a small Envis stone in his right hand as if his life depended on it, and it was one of the rare ones."

"Well I never," Ilona said laughing at the mystified expressions on the faces of her husband and son.

"What a waste of time and energy. He can't even keep it for himself, it has to be handed to the Vaga. I suppose it was his masculine pride that made him go searching, but saying that, he was lucky to find such a stone and even more lucky to be alive."

Ilona turned to her husband and son. "Dinner in fifteen minutes, so if you want a shower you'd better get a move on."

Ilona motioned Kathryn to stay. "Did you speak to Nadia?"

Kathryn nodded. "Yes, she did explain a few things, but I'd still like to have a chat with you tomorrow."

"Don't worry, I'll make sure of that. Off you go Kathryn; I don't need any help here. As I said, dinner in fifteen minutes."

~*~

Dinner was a leisurely affair. Ilona was thankful that Kathryn looked and seemed happier than earlier, and that Michael obviously didn't suspect anything. The chat with Nadia must have helped a lot.

"I'm taking Kathryn down the Black Lion for a drink. Are you two coming?" Michael looked at his parents.

"Not tonight," Richard said quickly. "Your mother and I have something to discuss."

"I'll help your mother clear the table and load the dishwasher and then we'll go," Kathryn said, stacking the plates onto a tray.

There was a guarded silence between Richard and Ilona until they heard the front door being closed.

"Come and sit down Ilona. I'll get you a drink. What do you want, brandy, whisky or whatever?"

"I'll have a brandy please."

"What mixer do you want, same as usual?"

"Please." Ilona sipped the brandy and tonic, waiting for Richard to start.

"I'm glad Philip was found. It would have broken Marjorie and James' hearts if anything had happened to him."

"Yes, it would," Ilona agreed, determined not to ask if Richard had accepted the post of Governor General. She made no attempt to keep the conversation flowing, apart from uttering a few words now and again when gaps occurred in Richard's monologue. Eventually Richard couldn't stand the atmosphere any longer. He looked at his wife, took a deep breath and said, "You know, don't you?"

Ilona nodded, her face was inscrutable.

"My mother told me this afternoon. Have you decided?" she enquired.

It was Richard's turn to nod.

"Yes, I have."

"Without discussing it with me or Michael."

Richard got up and walked to the window. For a few moments he looked at the tranquil view outside, then he turned and faced his wife.

"I've loved you for almost thirty years, twenty-five of which we've been man and wife. That day you came to me after your baby died, I never asked questions, but you knew I was always there for you if you wanted to talk. Even to this day, I don't know the whole story. I do know, however, that you only married me to get away from your father and the islands. I was fool enough to think you might learn to love me. You could have you know. If only you'd grieved for Morgan and your baby and then moved on, but you couldn't, or wouldn't."

Ilona opened her mouth as if to say something, but Richard carried on speaking as if he hadn't noticed.

"Yes, I have decided. I told Justin earlier today that it was a great honour and that I would be proud to accept. I'll be leaving shortly. What you do is up to you. Our tenancy lasts until the end of September, with an option to take out a longer lease at the end, but you know all this already."

"Since I spoke to my mother, I've done some hard thinking this afternoon. I won't stay here; the house will be much too big for me on my own. I don't foresee any problems in finding other tenants for the summer. Do you?"

"No," Richard agreed. "If you don't stay here, where will you live? You can't have mapped out your future in a few hours."

Ilona gave a small smile. "I'll live where you live, as any wife should."

Richard looked astonished and a delighted smile spread across his countenance.

"Do you really mean that?"

It was a rhetorical question, for he could see from the expression on her face that she meant it.

"Why now after all our years in exile?"

"It's time I went home and laid a few ghosts to rest," she said simply.

Richard came across the room and sat beside his wife. He drew her to him and kissed her gently on the forehead. "I still love you, you know," he said.

"I know you do. All these years, I've taken your love for granted, but not anymore. Suddenly today I felt ashamed at the way I've treated you. It's time I grew up."

They sat there silently for a while, each with their own thoughts, but it was a contented silence.

"My mother said a strange thing today." Ilona remarked.

"What was that?" "

"She said Leah had been speaking to my father on the telephone, and my mother is convinced she is trying to stir up trouble."

Richard was instantly alert.

"I wouldn't be surprised. It's not like Leah to speak to Drystan. Oh I'm too happy to think about my sister and her devious ways tonight, we'll deal with whatever mischief she is causing when it happens. There is nothing she could know that could hurt us, is there?" He looked at his wife questioningly.

"I can't think of anything, but Leah has always been fond of prying into people's lives, but as you say there's no point in worrying." Ilona turned her head and looked at Richard. "There is something I should have told you many years ago." Ilona took a deep breath. "Remember that day I came to you after I lost my baby."

"Yes, I remember. You were the last person I expected to see when I answered the door. You looked terrible, as if your whole world had collapsed, when of course it had. Losing Morgan was bad enough, but for your baby to die as well was a double blow. You never did tell me how he died, and I didn't want to pry."

"He didn't die."

Richard jumped up off the settee. "You lied to me then and lived a lie for twenty-five years! You told me he'd died."

"No, I said I'd lost my baby. You took it for granted he'd died. I meant to tell you, but every time I started to speak about him you changed the subject."

"Yes, but only because it was upsetting you to talk about it."

"In the beginning, I thought he was dead too." Ilona said. "Hallam came and informed me that he was. He told me that it would be better for my health to leave straight away. No one argued with Hallam. If he said we were to leave, we left. Leah returned to St. Elizabeth and I went to stay with Luke in Leil to recover my strength. About a week later, Hallam turned up and calmly announced that my son was alive and well and that he'd placed him with a couple who would be good and loving parents. He said he hadn't told me sooner because he didn't fully trust Leah to keep her mouth shut. Before he left he gave me a photograph of him."

"The man's just as big a monster as your father. Have you ever tried to find him?"

Ilona shook her head.

Richard had to ask, "Who else knows?"

"Hallam, of course, and the midwife, but she was quite old then so she may be dead. Anyway she wouldn't dare talk."

"Anyone else?"

Ilona looked up at her husband towering above her. "Please

come and sit down by me again. The only other people who know are my mother, Luke and Justin. Don't let this spoil our return to the islands," she pleaded. "I never meant to lie to you. I just didn't explain the meaning of my words properly. Oh Richard if you only knew how the memory of that day has haunted me. I only had him for such a short time." Ilona's voice faltered. "I didn't mean any harm by misleading you, but as the days went on, there didn't seem any point in telling you he was alive. Hallam had taken him to be adopted and I knew I would never see him again. Then I got pregnant and when they put Michael in my arms for the first time, it eased the pain so much, but I was sad that he had a half brother that he'd never get to know."

Richard returned to sit by his wife's side.

"It's a lot for me to take in. I still wish you'd trusted me enough to tell me. I can't say I'm not hurt by it, because I am, but you're right, we mustn't let it spoil tonight." He clasped his wife's hand. "Do you know, I think we've understood each other better tonight than the whole of the past twenty-five years. Let's put the past firmly where it belongs and go out and celebrate. We'll drink a silent toast to your first-born son and hope he's happy wherever he is. It's a lovely night. Fetch your jacket and we'll join Michael and Kathryn in the pub and tell them I'm returning to the islands as Governor General. What do you say?"

"Yes," she said. "Let's do just that."

Chapter 8

July

Dear Mum and Dad,

As I told you this morning on the telephone, I'm feeling a lot more cheerful than when I wrote to you last. You probably won't have received the letter yet as I only posted it to you yesterday, but I know you Mum, no matter what I told you on the phone, you'll still worry about me. I should never have posted the letter until I'd spoken to Mrs Vandrell. Please don't take any notice of what I said. It was all a big misunderstanding in one way. I couldn't tell you much when I spoke to you as Michael was in the other room and I didn't want him to know what his grandfather had done. I thought that Mrs Vandrell had hired a private detective to look into our family. Later that afternoon Nadia telephoned and I was able to have a chat with her. Luckily Michael hadn't arrived back from town and his mother left me alone. Nadia said that it was more likely Drystan Pendenny (that's Michael's grandfather, by the way) had arranged it. She also told me that I wasn't to worry and to tell Mrs Vandrell everything before doing anything stupid such as coming home, or worrying you, but by then it was too late, as I had already posted the letter.

Michael and I went down to the pub last night for a quiet drink. It was an old country pub, low ceilinged, with large oak beams. It was such a lovely evening that we sat outside. Ilona and Richard said they wouldn't accompany us, but they changed their minds and followed us down later. They had some good news to tell us. Michael's father is to be the next and last Governor of the British Tomayon Islands and they are leaving the Isle of Wight shortly.

Ilona told me that this was definitely their last move and that she was going home for good. Richard looked much happier than I've ever seen him look, although I don't know him all that well. I always had the impression though of a deep rooted sadness that showed in his eyes. We had quite a cheerful evening and I can tell you I was quite merry when we got back to the house, although in the back of my mind was the talk Ilona and I were to have this morning. I told her that Michael and I had decided to go to the islands in a few weeks time. Michael had told me that he was looking forward to meeting his grandparents and wanted to find out about his mother's country. Ilona did make an attempt to talk us out of it until after the wedding, but as she and Richard were returning, she could see it was useless. She did take me aside later when we were in the kitchen making coffee and warned me that I could lose Michael for a little while. She told me that she couldn't really explain her gut feeling, but that she knew her father and his manipulative ways too well, and that if she herself wasn't around at any time and I was worried, I should talk to her mother. Her mother knew exactly how to handle Drystan Pendenny. I was rather worried about what she'd said, but she couldn't put her feelings into words. She said that her instincts told her that her father was up to mischief, but neither she nor her mother knew what. She said that Michael might get seduced by the wealth, and more especially, the power his grandfather was able to wield on the islands and be swayed by this. I've decided that I'm not going to worry about anything, but deal with it, if and when, the time comes.

The next morning, Ilona sent Michael and Richard out of the way so that she could explain about the video. It was she who told me to phone you and put your mind at rest. I told her everything, even about what those girls had said in the club in Bath. She remembered Michael's previous girl friends and assured me that their finishing with Michael had nothing to do with her and I believed her. She also told me that Michael hadn't been serious about either of them, and neither were they about him, and if her father hadn't interfered, the relationships would have died a natural death given time. He'd done exactly the same thing, hired private detectives and after he'd seen them he'd sent them to Ilona for her to see. She said she didn't even bother to watch them, but taped over them. Her father had then bribed both girls to finish with Michael, one had a holiday in the Bahamas and the other received a very expensive make of car. Ilona managed to keep all of this from Michael and Richard. It was unfortunate this time, she said, that as her father was coming over for the silver wedding, he'd had the video sent direct to Ilona to keep for him. Then it had somehow got mixed up with the videos that Ilona had given to Mrs Malloy to put in my room. I was never meant to see it. She also told me that more than likely I would receive an offer of an exotic holiday or something expensive when her father arrived. Why he interferes in the life of a grandson he has never seen beats me. She made me promise not to tell Michael about any of this and I agreed. I told Ilona that I loved Michael and I would never accept anything to make me end our relationship. The only time I would do that is if I knew Michael wanted it to end.

As the video had been delivered to Ilona, Mr Pendenny hadn't even seen it or the written report, which until that time I knew nothing about. Ilona said she had no intention of reading the report or watching the video, but when Michael had told her that I was Welsh she couldn't wait to see what her father's reaction would be. I was rather annoyed when she made this statement, as I'm proud of my Welsh heritage, but then I remembered that Morgan Draymer, who was the cause of the feud, had been Welsh. That's another nail in my coffin, so perhaps he'll offer me a bigger bribe to finish with Michael. I'm only joking.

I'm going to stop writing now as Michael has found a perfect gift for his parents for their silver wedding. He went into town yesterday to do some shopping for his mother and to collect his father from the ferry, and found a silver salver that he thought they would like. It's awfully difficult buying presents for rich people who've got everything. Anyway he arranged to get it inscribed and we've got to collect it today.

I'll write you again after the party and let you know all about it. I'm glad we spoke on the phone. It was lovely to hear your voice. I was only sorry that Dad was out.

Love,
Kathryn
xxxxx

Chapter 9

Justin manoeuvred the car expertly through the narrow lanes. He couldn't wait to get on the motorway and already could feel the surge of power of which James' car was capable. James had no qualms about letting Justin drive his beloved car, for he knew he was a fast, but skilful driver and that his younger half brother was itching to get behind the wheel. There were no motorways on the islands and it was therefore rare that any speed could be sustained for a long period. There were small stretches of dual carriageways, but these were few and far between and the majority of the roads were narrow and winding, similar to those on which Justin was now driving.

There was silence in the car as they made their way to the Isle of Wight. Marjorie and James were giving thanks that Philip's accident hadn't been worse and both were wondering how much his grandfather had had to do with it. Ria had eventually telephoned to let them know what had happened and to reassure them both that Philip was shaken and bruised, but nothing more. Justin had no desire to talk. Since Richard had left, Leah and he had barely spoken to one another. He was sick to death of the rows between himself and his wife. He was certain that Marjorie and James were relieved that their house guests were leaving, albeit they still had to spend a few more days in each others company. He let himself concentrate on his driving to the exclusion of everything else, experiencing the thrill of the open road. Leah was in a silent rage with the whole world in general, but particularly with Justin. From the rear seat she looked at the back of his head with hatred and longed, with an intensity which should have alarmed her but didn't, that she had a knife she could plunge into his back. Her mind was in turmoil. In a pique of spite she'd telephoned Drystan Pendenny and told him certain things that had been better left unsaid. Half of her trembled inwardly, but the other half exulted in the thought of the storm that was about to break around their heads.

Ilona and Michael were at the front door to greet them as Justin pulled into the driveway. Richard had taken Kathryn out for a walk. He had told his wife point blank that he knew he was being rude to their guests, but he didn't care if he never saw his sister again. As there was nothing he could do about it this weekend, however, he would stay out of her way as much as possible. He was sure that Justin, Marjorie and James would understand.

Whilst Leah and Marjorie went upstairs to unpack, Justin took Ilona to one side and suggested she show him and James the garden. James declined, saying he would relax in the drawing room with a whisky and soda until dinnertime. Ilona looked in amazement at Justin who had never shown the slightest interest in gardening at any time in his life, but after telling James to give Marjorie and Leah a drink when they came downstairs, she allowed herself to be led outside.

Justin and Ilona strolled along the weed free pathways, Justin sniffing the roses and admiring the neatness of it all.

"What's that called?" He asked, pointing to some gaily-coloured flowers in an earthenware pot.

"How on earth should I know," Ilona replied. "I'm no gardener Justin as well you know. If you've only dragged me out here to ask asinine questions, I might as well go back indoors and see if Mrs Malloy needs any help in preparing the dinner."

Justin turned and looked back at the house. "It isn't that I've anything terribly secret to say to you, but I wanted to keep this conversation private. I took a chance that James wouldn't accept my offer to look around the garden. Leah has been speaking to father. I only found out by accident." He looked mischievous. "That's a lie. Since the row we had the other day, I've been expecting her to do something and I eavesdropped. It was a nuisance, I'd just heard her ask for father when James came in from the garden and I had to hurry away, so I never heard the rest of the conversation. Did Richard tell you about our quarrel."

Ilona nodded. "Yes, he told me last night after Michael and Kathryn had gone to bed. It was a terribly cruel thing you did to her, but it's done now and out in the open. You know Leah, you surely didn't expect her to take a revelation such as that lying down, did you?"

Justin didn't answer.

"I did know that Leah had been speaking to father. Mother told me," Ilona continued. "Richard and I talked about it yesterday and we decided that whatever she said, it's too late now. We'll just have to play a waiting game. Father will be here tomorrow and knowing him we'll soon find out."

"I hope he doesn't spoil your party."

"He probably will, but again I'm not concerned and I'm not going to get upset either. I think the longer I've lived away the better I understand him. He won't mean to upset me, but he has always thought he knew what was right for all of us. So far I've managed to keep Michael out of his net."

Justin sat down on the seat at the far end of the lawn. At the sides and overhead there was a trellis covered in a profusion of pink and yellow climbing roses. He patted the seat beside him. "Sit down for five minutes. These roses are pretty," he said. "Why are there pink and yellow coloured blooms on the same bush?"

Ilona laughed. "Don't start that again. However, I do know the answer this time. I asked the gardener the very same question recently. The rose is called Masquerade and when the flowers first appear they are one colour and then gradually they change to the other colour. I can't remember which colour comes out first. If you're that interested there are a few buds on the point of opening, you'll just have to keep popping down the garden to see for yourself."

Justin pondered this for a moment. "Weird," he said. "Are you sure?"

"Yes, I'm sure. I can't stay down here talking too long, but it is lovely to see you again."

"I'm worried," Justin continued. "I don't think Leah can have told father about you having the baby. There wouldn't be much point as she thinks he's dead. I enjoyed driving down here, and once I was on the motorway James' car handles so beautifully that I had the peace and quiet to think things over in my mind. I'm only guessing, but I think that it would have to be something to discredit Vonryn Santella, but what I don't know. That would get her in father's good books straight away."

"That's all right then," Ilona said, getting up. "It doesn't matter to us about Vonryn. I've never met him, although that will be rectified tomorrow as he's coming to the party with Nadia in place of Hallam Draymer."

"You're missing my point. If Vonryn can't be Vaga because of something in his past and James has stated categorically that his future is here in England, then that leaves only Philip and Michael. I think after Philip's outing on Envetta that rules him out so we are left with Michael. The more I think about it, the more I think I'm right. Michael has never met his grandfather and he won't know how to deal with him."

"You've got me worried now," Ilona was thoughtful. "I'll have to think of something if and when the time comes. Michael could never be Vaga. Father would be out of his mind if he thought that the people would accept someone who was born in Britain and lived his life here."

"I agree with you. How will you deal with the problem when you'll be here and Michael and Richard will be in the Islands? Richard told me that Michael was going over for a holiday."

It was Ilona's turn to smile mischievously. "You haven't seen Richard of course, so he couldn't tell you. I'm going home with him. Don't look so stunned. It's time I went back and faced the past."

Ilona was laughing as she retraced her steps to the house. She looked back once to see her garrulous brother silenced for once by her last statement.

As soon as Luke heard from his mother about Philip's accident, he'd packed a bag and hurried to Envetta to help in the search. It was a wasted journey, however, for when he arrived, he was told that Philip had been found alive and well and had been taken to St. Helena. Luke was in a dilemma. He hadn't intended travelling with his parents to the UK, but returning to Leil was pointless when he would have to leave almost immediately for St. Elizabeth airport. He decided it was better to meet his father before Ilona and Richard's party and if, as seemed inevitable, there was to be a quarrel, get it over with. He telephoned Stephen Laridon on St. Helena and warned him of his arrival and was reassured to learn that Philip, although a mass of bruises had no major injuries. At dinner that evening, he came face to face with his father for the first time since the meeting in Christenbech. There was no scene because Drystan refused to acknowledge the presence of the son he'd disowned. Ria was glad when the meal was over, but was horrified when Luke told her that he wouldn't be attending Ilona's party. She saw her husband disappearing into the library, and dragging a protesting Luke with her, she followed Drystan.

Defiantly she shut and locked the door firmly behind her, placing the key in her evening bag.

Drystan was standing with his back to the door, looking out through a large window at the sea and watching the waves as they broke over the rocky headland.

"Luke says he has decided not to go to Ilona's party," she said.

"That's right," Luke inclined his head in the direction of his father. "Not if he's going."

"We're all going," she said determinedly. "You Luke can phone your housekeeper and she can pack your case. I'm sure Stephen will send a small boat to collect it."

"There isn't time for that mother. We have to leave at 12 o'clock for the airport, but that isn't the problem. I brought a packed case with me. I thought perhaps father might have reconsidered and realised that the way Justin and I voted was no reflection on him, but that we did it for love of our country. I can see from his attitude to me over dinner that that isn't the case. I won't spoil Ilona and Richard's day for them."

Ria went over to her husband. She said quietly. "I've hardly seen my daughter in the last twenty-five years and I've never seen my grandson and that is your fault. I know you've disowned Luke and Justin for voting the way they did, but I agree with Luke, it was for the good of the Islands. For God's sake Drystan, can't you have a short truce for my sake?"

She turned to Luke.

"What's the opposite of disown Luke? You're good at English."

Luke smiled. "I don't know, I've never thought about it. Reinstate perhaps."

"It doesn't matter, reinstate will do. Can't you reinstate your two sons for a short time Drystan, for my sake? I've never asked you for much, but I'm asking this now."

Drystan thought for a few moments, then turned and looked at his wife and son.

"Very well, for the time we're with Ilona, I'll try and forget how Justin and Luke betrayed me, but can you imagine how it felt."

Ria patted her husband's arm and giving the key to Luke motioned him to leave the room.

"I know you're hurting now Drystan, but you'll realise one day that what they did was right."

~*~

Drystan Pendenny was strangely quiet during the long night flight to Britain. He had warmed slightly in his attitude to Vonryn, but that was only because Vonryn had been instrumental in rescuing Philip. It hadn't, however, prevented him from reading the small file that his enquiry team had rushed to him. He read the papers with carefully concealed enjoyment. It was amazing what an experienced team of operators could discover in such a short time. He carefully replaced the file in his brief case and locked it with a key that hung from a chain around his neck. He shut his eyes and leant back and relaxed. His wife watched as Drystan tucked the key inside his shirt. Unbeknown to her husband, she'd had a duplicate key for years. It was only a matter of time before she found out about the contents of the file. She was under no illusions about her husband, but she still loved the stubborn old man. She also loved her children and her stepson by Drystan's first marriage, and she was determined to prevent Drystan interfering too drastically in their lives ever again. He'd meddled enough in the past and it was time for that to stop. From the few hints that he'd dropped, Ria was convinced she knew what was going through his mind. He was going to try and overturn the vote, but how? Ria shut her eyes and tried to relax. There was nothing she could do on the plane. She would have to be patient and wait until she could persuade Ilona or Justin to get their father out of the way so she could read the file.

It was late afternoon before they arrived on the Isle of Wight and Richard and Justin were waiting to meet them off the ferry. Justin thought his parents looked very tired after their long journey and for the first time it hit him that they were getting old. His father had meddled in all their affairs since he could first remember, but he couldn't envisage life without him. For all that, his greeting to his father was a cold one but he turned lovingly to his mother and kissed her on her cheek. "Thanks for arranging a truce. Luke phoned me," he whispered. Out loud he said, "It won't be long and we'll be in Ilona's and then you can have a lie down before dinner."

Justin drove off with his parents and Philip, leaving Richard to follow with Luke, Nadia and Vonryn. The bodyguards followed closely behind in the two hire cars.

Richard's first impression of Vonryn had been a good one. He shook hands with a firm grip, but as Vonryn turned to help with the handling of the luggage, Richard was startled at Vonryn's resemblance to his own son Michael. They were both tall with dark complexions, albeit Vonryn's was deeper having lived in the hotter climes of the islands. Both had the same black wavy hair that showed copper highlights in the sunshine and the same high cheekbones, but when Vonryn turned to face Richard again the likeness seemed to recede. It was only in profile they seemed alike, but for some reason it disturbed Richard. There was no doubt that Vonryn was a handsome man with matinee idol looks, but thankfully this was offset by the square chin which in no way detracted from his appearance but which gave his face character. Luke and Vonryn looked around them with interest. For both of them it was the first time they'd left the islands.

"Everything looks so green," Luke said.

Richard agreed. He liked his other brother-in-law, in some ways more than he liked Justin. Justin was the clown and Luke the serious one, but they had both been there when Ilona was in trouble and needed them. It was many years since he'd seen Luke, longer than he cared to remember.

"This must be something of a record for you Luke," Richard remarked jocularly. "This is twice in a short space of time that you've left Leil."

"Yes, I'd better be careful otherwise it will become a habit. Seriously though," he added, "I'm to become Bishop of Mordeen soon. Father agreed the appointment before our quarrel and now he can't retract."

Richard was so surprised that he almost crashed the gears.

"Good heavens. Am I hearing right. What has brought about this decision? First Ilona decides to return home with me when I'm made Governor General, and you're leaving Leil."

"There are a couple of reasons."

"You'll find it a completely different life style."

"That's no problem. You see like Ilona, it is time for me to move on, but I'll miss all my friends in the village."

"They'll miss you. We may not have met much over the years, but your letters have always been so full of information that both Ilona and I feel we know most of the villagers. You describe them all so vividly. You've made that village prosperous, especially with the wine co-operative that you set up."

Luke smiled, remembering the struggle he had had establishing the co-operative. "Yes, that was great fun. I knew that I couldn't lose, not with father behind me. Of course none of the villagers knew I was his son. All the villagers knew, however, that Drystan Pendenny had a hand in helping matters along. In one respect I'm ashamed that I used the power of my family to get my own way, but it has brought prosperity to Leil and that is what counts. The business runs so smoothly now that it can function without me at the helm. In fact it has been able to do without me for many years, but I was happy there and didn't see any point in moving away."

Richard was amazed. "I'm surprised Drystan helped a village in the British Islands."

"Good PR Richard. Father's a master at that. He knew that when independence comes, the people there will recall how he helped them."

"Marjorie and James are going to have a shock when they see Philip. They know about the accident of course, but even I never knew how many colours you have in so many bruises." Richard said as he slowed down at a road junction.

"He's lucky to be alive," Vonryn remarked from the back seat. "It was a very stupid thing to do."

"I hear he found an Envis stone though."

"Yes, he did. Of course it has to be handed over to the Vaga as it is a rare one."

"Why do you think he did it?"

Luke answered. "I expect my father goaded him with the old story. Philip probably felt that if he did this then no one could call him a coward

"No one would ever have done that. If he had wanted to be Vaga then I could have understood it, but he didn't. Anyway, we're home, at least home for a short while more, then St. Elizabeth. You've got time for a rest before dinner. Don't worry if you fall asleep. One or other of us will give you a shout in plenty of time."

Richard turned the car into the driveway in time to see Marjorie's emotional reaction at the sight of Philip's multi coloured bruises. He heard Drystan praise the bravery of the rescuers and in particular Vonryn. He turned to Justin and grinned. They both knew how much it must have galled Drystan to praise Vonryn, but with him sitting in the rear seat they thought it best not to comment, but Vonryn said it for them.

"I know what you're both thinking," he said. "He must hate having to thank me for rescuing Philip. I'm sure he wishes someone else had done it."

"Vonryn," Nadia remonstrated. "You shouldn't say that."

"Why not?" Justin remarked. "Richard and I were thinking exactly the same thing."

Richard looked closely as Ilona greeted Nadia and Vonryn. They'd both met Nadia before when they were living in Bath, but this was the first time they'd seen Vonryn. Richard waited to see if Ilona noticed the likeness between Vonryn and Michael, but apparently she didn't, because the expression on her face remained one of a hostess greeting her guests. After all these years, Richard knew her too well for her to hide anything. It was only when they all went into the hallway and Vonryn removed his glasses that Ilona gave a slight gasp, which she quickly covered up by coughing.

"Are you all right?" Richard asked.

"Of course, something tickled my throat," she replied, and for the time being he had to be content and leave the matter to rest. She'd noticed something, Richard thought, but for the life of him he couldn't think what. If it had been the likeness between Michael and Vonryn, she would have noticed that when they were outside. He made up his mind to ask her about it the first chance they had of being alone.

~*~

Ilona looked around the dinner table that night with gratitude. So far, so good, she thought. Everyone appeared relaxed and her parents looked less tired after their siesta. The meal of chicken breasts cooked in a white wine and cream sauce and served with tiny new potatoes, broccoli spears and baby carrots had seemed to please everyone. This was followed by meringue nests of strawberries, pineapple and kiwi fruit, topped with Mrs Malloy's home made ice cream.

"The meal was delicious," Luke said. "Not too heavy. I find the older I get the less I can eat in the evenings, unless I take indigestion tablets before bed."

Everyone declined cheese and biscuits, but Justin helped himself to another glass of Chardonnay. Kathryn offered to go and make coffee or tea for anyone who wanted it as Mrs Malloy had gone home after stacking the dishwasher. They all adjourned to the drawing room, and as it was another pleasant evening, the younger ones decided to walk down to the pub in the village. Marjorie told James to get the car out and run them down as Philip must still be weak after his accident, but Philip declined saying that he was fit enough to walk, telling his mother not to fuss.

It wasn't until they were undressing for bed that Richard was able to question Ilona about her reaction to Vonryn in the hall.

"What made you gasp when Vonryn removed his glasses?"

Ilona was taking off her make up in front of the mirror in the en suite bathroom.

"It was his eyes."

"I couldn't see anything wrong with them. They seemed perfectly normal to me."

"There's nothing wrong with them. It's the colour, they're yellow."

"Are they?" Richard stopped to think for a moment. "I can't say I noticed."

Ilona had removed the hairpins and was brushing her shoulder length hair.

"He's Morgan's son," she said turning to look at Richard who was standing in the doorway. "He had yellow eyes too. Don't you remember?"

"I can't say I do. I don't make a habit of looking into men's eyes, women's perhaps."

"Don't make a joke of it. I know he's Morgan's son."

"Let me get this straight. Are you saying he is your son by Morgan; the one Hallam took for adoption. If so that would explain the likeness." Richard stopped speaking suddenly, but Ilona didn't seem to notice.

Ilona bit her lip. "He could be my son, or Morgan could still have been having a relationship with Barbara. Perhaps Morgan didn't really love me, perhaps he wanted to marry me because of pressure from his father." Richard digested this information in silence. He didn't tell his wife that Leah had voiced the same thoughts as to why Morgan had married Ilona.

"I'll be honest Ilona, when I met Vonryn today and he turned and I saw him in profile, he reminded me of Michael. In fact from the side they could be brothers, but when we were face to face again, the likeness had disappeared, that is apart from their colouring and height. What would you do if we could prove he was your son?"

Ilona looked surprised. "What could I do? I could hardly go up to this young man and tell him I'm his mother and I gave him away. Anyway the only infallible proof would be DNA testing. Whether he's Barbara's son by Morgan or my son, I wouldn't do anything.

He seems a nice, happy, young man, engaged to Nadia and obviously Hallam has trained him to be Vaga. I wouldn't want to shatter that happiness.

Richard turned down the duvet and climbed into bed. "Have you thought that perhaps he is Barbara and Vincent Santella's son? After all Vincent is descended from the Draymer line. The colour of the eyes could be a throw back, which only comes out in certain generations.

"Yes, you're probably right." Ilona switched off the light and after kissing Richard lightly on his cheek, she turned her back to him and was soon asleep.

Richard lay awake for a good while listening to his wife's steady breathing. He stroked her hair lightly and she turned in her sleep and snuggled up closely to him. He hoped he'd convinced Ilona that Vonryn wasn't her son, but he'd remembered Justin telling him about the meeting and how Luke and Justin had voted against their own father for Vonryn. He was convinced they had been voting for their own nephew and was sure his brothers-in-law knew the truth. Before he fell asleep he wondered if anyone had told Ilona about the way they'd voted. He hoped not, and decided to warn Justin and Luke not to say anything. If it was too late and someone had already told her, then there was nothing he could do about it. Richard wondered whether he ought to ask his brothers-in-law outright if Vonryn was their nephew, but before he came to a decision he fell asleep.

~*~

The day of the party dawned fine and dry but a heavy mist lingered over the sea. Mrs Malloy assured Ilona that once the mist had cleared it would be a lovely day. Ilona hoped that she was right, although it wouldn't make that much difference as everything would be under cover. A warm evening, however, would be a bonus. Mrs Malloy left after she'd drunk her elevenses and finished questioning Ilona's mother about her life on the Islands. The house was empty apart from Ilona and her mother. Leah and Marjorie had gone to the hairdressers and Richard had taken his father-in-law and brothers-in-law on a round trip of the island.

The young ones had taken their swimwear and announced that they wouldn't be back until late afternoon, weather permitting. They were going to laze on the beach and have a swim. As soon as Mrs Malloy had left the premises, Ria told her daughter to come upstairs to their bedroom. Once inside she unlocked her husband's briefcase.

"Should you be doing that?" Ilona queried.

"You know your father Ilona. He will only tell me things when he feels like it. I don't make a habit of this, only if I feel the family might be threatened."

"Is it anything to do with Leah's phone call?"

"I won't know until we read the contents of the file he has locked away."

Ria took out the small file of papers and read it through.

"It's as I thought. He has something against Vonryn, at least against his parents, but that amounts to the same thing in the end."

"Let me see." Ilona took the papers from her mother and studied them carefully.

"It's what I suspected. Vonryn isn't Vincent Santella's son. I remember years ago, Leah was on holiday in New York. She came back before I married Morgan. If what she says is true, and according to this report it is, then Vincent was living and working in New York and couldn't possibly be Vonryn's father. So for all Morgan said he loved me, he was still sleeping with Barbara and she must have persuaded Vincent into accepting Vonryn as his son."

"Was Vincent married to Barbara at that time?" her mother asked.

"Yes. It was very sudden. Morgan ended the engagement and she and Vincent were married almost immediately afterwards. She must have been pregnant and that's why she rushed into it."

"He could be your son," Ilona's mother said gently. "Have you thought of that?"

"Yes, Richard and I talked about it last night, but I prefer to believe that he is Barbara's son. I suppose this means that father intends to tell Vonryn this fact sometime during my party."

"Undoubtedly. He'll enjoy doing it. What it will do to that young man I don't know, but he won't be eligible to succeed Hallam Draymer now unless Barbara admits that Morgan was the father."

"I can't see her doing that."

Ria carefully locked the briefcase and returned it to the wardrobe. The two women descended the wide staircase lost in their own thoughts.

Ilona went into the drawing room and poured herself and her mother a sherry.

I feel I could drink something stronger, but it's too early in the day. Do you think father has visions of Michael being the next Vaga?" Ilona asked.

Ria sipped her sherry slowly.

"Of course. That is the whole point of this exercise. Over the next few days your father will destroy Vonryn and charm Michael. We can't interfere too obviously, but try not to worry. I'm sure Michael won't be fooled for long. Surely he can see that an outsider couldn't be brought in."

"I agree with you, but before then a lot of damage will have been done. I can't see anyone coming out of this unscarred. Did father see the video about Kathryn? I left it out for him."

"Oh yes, he watched it last night before we went to sleep. There's no way he'll want that marriage to go ahead. I should imagine that he has Nadia in mind for Michael."

"But she's engaged to Vonryn," Ilona protested.

"Don't be naive Ilona, when has a little thing like an engagement ever stopped him, and of course with a scandal concerning Vonryn about to break, the engagement may be called off anyway."

Ria laughed suddenly and Ilona looked at her mother enquiringly.

"I was only thinking dear what your father would say if he knew about your marriage to Morgan and your subsequent pregnancy."

"Yes, you're right. I still can't believe that we managed to keep it from him and his secret police."

"Well we did, be in no doubt about that. All hell would have broken loose years ago if he'd found out. The only fear I had," Ria continued, "was that someone searching the records for ancestors would come across the information by chance.

"They wouldn't come across the marriage certificate," Ilona replied. "After Morgan's death Luke swore an affidavit for the Records Office that a batch of blank marriage certificates had been destroyed by fire so it wouldn't show in the main register kept in St. Elizabeth. Luckily Luke didn't carry out many weddings and he only sent off records every six months. I expect Hallam arranged something similar in Envetta about the birth certificate, which would have been easier for him as the baby was born there and not in the British Islands. The only danger was that the marriage is in the church's own record book. We intended to face father with the truth about our marriage, but what was the point after Morgan died. People visiting local churches and going through their registers might come across something, but with everything on computer why go to the time and trouble of traipsing around the islands."

"Where are the originals?" Ria asked a worried expression on her face.

"Don't worry mother, they're well hidden."

Later in the afternoon, before she dressed for the party, Ilona went to inspect the marquee. The caterers had done an excellent job. It was to be an informal buffet style meal. Long rectangular tables were being laid out with food to suit all tastes from the exotic to vegetarian. Ilona had insisted that although she wanted a buffet style meal, she also wanted somewhere her guests could sit down comfortably to eat. She didn't want her guests to have to try and do a balancing act whilst they juggled with trying to eat and drink and only two hands to hold everything. It was peaceful in the marquee and she sat for a few minutes savouring the tranquility. She didn't feel as confident now as she did earlier in the day when she had spoken with her mother, but she resolved firmly to put her worries aside for one evening.

Chapter 10

July

Dear Mum and Dad,

As promised, I'm writing to let you know how things are going here. Before that, I'll tell you about THE FAMILY. The capital letters aren't a mistake, that is how I think of them. Luckily, I met them in stages as I was very nervous. The first to arrive was Ilona's brother, Justin and his wife Leah. They travelled down in the same car as Ilona's half brother, James and his wife, Marjorie. This is where it gets confusing. Ilona is married to Richard, as you already know, and Richard's sister, Leah, is married to Ilona's brother, Justin.

I'd noticed that Richard seemed restless all morning, and it was almost time for them to arrive, when he suddenly announced that he was going for a walk and did I want to go with him. I didn't know what to do, as it seemed rude to leave Ilona and Michael to greet their guests, but I saw Ilona nod her head at me and I agreed. Richard strode out very quickly and I had a job keeping up with him, but I didn't mind being quiet as I had plenty to think about. It was another lovely day, the sun was shining out of a cloudless blue sky and the grass was springy under our feet as Richard walked and I galloped along behind him. Richard, being a kind man soon noticed that I was having difficulty keeping pace with him and he apologised and slowed down. He suggested we sit down on a rock and have a breather and we both gazed silently out to sea, lost in our own thoughts. I racked my brain for something to say, but unlike me, I couldn't think of anything. It was he who eventually broke the silence.

"She's my own sister," he said, "And I can't stand the sight of her." He looked straight at me as he said this, as though he wanted to know what impression his statement had made on me.

To be honest, I didn't know how to reply. I think I said something like, 'Oh'.

"Kathryn," he continued, "If she's rude to you, and she probably will be, try and ignore it. Remember we're not all like her in this family. I can't tell you much about what has happened in the past, because other people's secrets are involved, although if you marry Michael and go to live in the Islands, you will probably hear rumours. I'll just say that she has become a bitter woman, different in all ways to the little sister I knew and loved. I know that she has been trying to make trouble within the family and I'm worried. It might all come to a head this weekend, but I want you to remember what I said. If she's horrid to you, it's nothing personal."

I nodded and gave him a weak smile. I was dreading the weekend more than ever now. However, when I did meet them over dinner, it wasn't as bad as I'd expected. Apart from Leah, they all seemed genuinely pleased to meet me. Leah seemed to look through me in a supercilious way, but it was true what Richard had said, she didn't single me out, because she didn't make any effort to talk to the others, and she completely ignored her husband, Justin. This didn't seem to bother him at all and it definitely didn't affect his appetite.

The following day Michael's grandparents arrived. Richard and Justin took two cars and went to meet them and the others who were arriving from the Islands. Michael didn't go, as there wouldn't be room in the cars, although I could see he was excited about their coming. Justin was the first to arrive back with Michael's grandparents and also Philip, Marjorie and James' only son. Philip looked terrible. He was a mass of bruises. By all accounts, he'd had an accident and was lucky to be alive. He seemed very nice, about Michael's height, but different hair and skin colouring, being fair skinned, and his hair had been bleached by the sun so it seemed almost white. He mother was awfully distressed when she saw the extent of his bruising, but he jollied her along, saying he felt fine.

They were just on the point of entering the house, when Richard drove up with his brother-in-law Luke and Nadia and her fiancé Vonryn. I was so pleased to see her and Ilona gave me the task of showing the younger members of the party to their rooms. I helped Nadia unpack and we were able to have a good chat. She was a bit puzzled by an expression on Ilona's face when she was talking to Vonryn in the hall. I told Nadia that I hadn't noticed anything, but I could see it bothered her. We chatted for a while and she told me that the videotape was typical of Drystan Pendenny. She said that in a way it was only like Dad asking about Michael's prospects. Perhaps it's the way they do things in those sort of families, but I still feel it was an invasion of privacy. I had the feeling that Nadia felt I was making a mountain out of a molehill, so I dropped the subject and we talked about other things, such as me visiting her in the near future. I'm really looking forward to that.

The evening went off all right. Thank goodness Michael's grandfather wasn't sitting next to me. I think I would have found it difficult to make polite conversation, and from what Ilona said, he would be delighted to know he was getting to me. Instead, Ria, Michael's grandmother, was on my right and Justin on my left, with Luke and Nadia sitting opposite. Justin is a terrible tease. I think I blushed a few times. You know how easily I blush. I didn't mind his teasing though, he meant it kindly and made us all laugh. Ria seems very kind. I didn't know whether to call them Mr and Mrs Pendenny, or whether I ought to address them by some other title. I'd meant to ask Ilona or Richard earlier on, but I forgot all about it. I managed to evade the issue for a while, but when everyone else was talking, apart from Ria and myself, I asked her. She said for me to call her Ria and said the correct way to address her husband was Larn, unless he suggested anything else. She also explained that long ago in the islands, only the men had titles and the women were known by their Christian names followed by wife of or daughter of. I asked her why in these more modern times the women weren't given a title. She laughed and said that as her husband was the only surviving holder of the ancient title of

Larn and the Vaga was a widower, she didn't think she'd command much public support to give her a title, and anyway, she added, there were much more important exciting developments due to take place in the near future.

After the meal, all the younger set went out for a drink. Again it was a lovely evening and we managed to find a table outside. We were all talking generally and enjoying ourselves, when Vonryn tore a strip off Philip for being such a stupid fool and going to Envetta. Philip flushed a bright red colour and I thought there was going to be a row, but there wasn't. Philip apologised for the trouble he'd caused and blamed it on his ignorance of the island where he'd had the accident. He thanked Vonryn profusely for saving his life, which embarrassed Vonryn and he told Philip that as far as he was concerned the incident was closed forever.

The following day we younger ones went off to find a secluded beach, as Philip was self conscious about his bruises. We took a picnic with us and spent many hours swimming and sunbathing. I was feeling more relaxed, knowing that I only had the party and then breakfast the next day to get through. As so many people were coming to the party, I could easily keep out of THE FAMILY'S way.

In the evening, Nadia and I went downstairs together. I'd told her earlier on that I needed moral support. The marquee was huge and was decorated with masses of fresh flowers, the scent from which filled the air. Tables creaked under the amount of food on them, ranging from the exotic such as caviar (which looked like miniature sheep droppings to me and which I didn't try) to something as mundane as chicken legs. I wore my black and white cocktail dress. Remember you were with me when I bought it in Cardiff. Nadia was wearing an evening trouser suit in the palest shade of green. I'm not going to describe the dresses that all the women wore, although I know you'd be interested. What I will do is send you some photographs taken at the party. There was a photographer present, so I'll order some to show you. I think I told you that we'd bought a silver salver for a present, but I can't remember if I said that we'd had it engraved with a map of all the Islands. Both Ilona and Richard were delighted with it, or so they said. After the meal Richard and Ilona's father made short speeches, thank goodness. There was a small space left in the centre of the marquee for dancing and a small band had been hired. Ilona and Richard took to the floor and started off the dancing to the tune of the Anniversary Waltz. They looked very happy. I hope that Michael and I will be as happy as them on our silver wedding day. Once the dancing started, people seemed to drift from table to table and out into the garden, as it tended to get stuffy in the marquee, and outside the evening air was still warm. As I only knew a handful of people there, I had a few dances with Michael and Vonryn and was content to sit and be an observer. I was doing just that when Mr Pendenny (I'll call him that in future instead of Larn) came and settled himself in the chair next to mine. He was all smiles.

"I haven't had much of a chance to talk to my grandson's fiancée," he said.

I agreed and stayed quiet not knowing what to say to him. If I hadn't known he'd commissioned the videotape, I would have fallen for his charm, of which he has plenty. He asked questions about my work and my family. As he already knew all the answers, I felt it was a rather pointless exercise, but he seemed so genuinely interested that I realised I was starting to like him. I was just beginning to relax and feel that he wasn't as bad as everyone had painted, when he dropped his bombshell. As he got up to go he remarked casually. "I've had a long chat with Michael. We've got a lot of years to catch up on you know." He looked straight at me and for a fleeting moment I felt sorry for him, until he carried on. "I told him you'd understand when you knew that Michael is flying back with his grandmother and me next Tuesday. It's such a shame that you have to go to work on Monday, but I'm sure we'll be able to arrange a visit soon. I want Michael to stay a long time and really get to know the Islands." He patted my shoulder and then walked away leaving me speechless. I was furious with Michael for agreeing to go without me and for not even bothering to talk it over with me first. I was also furious with his grandfather.

It looked very much as if he thought I could be written off without even being offered a bribe - not that I want one of course. I couldn't see Michael anywhere inside, so I tried looking for him in the garden. He was talking to his grandmother and as I approached, I heard her say, "It isn't that I don't want you to come and stay with us Michael, I do. I can't think of anything I'd like better, but why don't you wait until Kathryn can travel with you?" She saw me approaching and said, "I'm sure Kathryn will agree with me that you should wait." Deep down that is what I wanted, but I could see the little boy stubborn look creeping over his face. "I do and I don't," I said. "I really want to visit you Ria, but I'll travel out on my own in a few weeks and Michael can spend time alone with you both first." Michael's face lit up and he kissed me on the cheek before rushing off to tell his grandfather that I didn't mind. Ria and I looked at one another. "In one way that was a wise move for such a young person," she said and taking my arm she guided me along one of the garden paths. "Take my advice, however, and don't leave it too long before you arrange to take your leave." I told her that I could probably get away in about a fortnight, and she nodded. "Try not to worry about Michael," she said. "I'll keep an eye on him for you and I'll look forward to seeing you soon." She made to go back into the marquee but then turned and said something strange. "Of course," she said, "The outcome in the end rests with Michael and what he really wants. I can only do so much."

I hadn't been worried before, just annoyed that Michael was going to the islands without me, but now my mind was imagining all sorts of scenarios. I wondered if I should go back and find Michael and tell him that I didn't want him to go without me, but I was frightened, because I don't know if he would have taken any notice.

That's how things stand at the moment. I'm returning to Bath alone and Michael flies off to the Islands. I'm finishing this letter before I get into bed. I'm leaving straight after breakfast tomorrow. Michael is obviously staying here until Tuesday. I don't know what Justin and Leah are doing, but they're not going back to Bath, so

James told me that there's no need for me to catch a train. I can go back to Bath with them. I was glad of that because I don't know how regular the Sunday trains are. I'll phone you tomorrow evening from my flat.

Love,
Kathryn
xxxxx

Chapter 11

Ria was happy. The weekend was going much better than she'd anticipated. So far there had been no trouble between her husband and two sons. She watched Ilona and Richard as they danced to the strains of the anniversary waltz. They seemed at last to have found happiness together after twenty-five years. She sighed contentedly, but still felt a little sad knowing that Tuesday would soon come and the family would once again be parted. This time, however, it wouldn't be for long. When Justin had phoned her with the news that Richard had accepted the post of Governor General, she was frightened that Ilona would chose to stay in England, but to Ria's amazement and delight she hadn't. At long last her daughter was coming home, albeit to live initially on another island, but there wouldn't be thousands of miles between them, only a small stretch of sea.

She sat quietly watching as more dancers joined Ilona and Richard. It was a very pleasant evening and although the sun had gone down the heat of the day still lingered. She saw Justin approaching and he beckoned her to join him on the dance floor.

"Come on mother, shake a leg," he said.

Ria groaned. "That is definitely not the correct way to ask a lady to dance, but I'll accept, that is if my arthritis will let me." She took his arm and allowed herself to be led onto the dance floor.

"You should be dancing with Leah and not your mother," she remonstrated.

His face tightened. "I don't think so," he said. "We've definitely reached the end of the road." He stopped dancing suddenly. "Come out into the garden, we can't talk privately here." He took her elbow and guided her out of the marquee. They sat on the same seat where Justin had talked to his sister a couple of days earlier. Although he had said he wanted to talk, he remained silent for a few minutes, as though deciding what to say. Ria wondered if he wanted to tell her about his quarrel with Leah. She decided to make it easier for him.

"I know you had a vasectomy and I know you never told Leah. That was a cruel thing to do. Every month she kept hoping that she would be pregnant. Many a time she came crying to me, but I never told her."

"How did you know? Oh never mind, don't tell me. Sometimes I think you know more than father does. Between the two of you, I doubt if I have a secret left. The fact is I made a conscious decision many years ago not to have children."

"Why?"

"I had my reasons."

"If that is all you brought me out here to say, I might as well return to the marquee." Ria made as if to get up off the seat, but Luke restrained her.

"I'm not finding this easy. I want you to think well of me, and I have treated my wife badly, but it has been six of one and half a dozen of the other. I intend to ask Leah for a divorce, and when I do, God only knows what lies she'll come out with, so I want you to hear the story from me first. It started after Ilona and Morgan were married secretly in Leil by Luke. Leah as you know purported to be Ilona's best friend at the time so she was one of the witnesses, although even then there was a trace of the green eyed monster in the relationship. Everything would have been fine if Morgan hadn't been killed in that motoring accident. Father would have had to reconcile himself to the marriage eventually. Ilona and Morgan could have stayed with Hallam on Zerrebar and father couldn't have touched them," Justin paused. "Did you know that Hallam accused father of having a hand in Morgan's death? Do you think he had anything to do with it?"

Ria shook her head. "He had nothing to do with it, I can assure you. Strange as it may seem, he didn't know about the wedding. If he had, do you think he would have kept silent? Hallam would have heard his roar of anger in Zerrebar."

Ria shivered. After the stuffiness of the marquee, it felt chilly sitting out in the garden.

Justin removed his jacket and draped it around his mother's shoulders. "I shouldn't have dragged you out here. There isn't much to tell you really. Morgan was dead and Ilona found out she was pregnant. Luke, Ilona and myself fell to pieces. We didn't know what to do and you took over. Remember?"

Ria remembered only too well. How to handle a distraught, pregnant daughter who wanted to tell her father the truth about her marriage to Morgan Draymer. She'd managed to calm Ilona down long enough to point out that without Hallam Draymer's support, her father would destroy the marriage records and insist on her having an abortion. Ilona had eventually agreed that Ria should ask Hallam for help, and between them they'd devised a plan. Ilona was to start a quarrel with her father and then run away to Zerrebar. In her emotional, grief stricken state it wasn't necessary to stage-manage a quarrel, one was inevitable. The difficult part was impressing on Ilona the necessity of keeping a check on what she actually said to her father. The morning after the quarrel, a maid had reported that Ilona's bed hadn't been slept in and that there was a note on the pillow. Drystan had read the note in silence, and then flung it across the breakfast table for Ria to read. Ria was slightly surprised that there wasn't more of a reaction. He'd finished his breakfast in silence and as he was leaving the room, he turned to his wife and said. "She'll come running back before long with her tail between her legs, you'll see. I'm not going to do anything, but I want you to check that she reaches there safely."

Drystan's reaction to the news baffled Ria, but once she'd talked with Ilona and told her husband that his daughter was safe and well and staying with Hallam, he nodded.

"Hallam and I have been at loggerheads since we were boys, but I feel for him, losing his only son. Ilona too must have time to mourn and they can help each other."

Ria looked at her husband in amazement. He did have a heart

after all. It lay beating somewhere beneath layers of pride and ambition, but he destroyed this notion by his next remark.

"When she comes back," he said, a calculating look on his face that she knew so well, "She'll have forgotten about Morgan Draymer, and then one day when Hallam dies, I intend to see that James becomes Vaga."

Ria knew she had to be careful that her phone calls to Hallam weren't monitored. Fortunately she was the one person Drystan trusted, and as she still loved him, she didn't want to destroy that trust, nor did she want to find out if he would forgive her. She doubted if he would. The first phone call to Hallam she'd made when Drystan was within earshot, but thereafter she'd used a telephone kiosk when she was in Mordeen. If anyone had seen her that too would have looked decidedly peculiar so she had to be forever on her guard. Hallam had had Ilona moved to the stronghold of Envetta. During certain months of the year and even sometimes in summer, the interior of that island was a dreary damp world and for company Hallam arranged for Leah to come back from New York to stay with Ilona, for which she'd been well rewarded.

"Leah blackmailed me into marrying her," Justin continued. "Oh, I could have said no, but I thought Ilona had gone through enough, and I knew that if father found out how you'd betrayed him, he would never have forgiven you, so I agreed. At the time, I was a little in love with Leah, she was very attractive, and I thought we could make it work, but she changed. Her jealousy of Ilona grew worse over the years, and when Ilona married Richard with father's blessing, instead of bringing them closer as sisters-in-law, it was as if Leah hated her. Thank God Leah thought the baby was stillborn."

Ria was getting impatient. "Why did you bring me out here to tell me things I already know."

"She found out a few days ago that I'd had a vasectomy without telling her and that I'd done it deliberately to prevent her ever having a child."

The few clouds that had obscured the moon drifted away, and

moonlight shone on her son's troubled face.

Ria put her hand over his. "I'm sorry she's found out. I suppose you were quarrelling as usual."

Justin nodded.

"What I've never understood is why you did it. Perhaps if you and Leah had had a family things would have been better between the two of you."

"It wouldn't have made any difference."

Ria took Justin's coat off her shoulders and handed it back to her son. She looked him straight in the eyes and it was Justin who averted his gaze first. Then clearly she saw that she had been right earlier on. The whole thing fitted, Vonryn Santella was Ilona's son. A rush of emotion flooded through her. She had often wondered about the whereabouts of her other grandson. Fate had been unkind to her, two grandsons that she'd never seen growing up, but now in the space of a weekend she'd met them both.

"Why did you and Luke vote for Vonryn Santella?" she asked casually.

"He's the best man to lead this country forward."

"I agree with you there, but you're lying to me. I could always tell when you were lying; the look on your face always gave you away. You knew and probably Luke knew that Vonryn Santella is my grandson. Ilona doesn't realise it yet, but she has noticed the likeness to Morgan and is now convinced that Vonryn is Morgan and Barbara's son."

Justin shook his head. His mother never ceased to amaze him.

"How did you work it out?" he asked incredulously.

"Quite easily now I have more facts. Leah has informed your father that Vincent Santella couldn't be Vonryn's father and after meeting Vonryn, the colour of his eyes and the family likeness is such that he is definitely Morgan's son. He is my grandson, isn't he?"

Justin's silence was all the confirmation Ria needed. She turned and walked back into the marquee leaving a stunned Justin sitting alone with his thoughts.

Returning to her table, she noticed with relief that her gin and tonic hadn't been removed. Her hands were trembling as she raised the glass to her lips. How could Justin have been so stupid as to antagonise Leah? Drystan would undoubtedly tell Vonryn that Vincent Santella wasn't his father. She thought quickly. Was it too late to prevent Drystan telling Vonryn and if not was there anything she could do? Although she was seething inwardly, her mind was cool and calculating. She doubted if she could stop Drystan. It might even now be too late as there was no sign of Vonryn or her husband and hadn't been for quite some time.

Luke was dancing with his sister, when he noticed that his mother looked unwell. Ilona and he left the dance floor and persuaded Ria to leave the marquee and return to the house. Despite her protests that she was fine, five minutes later she found herself ensconced in a comfortable armchair, and Luke propping numerous cushions around her.

"No more cushions Luke, please," she pleaded. "There soon won't be room for me in the chair."

"I'm going to make you a cup of tea," Ilona announced and departed to the kitchen.

Ria watched as her daughter closed the door and then turned to Luke.

"I know Vonryn is Ilona and Morgan's son," she said abruptly. There wasn't time to lead into the subject gradually.

Luke gasped. "Justin had no right to tell you."

Ria could feel the anger rising within her. "No right! Between you all, I've been deprived of two grandsons, but that's the least of my worries. About ten minutes ago, I told Justin that Leah has proof that Vincent Santella isn't Vonryn's father."

"I know, Ilona has already told me. Even at a silver wedding party, this family can't escape from intrigue. Ilona thinks that Morgan was having an affair with Barbara before and just after their marriage."

"Never," Ria said emphatically. "We know the truth and once Ilona thinks rationally about this, so will she. That young man was too much in love with Ilona to do that. It was obvious to everyone who saw them together that his feelings were genuine. It must be old age," Ria mused. "I should have made the connection when you and Justin voted for Vonryn. I'm only surprised that Drystan hasn't, though if Leah thinks the baby died, there would be no reason for her to mention the marriage or the baby. I suppose your father thinks that you're both doing it, as always, to go against him at every opportunity." Ria paused waiting to see if Luke had anything to add to her speculations, but when he didn't answer, she continued.

"Why didn't you marry Ruth Graham? It was obvious that you loved her."

Her son looked startled. "That's ancient history," he said. "Anyway, how did you know about her? You never visited Leil or met her and I never told you anything when I came home."

Ria smiled enigmatically. "It's not only your father who has his spies."

"It wouldn't have been fair to marry her. I would have stood in the way of her career living in Leil."

"You and Justin are complete idiots. You've wasted your lives. Justin letting himself be blackmailed by Leah for nothing. With Morgan dead the marriage didn't matter anymore and Leah believed the baby was dead so the hold over Justin was minimal." She stopped speaking for a moment and thought. She could understand why Justin had let himself be blackmailed for her sake, but why had Luke stayed in Leil and never married Ruth, then the truth dawned. "I see it all now," she said slowly. "You both sacrificed the chance to have children and loving marriages to ensure that the Islands would be united eventually under one man. You were taking a very long-term view, one that might never have come off. Was it worth it?"

Luke smiled. "Oh yes. It was definitely worth it. Don't you see mother, we knew independence would come one day and our sacrifice was so small compared with a peaceful transition to life under one Vaga. Also my continuance as a priest at Leil made sure that no other man would ever see Ilona and Morgan's entry of marriage. I couldn't erase the record in my church, but there's no copy in the Records Office, and I think I've stayed long enough to make it unlikely that people will notice it, not unless they are actually looking for such an entry."

"You are all fools and I don't mean just you and Justin, I include Hallam in that statement. Your father has proof that Vincent Santella isn't Vonryn's father. Leah provided him with that bombshell and Ilona believes Vonryn is Barbara's son by Morgan. Already it is a complete shambles and this is before independence."

"Ilona has the Birth and Marriage Certificates well hidden. I'm sure that once Barbara and Vincent Santella tell the truth father won't mind, at least once he recovers from the shock; Vonryn is his grandson for heaven's sake."

Ria sighed. "There are two things you haven't considered, the first is that your father now wants Michael to be Vaga, which would be a huge mistake. I'm sure eventually even your father, stubborn as he is, would realise this and with all the proof you have he would accept Vonryn as his grandson and I truly believe that under Vonryn the populace of the British Islands would agree to join with the remaining islands."

"What did I tell you," Luke interrupted. "Problem solved."

Ria continued as if Luke had never spoken. "The second thing you haven't considered is the human factor."

Luke looked puzzled and both Ria and he failed to notice that Ilona had been standing in the doorway for some time listening to their conversation. Her hands were shaking and it seemed as if she were about to burst into tears. Luke hurried to her side taking the tray away from her and placing it on a small table. He poured three cups of tea and handed a cup each to his mother and Ilona, who was now seated on a sofa opposite. Her face was ashen.

It was obvious that Ilona had heard them and Luke felt it was time for the truth to be finally told, so he carried on his conversation with his mother.

"You were saying mother, something about the human factor. I don't understand."

Ria hesitated for a moment, but realising Ilona wouldn't be satisfied now with anything less than complete honesty, resumed speaking. "You should know about the human factor. Shame on you Luke and you a priest." Ria remonstrated. "At the moment Vonryn is to be the next Vaga. This was decided by a majority verdict of the Islands' Council. He believes that he is a Draymer by virtue of Vincent Santella's distant relationship to Hallam. Your father is going to destroy that young man by telling him that the man who raised him isn't his father, and that the woman he believes is his mother is an adulteress. Those facts alone are bad enough without telling him that Barbara isn't his mother."

"Hallam always intended he should be told one day," Luke said.

"Then he should have told him when he was a small child and made a story of it, not this way."

"He must never be told," Ilona spoke for the first time since re-entering the room. Her voice was unnaturally shrill. "When Hallam told me he was alive, I was glad. Hallam promised me that my son would be placed with kind people and have a happy and contented childhood with a good start in life and I won't have this destroyed." Her face softened. "I'm glad I know the truth and that Morgan didn't continue his affair with Barbara."

Her mother snorted. "How you ever believed that I'll never know." She looked across at her daughter's stricken face. "It was obvious that Morgan was besotted with you." Ria reached out for her cup and drank the warm tea gratefully. "I'm getting too old for all these intrigues. All I ever wanted was a quiet family life. You two had better return to the party. People will be wondering why you've disappeared. If they ask about me, say the heat was too much for me in the marquee, but that I'm feeling fine now. I don't want anyone else coming fussing around."

"We'd rather stay here with you," Luke argued.

"Don't be silly. I wasn't ill or anything, just shocked. Anyway, I need time to think. I'm just going to sit here for a while longer, drink my tea, maybe have another cup, and relax. I'll return to the party soon."

"If you're sure," Ilona looked more composed now and she bent to kiss her mother. "We'll leave by the French window."

Ria felt a cold draught of air as Luke and Ilona opened the

window and stepped out into the night. After they'd gone, Ria finished drinking her tea, and putting the cup down walked across to the window. She looked out into the semi darkness of a summer night, and gazing upwards wondered at the myriads of stars sparkling in the sky. They were light years away and made troubles on earth seem trivial in comparison with the vastness of space. She turned as she heard the door opening. It was her husband. He hurried over to her and there was a concerned look on his craggy features.

"I wondered where you'd got to and I was just starting to look, when I met Luke and Ilona. They told me where you were. Ilona said she'd made you a cup of tea. Are you ill?"

"No," she replied, "I'm not ill. It was the heat and noise in the marquee got to me."

"That's all right then," Drystan seemed relieved. Ria smiled inwardly. She knew Drystan loved her, but she also knew that now he was sure there was nothing ailing her, he could return to his planning and scheming.

She turned once more and looked at the night sky. "Do you remember when the children were small and the fun we had?" She asked.

He looked bewildered. Women were funny creatures, he thought.

"Of course I remember. They were good times."

"Remember as they grew older and started to think for themselves how it all started to go wrong." He was standing close by her side, and she clutched at his sleeve. "We've only just found Michael. Please don't make the same mistake with him."

"I don't know what you mean. I only ever wanted what was best for them."

Best for you, Ria thought. Tonight she didn't want to argue, but she had to try. "Of course you know what I mean," she replied sharply. "You're going to try and manipulate him and Vonryn into doing things the way you want."

Hallam smiled at her and the blood in her veins seemed to turn to ice. She knew it was too late. "I've already had a long chat with Vonryn and I'm sure we understand one another." Drystan peered through the window. "I think that's Michael over there. I'm going out to try and persuade him to return to Innisver with us next Tuesday instead of waiting."

"And Kathryn?" Ria questioned.

"Of course Kathryn must visit us," he said as he stepped through the French windows onto the terrace. "That is when she can get time off from work."

So that is his game, Ria thought. No obvious opposition towards Kathryn, that would only antagonise Michael. However, sweet reason was going to be a good deal harder to deal with than outright hostility. If she wasn't careful, she would have Michael thinking of her as the enemy. For a few seconds she watched her husband and grandson chatting. She noticed with wry amusement that Drystan was doing most of the talking. It was too dark to see the expression on Michael's face, but from their body language, it seemed as if everything was going Drystan's way. Turning from the window, she wondered idly if the tea in the pot was still warm. She poured herself another cup, and grimaced as she sipped the now lukewarm liquid, but decided that it was just about drinkable. Flinging a few of the cushions off the chair, she sat down and leant back. She wondered what, if anything, she could do. I'll have to play it by instinct, she decided. I'll finish my tea and then I'll have a chat with Michael and then Kathryn. Having arrived at this plan of action, she was just starting to relax when she heard the sound of the door being opened. This is getting ridiculous, she thought. It's busier here than in the main square in Mordeen. Who could it be this time?

"I'm so sorry Ria L'Innisver. I didn't mean to disturb you. I was looking for a quiet place to be on my own for a while."

Ria turned to face the intruder, but she already knew that it was Vonryn. No other man at the party would address her in such a way. Most of Ilona's guests would have addressed her as Mrs Pendenny.

Vonryn made as if to leave.

"Don't go Vonryn, stay a few minutes and chat, and please

drop the L'Innisver and call me Ria. Two escapees should never stand on ceremony with one another."

"As you wish," he said abruptly in a cold voice. He didn't sit down, but paced restlessly.

"I suppose you know why I need a place to be quiet and to think. I expect the Larn tells you everything."

Ria evinced a surprise she didn't feel. She wasn't lying when she replied that Drystan hadn't told her anything, he hadn't. She wouldn't have known anything if she hadn't snooped in her husband's briefcase. She hoped fervently that her acting would be up to scratch.

"I don't know what you mean. Drystan tells me very little. Has he upset you in any way?" She enquired artlessly.

He laughed bitterly. "That is the understatement of the century." He sat down suddenly on the sofa, but remained on the edge, as though poised to flee at any moment. "Your husband," he emphasised the word husband, "Calmly informed me tonight that he had irrefutable evidence that Vincent Santella isn't my father. He then went on to ask when I'd be letting the Islands' Council know that I was ineligible now to become Vaga."

Ria felt desperately sorry for Vonryn and angry with Drystan for doing this to their grandson. "What did you say to him?" she asked.

"I amazed myself. I stayed quite cool, although inwardly I was seething. I told him that I wanted to speak to my parents first, and more especially, the Vaga. Once I knew the truth, I would then take appropriate action. I also said that I felt I was the best person to unite the islands, and that why should an accident of birth be the main criteria to be Vaga."

Ria bit her lip to stop herself laughing. "Drystan must have loved that. I agree with you about the hereditary bit. I mightn't have agreed with you a few years ago, but now with independence looming, I think that perhaps the Vaga should be like a President and voted for by the people. It will probably come some day." She paused. "Have you thought that my husband might be lying?"

"Oh I thought of it, but I know he's not lying. He wouldn't

make such a statement without having proof. What would be the point?"

Ria nodded. "You're probably right, but I beg you don't do anything in haste. You are the right man for the Islands and you will make an excellent Vaga."

"Would have made an excellent Vaga. I'm positive the Islands would have accepted me, and the transition to a united country would have been peaceful. I hope that doesn't sound as though I'm bragging."

Ria was quiet for a moment. She wanted to choose her words carefully. "Listen to me Vonryn. This is the 20th century, nearly the 21st. I know I shouldn't be saying this, especially as I married into the Islands' second family, but the fact that you may not have Draymer blood coursing through your veins shouldn't matter. I'm sure Hallam has trained you well. My advice is don't give in without a fight."

"That's heresy coming from you," he said. Ria was pleased to see that she had managed to get a weak smile from Vonryn.

"I'll do as I said. I'll go home and discuss it with my parents and Hallam and we'll see. At the moment though, I don't much care what happens back home. Going round and round in my head is the fact that the man I've called father all these years isn't. I don't know if I want to find out who my biological father is, but what I've got to find out is why they lied to me all these years."

He got up from the sofa and once again started pacing back and fore.

"Stop that for heaven's sake," Ria commanded. "It won't do you any good and will only wear out the carpet, leaving Ilona and Richard to foot the bill for a new one when their tenancy ends."

Vonryn laughed out loud. "Do you know, I'm glad I wandered in here. I was feeling nearly suicidal when I came in, but you've made me feel much better."

Ria also stood up. "Good, I'm glad of that. Now will you escort me back to the party, or would you rather I left you here on your own to mope."

Vonryn opened the French windows and then offered her his arm. "I'd be delighted," he said.

As they walked across the lawn, the grass soft and springy beneath their tread, Ria noticed Michael standing alone by the entrance to the marquee. She smiled at Vonryn. "I can see my grandson over there and I want to have a chat with him. You go and find Nadia and try to enjoy the remainder of your stay here. I know it won't be easy, but do try."

He inclined his head and taking her hand he raised it to his lips. "I'll do my best to follow your advice."

She started to make her way over to Michael. I ought to start a counselling service, she thought, and if Drystan ever finds out the part I played in everything, I'll be my first client. My marriage and my whole way of life will be over and I'm much too old to start again.

Chapter 12

Vonryn felt a sense of relief that the weekend was finally over. Sunday had seemed endless trying to smile and make small talk. All he wanted was to return home and confront his parents, or the people he'd always taken for granted were his parents. He'd managed to avoid Drystan Pendenny during the day, with the exception of meal times, and he made sure that for the drive to Heathrow airport on the Monday, he was in the second car with Nadia and Luke. As the plane taxied along the runway preparatory to take off, he tried to make sense of what he'd been told. It was a night flight and most of the passengers would be only too glad to doze. As the plane levelled out, he opened his eyes and smiled at Nadia, kissing her lightly on the forehead.

"I think I'll try and sleep for a while," he said. "I'm tired, it's been a long day after a hectic weekend."

Nadia returned the smile, but she was concerned. There was something wrong, something had happened over this short weekend that she couldn't put her finger on. Everyone, including Drystan, had been polite to Vonryn, and up until the party he had been his usual self, relaxed and happy in company, and to all intents and purposes thoroughly enjoying himself.

The cabin crew came around, handing out pillows and supplying hot drinks to those who wanted them. They both refused drinks, but accepted pillows. Casting a surreptitious sidelong glance at her fiancé, she saw that his eyes were shut, not because he wanted to sleep, she was sure of that. Her instincts told her that it was best not to probe, so resting her head on the pillow; she shut her eyes and pretended to sleep as well. She hoped that during the week they planned to stay with Ruth, she'd be able to find out what was wrong.

The aeroplane made its steady way through the darkness, and only the sound of the engines and a few snores pervaded the cabin. The sound of Nadia's steady breathing told Vonryn that she had eventually fallen asleep. He opened his eyes and glanced down fondly at his fiancée. He resisted the desire to stroke her long black hair, but gently pushed back a strand that had escaped and fallen over her face.

Alone with his thoughts, the flight seemed interminable. He was under no illusion that if his parentage was in doubt, their marriage would not be allowed, no matter how much in love they were. They could of course give everything up and leave the islands. Nadia was no socialite, but she had always enjoyed and taken for granted a privileged lifestyle. He imagined them several years on, living in exile in reduced financial circumstances. They'd need a very strong love to overcome that and how long would it be before one or the other started apportioning blame. He was glad when the cabin crew came around with breakfast, knowing that once the meal was over it wouldn't be long before the plane started its descent prior to landing at St. Elizabeth airport.

"I wish you could spend more than a week at Ruth's instead of rushing back to Zerrebar," Nadia said. "Sometimes I wonder if you really want to be with me, it is as if you're happier when we're apart. It doesn't have to be like this. Why don't we just tell everyone that we're bringing the wedding forward?"

Vonryn squeezed her hand tightly. "Don't be silly Nadia, you know I want to be with you, but we're not an every day average couple. We both have responsibilities and as you know preparations are underway for a spring wedding next year." He took a deep breath. "I don't know quite how to say this, but I'm going to have to alter our plans. You'll have to apologise to Ruth for me, but as soon as I get off this plane, I'm boarding the next available one for Quan Tomay. Please don't ask me why. I have a very good reason which I will tell you as soon as I'm able."

Nadia gave Vonryn a long hard look, started to say something, but then changed her mind. She patted his hand comfortingly. She was right there was something definitely wrong.

As they'd been flying west, it was still nighttime when they landed at St. Elizabeth airport. The plane taxied along the runway, and the passengers waited patiently whilst arrangements were made so that they were able to disembark straight into the terminal building. Vonryn walked swiftly towards passport control. This was only a formality, as customs had been notified that the Larn of Innisver and a party of friends and relatives were on board. Although Lorentia was still technically under British control, with independence looming, it was in everyone's interests to treat such a powerful man as Drystan Pendenny with respect. They knew he was the type of man who would remember the smallest insult and repay it in full measure. Nadia had to quicken her step to keep up with Vonryn and her resolve not to say anything to him collapsed. "I wish you'd tell me what's worrying you."

Vonryn stopped suddenly and Nadia nearly collided with him. She stumbled and he managed to catch her before she fell. "I promise you that once I know the truth I'll tell you." Over Nadia's shoulder he saw Drystan and the others approaching. There was a self-satisfied smile on Drystan's face and Vonryn turned away. How he disliked that man. He would have loved to punch that smile off his face, but he knew he never would.

The burst of camera flashlights hit them as they turned the corner from passport control. This was most unusual as normally the Pendenny family went travelling with the minimum of attention. Ria raised her hand to shield her eyes from the glare, and both Michael and Luke hurried to her side, taking one arm each to steady her. The presence of journalists and photographers was so unexpected that the three bodyguards who had been with them in the Isle of Wight were completely taken by surprise. They were trying desperately to keep the journalists and photographers at bay, but without much success. One guard was on his mobile phone trying to get help from the airport police. Drystan for all his seventy odd years was still a match for them, however. Vonryn, though shaken at some of the questions being fired at himself, was still able to admire the coolness of the old man who barked authoritatively at the journalists, and made no attempt to push past them or shield his eyes from the glare.

"Our party is very tired after our long journey. If you will kindly allow my wife, Miss Laridon and my grandson to pass, I will remain with my son and Vonryn Santella to answer whatever questions you may have to ask."

The journalists reluctantly cleared a pathway and Ria, leaning heavily on Michael's arm, walked slowly through the terminal. Before she went through the door she turned and looked at her husband and Vonryn, a worried look clouded her features.

Questions were being fired from all directions at both Drystan and Vonryn, but the one question they all wanted answered was directed at Vonryn.

"Is it true that you were adopted?"

Nadia who hadn't left the terminal with Ria and Michael was still within earshot of the journalists and she managed to see the stricken expression on Vonryn's face as a reporter pushed a microphone in his face. He made no effort to answer the question and Nadia longed to rush to him and put her arms about him, but knew that that was the last thing he would have wanted.

Reluctantly she turned to leave the building. She knew now what was troubling him, but she couldn't make sense of what she'd heard. No wonder Vonryn had been in such a strange mood.

"Why have you brought your grandson back with you from the UK?"

This question was addressed to Drystan, but he was given no chance to answer before other journalists were firing more questions.

"Is your son-in-law to be the next Governor General?"

"Can Vonryn be the next Vaga if he's adopted and will the Islands' Council have to meet again?"

Drystan smiled ironically. He was sure that Leah was at the bottom of this. He should have realised that a troublemaker such as she, was bound to approach the media. He hadn't intended to go public as soon as this, but he couldn't undo what had already been done. He sighed. It was no good evading the Press, that would only make them more determined. He was used to thinking quickly and now he had to turn an awkward situation to his advantage. He knew he could do it. He raised a hand and the reporters fell silent.

"I'm too tired to answer any of your questions, but I will make a statement and in it try to answer the questions you've fired at me. I'll start with the easiest one first. Yes, my son-in-law, Richard Vandrell, is to be your next Governor General. The appointment had nothing to do with me, but in my eyes and in the eyes of the British Government he will be an excellent Governor General. The fact that he is also my son-in-law is irrelevant." He scanned the faces of the journalists and photographers. Although a motley bunch, they were all fairly young. "Looking at your faces, I would say that you're all too young to remember when Richard Vandrell's father was Governor General here, but he was well loved and respected. I'm sure you must have done your homework and found that out for yourselves. The only other question I can answer positively is about my grandson, Michael. There is nothing sinister in me bringing him back with me. He has lived all his life away from the Islands and he felt it was time to find out where his roots are. Also as you said, his father is to be Governor General so he will be making this his home until independence, and who knows, after that he may decide to stay permanently. I'll pass you over to Vonryn Santella and he can answer the other question you have asked."

They all looked at Vonryn and waited expectantly to hear what he had to say.

"I really don't know what to say to you today. I learnt a couple of days ago that there was a rumour going around that I had been adopted at birth."

"Did you telephone your parents and ask them?" a young reporter enquired.

Vonryn shook his head. He was amazed at his own coolness. It was as if it was a different person answering the questions and that his real self was an onlooker watching as events unfolded. "Although I was devastated at this rumour, I felt it wasn't something that should be discussed on the telephone. These last few days have been extremely difficult for me and all I want at the moment is to go home and find out the truth for myself.

Whatever the outcome, I have no doubt that the press will be informed in due course. As to whether I can still be Vaga if I was adopted; I don't know. Your question about another meeting of the Islands' Council is one that I'm unable to answer. I should imagine, however, that if I am ineligible then there will have to be another meeting."

At this stage, Luke moved forward and indicated to the guards and other airport security staff who had by this time arrived on the scene that the informal interview was over.

The journalists were not completely satisfied, but they sensed that they now knew as much about everything as the people they'd questioned, and half-heartedly cleared a pathway through their ranks.

Vonryn walked with the others to the exit of the terminal building. He would try and make himself inconspicuous until the reporters left, then he could go back inside and enquire about the next flight to Christenbech. Once outside, Drystan said a curt goodbye to Vonryn, who just nodded his head in reply and they went their separate ways. It seemed as if Luke were about to go after Vonryn, but his mother who was waiting with Michael in their limousine called out to Luke that she wanted him to travel with her. Vonryn smiled to himself. He knew Drystan wouldn't be happy with that, and would find it hard to forgive his sons for voting against him. Undoubtedly a truce had been called that weekend for Ilona's sake.

It was just beginning to get light and a faint pink glow was starting to show on the horizon. Vonryn knew from experience that soon the coolness of the early morning would be replaced with the heat of a summer's day and he longed for a quick shower, a cup of black coffee, and eight hours sleep without the noise of engines throbbing in his eardrums. Another large limousine drew up. Vonryn was so engrossed in his own thoughts that he didn't hear it pull up. He wasn't expecting to be met as the plan had been for him and Nadia to stay the week with Ruth Graham in her residence. Not seeing any sign of Nadia when he'd left the terminal, he'd presumed that she'd left without him. Already the rats were deserting the ship, he thought. She must have heard those reporters ask him if he was adopted. He looked down at the car with some annoyance. He definitely didn't know the chauffeur who was driving, but then he saw that Nadia was sitting in the rear of the car. The chauffeur made to get out of the car to open the door for him, but he motioned to him to stay where he was. Nadia opened the window. "Get in Vonryn," she said. "You know we'd planned to spend a week with Ruth and as arranged she's sent her car to meet us. It wouldn't hurt for you to spend at least one day with us, especially now we know what was worrying you."

"No," he said. "I'll see Ruth again, but I want to get straight home to meet my parents. I'll go and find out what time the next flight is to Christenbech and then I'll be on my way. You can arrange to have my luggage sent on if you will."

"I wish you'd change your mind," another female voice said from the depths of the car.

Vonryn peered inside and saw another older woman sitting beside Nadia. He hadn't realised that there was another passenger in the car.

"Please reconsider Vonryn," she pleaded. "A shower and a shave and then a few hours rest won't make all that much difference to the questions that are going round and round in your head. Anyway, the Vaga's Personal Secretary telephoned me yesterday evening to say that the Vaga's yacht will be docking here this afternoon at about two pm. As you might expect these rumours have reached him and he is anxious to speak to you. Your parents and the Vaga will be on board and you'll have all the privacy you require to discuss this chain of events. I've arranged for a hire car to deliver you to the docks precisely at that hour. What do you say?"

Vonryn suddenly felt exhausted and realising that there would be nothing to gain in insisting on flying to Christenbech immediately as the yacht would already be on its way to St. Elizabeth, he opened the car door and got inside. Almost at once the chauffeur pulled away and within ten minutes they were inside Ruth's bungalow. Her housekeeper greeted them and, set out on the verandah table, were jugs of iced coffee and freshly squeezed fruit juice. In the centre of the table was a large glass bowl filled with fresh fruit. The sun was now well over the horizon and already there were small boats putting out to sea. Nadia and Vonryn sipped the iced coffee gratefully, but declined anything to eat. Whilst Nadia went to have a shower, Ruth poured Vonryn another drink and they sat quietly for a few minutes both deep in their own thoughts. It was Vonryn who first broke the silence.

"I wasn't expecting that reception of journalists and photographers at the airport," he said. "How did they find out?"

"I really don't know," Ruth replied. "A few years ago anything that happened on the other islands wasn't newsworthy, but of course now that independence is near, whatever happens to either the Vaga or the Pendenny family is reported. I'm not giving away any secrets when I tell you that the government has decided to hold a referendum to allow the people to decide if they want to join with the other Tomayon Islands or stay separate from them."

"Any idea what the general feeling is?"

Ruth thought for a few seconds before replying.

"I think the majority of the people are undecided. The islands have co-existed fairly peacefully for many years under the present arrangement. Since the meeting of the Islands' Council, which I attended as a guest observer, I've given this matter a lot of thought. Gregory Rollins, the last Governor General, opened my eyes to the fact that there could be bloodshed if the transition isn't handled sensitively. I and other members of our government have talked with various members of the governments of Innisver and Quan Tomay and the majority view was that with both the Vaga and the Larn of Innisver in agreement over you becoming the next ruler, it would seem as if the Islands were starting anew with a young Vaga at the helm. Tentative talks have already started between the respective governments."

Although Vonryn was desperately tired, he was interested.

"What changes do you envisage in the way the Islands would be governed?" he asked.

"None for the foreseeable future. Each would keep its own members of parliament, and its own laws, but you would be the figurehead that would cement them together and in the future hopefully all the laws and tax raising could be made uniform. I can't, however, see any island wishing to give up its seat of government. The only way forward perhaps would be to have a federal parliament, but I'm sure there'll be arguments as to where this should be based."

"That's an interesting theory and one which I'm sure could work in the future. As to a site for a new federal parliament, I would have thought Kalima would be the ideal site, as although it was leased by the British to the Laridon family, it has always been seen as neutral territory."

"It's a good idea of using Kalima and in an ideal world everything would go smoothly, but apart from dozens of minor problems, we do have one rather major problem."

Vonryn interrupted her, a rueful expression on his face. "I know, the question of my birth and was I adopted? Ria Pendenny said to me that my birth shouldn't make any difference as I've been trained for this since the day I was born."

"I agree with her," Ruth replied. "We can't, however, have two systems. Since I attended the Islands' Council meeting, I've read up on the islands' history, of which I'm ashamed to say I was quite ignorant. As it stands, the position of Vaga is a hereditary one down through the Draymer or Pendenny bloodlines. The last thing we need at the moment is a dispute as to who should inherit the title. The people on the British islands might question the need for a Vaga and feel they would prefer a President. We're sailing dangerous uncharted waters here and the sooner this question of your adoption is sorted out the better." She paused momentarily.

"I feel there's something I'm missing, but can't put a finger on it." She wasn't talking to Vonryn anymore, but just thinking aloud. "What made Hallam Draymer agree to Barbara and Vincent Santella adopting a baby without the fact being made public. He must have agreed, they wouldn't have done it otherwise. When Morgan Draymer died, the next of kin was Vincent Santella and his descendants, with Drystan Pendenny arguing that his bloodline had prior claim. Personally I think Drystan may have had a point there, although it would need a genealogist to research the family trees. Even if you were legally adopted, Drystan could still argue that you aren't descended by blood from either the Draymer or Pendenny families. The rumour going around is that your natural parents are your mother and Morgan Draymer. Now that would make sense all round."

"I wish I had some answers. Hopefully by this time tomorrow, after I've seen my parents, I'll know the truth."

"We're all going around in circles at the moment trying to discover the truth, but whether the Vaga and your parents will tell you is another matter. Don't forget, if you ever want my help just let me know."

"Thank you Ruth, I'll remember that. I've got a gut feeling that I'll be knocking on your door sooner rather than later."

At that moment, Nadia came out on to the balcony, ensconced in a soft towelling robe. She came over to Vonryn and leaning down kissed him gently on the forehead.

He smiled up at her. "What was that for?"

"Just saying my goodbye to you now. I'm so tired, I've just got to get some sleep, and I may not surface before you leave."

Vonryn started to speak, but Nadia placed a finger on his lips. "Don't explain. Both Ruth and I understand you won't be staying here for a week as arranged. Neither of us expect it under the circumstances. You go and talk to your parents and we'll keep in touch over the phone. I'll either be here or at home in Kalima. If you want to come back to stay with Ruth at any time, I'm sure she'd only be too happy to have you."

Ruth nodded in agreement. "I've already told Vonryn that he is welcome here any time, and that if he wants a bolt hole to escape to, all he has to do is telephone me and even if I'm away, he can stay here. Maria, my housekeeper can look after him."

Ruth showed Nadia to her bedroom and once Vonryn had also showered and shaved, he too retired to sleep for a few hours, Ruth promising that she would wake him in plenty of time for a light meal before the car came to collect him.

Silence descended on the house and Ruth took advantage of this to look at her correspondence and dictate some replies. At twelve o'clock she paused for a light meal of salad and chicken breasts that Maria insisted she eat. She was just wondering whether it was time to awaken Vonryn, when he appeared on the verandah. He looked much more cheerful than he had earlier and accepted the offer of a chicken salad, eating it with relish.

"Coffee or tea?" Maria enquired.

Vonryn smiled at the housekeeper. "Tea please, Maria."

At precisely a quarter to two, the hired car pulled into the driveway. Ruth opened Nadia's bedroom door quietly, but she was sound asleep.

"Don't wake her. We've already said our goodbyes." Vonryn said. "Tell her I'll telephone as soon as I know something definite."

"I will," Ruth agreed. They walked out to the waiting car. "I'm glad we've finally met," she said, kissing him lightly on the cheek. "I was beginning to think we were destined never to. I hope the next time will be at your wedding."

The chauffeur opened the door of the car. Vonryn took Ruth's hand in his. "If things go wrong, be there for Nadia won't you?"

Ruth nodded her head.

"I know and you know that there may not be a wedding if I'm adopted," Vonryn continued. "I don't think Nadia has realised how much our lives may change because of that fact."

"She hasn't. I realised that when I met her at the airport."

Ruth waved until the car was out of sight, then she returned to the bungalow. She picked up a pair of binoculars on her way through the lounge and returned to the verandah. She watched as the maroon Daimler wound its way around the narrow winding streets down to the harbour. Occasionally she lost sight of the car, but finally it reached the harbour and she saw Vonryn alight and board a yacht that was flying the Draymer flag. Sighing she put the binoculars down and feeling in need of it, she poured herself a brandy, topping it up with tonic water.

~*~

136

It was no surprise for Vonryn that both his parents and the Vaga were on deck to greet him. His mother started to put her arms around him, but his father put out a hand to restrain her. Vonryn made no move to kiss her, which under normal circumstances he would have done. It was Hallam Draymer who spoke first.

"Let us go below," he said. Silently they followed him and settled themselves in the comfortable armchairs in the lounge. Without asking, Hallam poured out drinks for everyone. Barbara shook her head as Hallam handed her a brandy, but he still put it down on the table in front of her. Suddenly she leant forward and lifting the brandy glass drank its contents in one go. Vincent opened his mouth to remonstrate with his wife, but decided against it. Vonryn heard the engines roar into life and the yacht slowly made its way out into the Brenin Straits. He got up and watched as St. Elizabeth receded into the distance. He thought of Nadia still sleeping peacefully in Ruth's bungalow high on the green hillside that overlooked the harbour, and knew that for all their sakes he had to resolve this matter as soon as possible. He turned to face his parents and the Vaga.

"We can sit here in total silence until the yacht reaches Zerrebar or you can tell me the truth." He sat down again in an armchair and looked at them expectantly. "Well, what is it to be?"

"The mistake we made was not telling you the truth when you were a child." Hallam spoke first.

"I agree with you wholeheartedly, but what is the truth? It has to come out now that the Press knows. They'll carry on digging and digging and maybe only arrive at half truths and innuendoes, which will be much worse."

Hallam looked at Vincent and Barbara questioningly. They nodded their heads.

"Vincent and Barbara aren't your natural parents, but you were only a few days old when they had you. Apart from not telling you earlier, I really can't see why this fact has created such a bombshell. Under normal circumstances my son or grandson would have become Vaga on my death, but as I have neither, I have the right, under the Islands' law, to appoint a successor so long as he is related to me to the seventh degree. Although you were never legally adopted, you were raised by Vincent from under a month old until eighteen years of age, and according to Island law this means you are entitled to call yourself his son and therefore related to me and eligible to be Vaga."

Vonryn swallowed hard and thought for a few seconds. He looked across at the older man and then at his parents. The three of them sat quietly as if frozen in time, willing Vonryn not to ask the inevitable question.

"I know it's pointless asking for the names of my parents. If you'd been going to tell me you would have already done so. There are a few things that still puzzle me though. Shall I tell you all what I think is the true story. I think I have every right to be Vaga because my mother was having an affair with Morgan Draymer after she married my father. Am I right Grandfather?"

Hallam Draymer's silence was enough evidence to convince Vonryn that his assumption was correct. "You don't think that Drystan Pendenny will take this lying down do you? He'll whittle away at the heart of things with the help of the Press and his investigators and he'll discover the truth."

Vonryn turned to his mother and looked at her scornfully. "You betrayed your husband, who obviously forgave you, and then lied to your son all these years, but you're still my mother and I won't have your name dragged through the mud."

Vonryn drained the dregs of brandy that remained in his glass and stood up. "I'm going to spend the remainder of this journey in my cabin and I won't be joining you for the evening meal. When we arrive in Zerrebar I'll draft a formal statement to the effect that now I know I am adopted, I feel I have no right to succeed to the title unless the Islands' Council votes unanimously for me."

Barbara caught hold of him by the arm. "Please stay with us and talk."

He brushed her hand away as one might brush off an annoying fly. "As far as I can see there is nothing else to be said. The next few days are going to be traumatic. I've got to explain to Nadia why I am breaking off our engagement and then I must decide what to do with the rest of my life."

~*~

Later in the evening Vonryn left his cabin and dined with the Captain, who didn't seem surprised, so it was obvious that everyone was talking about the matter. It was a silent meal and after they'd finished eating, Vonryn made his excuses and went out on deck. It was a warm evening with a gentle breeze blowing the scent of flowers over from the land. He looked at the dark water beneath him and thought how easy it would be to slip over the side and disappear for good, but his innate common sense told him that that was not the way forward. The windows of the lounge below were open and in the stillness of the darkness, the voices carried upwards. It wasn't possible to make out complete sentences over the sound of the engine, but snatches of conversation floated towards him and unabashed he strained to listen. He didn't like eavesdropping, but if this was the only way to find out the truth so be it. He heard his mother's voice, high-pitched and almost hysterical. "All these years of lying and deceit. He'll never forgive me."

He listened as his father tried to calm Barbara. "You know Vonryn could have been in danger Barbara. Once he calms down, he'll stop blaming you and realise that we have been good parents to him." He must have succeeded in his attempt to placate his mother, for no matter how hard he tried, all he could hear was the murmur of voices.

He felt so confused. They had been good parents to him and obviously his father had forgiven Barbara, but the question was could he? He was sorry now that he'd had a nap at Ruth's, because he didn't feel tired and he longed to fall into a deep sleep where he wouldn't have to think. In the end he returned to his cabin and lay on the bed, where he did fall into a restless sleep. The next morning he breakfasted in his cabin and stayed there until the yacht was ready to dock on the island of Zerrebar. This had to be timed carefully, as twice a day a phenomenon occurred and the waters instead of receding from the island parted in front of it, revealing a causeway connected to the mainland. It was a sight that many islanders came to watch and marvel over.

As Vonryn had stated, the next few days were traumatic. Nadia had refused to consider their engagement over, begging and pleading with him over the phone to reconsider and even threatening to come to Zerrebar. In the end Vonryn spoke to her father, who realised straightaway that their marriage was probably no longer viable and promised to make sure that Nadia didn't do anything stupid. During the week that followed, Vonryn ate and slept as if nothing had happened. He was polite to his parents and the Vaga, staying out of their way as much as possible. After much persuasion he'd agreed not to refuse the succession, at least for the foreseeable future. He knew that his destiny was in the hands of other people and that he was virtually powerless to do anything. Every day he had the groom saddle his horse and he rode over the small island past the few isolated estate farms and military barracks that made up the community on Zerrebar, to a small secluded beach where he swam and sunbathed and idled the hours away. He knew this way of life couldn't continue, and one morning before sunrise he packed a few clothes in a holdall and at low tide he drove his car over the causeway. He didn't know where he was going, or what he was going to do, but he did know that he had to leave.

Chapter 13

Michael kissed Kathryn goodbye and he and his parents stood and watched as James drove away. Kathryn, who was sitting in the rear seat with Philip, was smiling bravely and continued to wave until the car turned the corner and her fiancé was no longer in sight. As soon as they'd gone, Michael started to feel guilty. He knew that Kathryn's smile had been a front and that she was close to tears. His grandmother's silent accusing looks over breakfast hadn't made him feel any better. He comforted himself, however, with the thought that they wouldn't be apart for long as he was sure Kathryn would waste no time in arranging her holiday.

Over lunch Justin announced that he and Leah would be leaving as soon as they'd eaten. In answer to Ilona's question as to where they were going, Justin seemed a little vague. He mentioned something about London and then turned to his mother and said that he was thinking of cutting his holiday short, and she wasn't to be surprised if he turned up in Innisver shortly. "That will be great," Michael said enthusiastically. "You and Aunt Leah can show me around when grandfather is busy."

"I'd love to show you around Michael, but I'm not sure what Leah will be doing." Justin looked at his wife with barely concealed hostility.

"What about the car you had in Bath?" Richard asked. "Was it a hire car?"

Justin nodded. "Yes, if it had been mine, I'd have driven down in it, but it never seems much point in shipping your own car over. Financially it doesn't make sense."

Michael offered to drive Justin and Leah down to the ferry, and was thankful that it was a short journey, as conversation was

141

desultory. Leah strode off without a backward glance or goodbye to Michael. Justin raised his eyebrows as he and Michael got the cases from the boot of the car.

Justin shook Michael's hand. "I'm glad you've met your grandmother at last. You'll never know how much it meant to her."

Michael noticed that no mention was made of the fact that it was the first time he'd met his grandfather but he didn't say anything. Over the weekend he'd gathered that things weren't right between his grandfather and uncles, although there had been no open quarrels. Justin paused as if deciding whether to say something. "I know you won't listen to me." He looked long and hard at his nephew and there was a troubled look in his dark eyes. "I never did when I was your age so why should you. If you really love Kathryn don't go to the Islands. Marry her first and then go together. I'm certain my father has plans for you, especially since..." He stopped speaking suddenly. "I can't say anymore, but take care and remember what I've said. If you really love Kathryn hold on to her."

Michael laughed. "Everyone seems intent on warning me about grandfather. I don't know why. He has been kind to me this weekend and I feel I've known him all my life."

"The bitterest pill comes sugar coated, and you may not realise it until you've swallowed it." Justin picked up the cases and followed his wife to the waiting ferry.

Michael watched the ferry leave and then wandered around Ryde feeling at a loss to know what to do. Vonryn and Nadia had gone off somewhere on their own. They had halfheartedly suggested that they wait for Michael to return from the ferry so that he could accompany them, but he'd declined. He didn't want to play gooseberry. His parents and grandparents had been relaxing in deck chairs on the lawn when he'd left, and probably all of them would have dozed off by this time, he thought.

On the way back, he mistook a turning and lost his way amongst the high hedged narrow country lanes, but he had plenty of time so didn't worry, reckoning that sooner or later he'd come to a main road with a signpost. Eventually he did and in no time at all he was home again. Parking the car in the driveway, he quietly made his way around the house. He was right in thinking that his parents and grandparents would be dozing in the warm sunshine. He was bored. Perhaps I should have gone back with Kathryn, he thought. What could he do until teatime? Afterwards would be all right. He'd jolly well play gooseberry and coax Vonryn and Nadia to go down the pub, that was if they needed coaxing. He decided that as there was nothing else to do, he might as well finish packing. If he was going to stay for a while in the islands, he would need another suitcase at least. Remembering there were some in the attic, he slowly climbed the stairs, recalling all the years of travelling he'd done with his parents. This family lives out of suitcases, he thought, but hopefully Kathryn and I will break the mould and settle down in one place. I expect my mother has only just put all our clothes away in the wardrobes and here we are already moving on again.

The attic was fairly empty apart from a number of trunks and suitcases and the boxes he'd carried up there before the party. He noticed that one of the boxes had split slightly and his eye lit on a leather bound photograph album. He opened it and saw that it contained photographs of when he was young and the houses he'd lived in when he was growing up. He smiled and thought that his grandparents would love to see these photographs. They wouldn't have time whilst they were here, but he could pack the album and they could all look at it and have a good laugh when they arrived in Innisver. He tucked the album under his arm and carried it and two suitcases to his bedroom. As he was returning to his room, he saw his Uncle Luke climbing the stairs.

"I thought you were sleeping off your lunch with the others," Michael said.

Luke shook his head. "No I wanted to see more of this beautiful island, so I took myself off for a walk. It was very enjoyable. I had no destination in mind; I just wandered. I also wanted to stay out of father's way. You know he disowned me and Justin?"

Michael looked surprised. "I did sense a few undercurrents,

but I didn't think it was anything serious."

Luke crossed to the window and looked out. "He called a truce for this weekend Mother persuaded him for your mother's sake. Oh it will all blow over eventually. At least I think it will." He looked despondent for a moment. "I don't like going against him. He is my father when all is said and done, but I had to do what I did," he said cryptically.

"And that was?" Michael enquired politely. He wasn't really listening, but he had taken a liking to both his uncles and ought to show some interest in their lives. He deliberately brought his mind back from his packing and waited for Luke to answer.

"Justin and I voted against him in a meeting."

"I think I heard my parents mention something about that. It was to do with Vonryn being Vaga wasn't it? Surely grandfather won't stay angry for long over such a trivial matter."

A smile hovered around Luke's eyes. It was obvious that Michael attached no significance to any of it and had no inkling of his grandfather's character.

"I'm sure you're right Michael. It was quite unimportant and will soon be forgotten."

Luke noticed the suitcases that Michael had laid on the bed and he perched on one corner of the bed, watching as Michael haphazardly flung clothes into the cases.

"I thought after all the years your family have moved, you'd be better at packing than that. Here empty it out and start again. You get what you want from the wardrobe and drawers and I'll give you a hand."

Michael handed his uncle his clothes and Luke neatly rolled each article and stowed it away in one suitcase. The smaller items he pushed down inside Michael's shoes. "There," he said as he snapped shut the lid of one case. "Maximum usage of space. Have you got the idea now, or do you want me to do the other one for you. Considering you're the one who was always on the move and I've spent most of my adult life in one place, I'm a better packer than you."

Shamefacedly, Michael grinned at his uncle. "Thanks," he said.

"Mother or the daily always did my packing for me, but I've got the idea now and I'll redo that one over there on the chair. I may not even need a third case now."

Luke noticed the photo album that Michael had flung down and idly flicked through the pages. Michael observed that although his uncle seemed to be giving only a cursory glance at the snapshots, there was a thoroughness about the manoeuvre that was more than just curiosity. Luke seemed satisfied at what he'd seen, and placing the album on the bed, he watched as Michael repacked the first suitcase.

"Are you looking forward to going to Innisver?" he asked his nephew.

Michael's face lit up.

"Very much. Mother told me a little about the islands when I was growing up, but not enough. In the back of my mind was the thought that one day I'd go and see for myself. I'm only sorry that Kathryn can't come with me straight away."

"She could if you waited."

"I know, but she understands how important it is to me. Anyway we'll be married shortly and hopefully living in Innisver, so it's best that she has time with her family before we move."

"Have you discussed living in Innisver with her?" Luke enquired.

Michael looked surprised. "No, I just took it for granted. Perhaps I shouldn't have. What do you think?"

"I think it would be a good idea to ask her what she'd like," Luke said drily. He got up off the bed and made to leave the room, but then turned back. "I hate to disillusion you, but I feel your marriage depends on what my dear father has in mind for you both. My advice to you would be to stay in England until you're safely married, but I don't suppose you'll listen to me."

Michael looked up from his packing. "Not you as well. I had Justin on to me when I dropped him off at the ferry saying almost the same as you. Nothing is going to stop me from going to Innisver. My mind is made up."

Luke looked resigned. "I thought you'd say that." He smiled down fondly at his nephew. "You and Kathryn must come and see me at Leil. I won't be there for much longer. I'm to be made Archbishop of Mordeen Cathedral which is adjacent to Innisver Castle. If it hadn't been announced to everyone, father would have made sure that the appointment went to someone else. However, that's irrelevant. What is important is that I'd very much like you and Kathryn to come and see where I've lived for most of my life."

"We'll look forward to that. I'll accept for both of us, without asking Kathryn."

Luke laughed, and his usual sombre face lit up. "Touché," he said and with a wave of his hand left the room.

~*~

The flight over was smooth and Michael thought he'd be too excited to sleep, but soon he felt his eyelids becoming heavy and he dropped off. It was only when the cabin crew were bringing round breakfast that he awoke. He peered out of the small window to see if he could get a first glimpse of the islands, but it was still dark. Shortly after breakfast, the plane started its descent and it wasn't long before the wheels touched the ground and the passengers waited patiently to disembark. It was a shock to everyone when the reporters and photographers surrounded them, their flash bulbs blinding them momentarily and the reporters shouting questions at his grandfather and Vonryn. Michael had seen things like this on the television, but having it happen to him was a frightening experience. Protectively he put his arm around his grandmother and he and Luke supported her until Drystan demanded that they allow his wife and grandson to leave. Nadia followed them outside and once there in the cool air, Michael felt his grandmother relax. The airport police helped them into the waiting limousine and not long afterwards his grandfather joined them for the short journey to the harbour. His grandfather made no attempt to get in the car and seemed to be having an altercation with Luke.

"I'm coming back to the castle with you," his uncle was saying determinedly. "I want to spend time with my mother and you know very well, I have to see the church dignitaries about my new appointment as Archbishop of Mordeen."

Michael noted with some surprise the furious expression on his grandfather's face. "If I could overturn that appointment, I would," Drystan's voice rose in anger. His grandmother, who had been lying back against the seat, her eyes shut, opened them and called out to her husband.

"Drystan please. I want to get away from this place and those reporters. If we don't hurry, they'll follow us and the questions will start all over again."

Drystan's face softened as he looked at his wife. "I said I'd call a truce for the weekend and you can't deny I was pleasant to both Luke and Justin, but after their betrayal at the meeting, enough is enough. They aren't my sons any longer."

Ria sighed. "Don't be a fool Drystan."

Michael waited for the explosion from his grandfather at being called a fool, but none came.

"Don't you see," Ria continued. "What was voted for at the meeting is now irrelevant after the news of Vonryn's adoption."

Dawn was now creeping across the sky, and Michael was able to see a satisfied smile creep across his grandfather's face. "You're right as usual," he said getting in the car. He looked at Luke who was hovering outside. "Get in for heaven's sake. You might as well come and stay for a few days. It's still your home and I can be magnanimous in your defeat. That doesn't mean I've forgiven you, because I haven't."

Luke lifted his eyes to heaven in exasperation and Michael wanted to laugh. His grandfather was behaving like a two year old, but then he thought of some of the things he himself had said and done over the years, and realised that he had inherited many of his grandfather's traits. It was a sobering thought.

Luke climbed into the car and Drystan motioned the driver to move away. Ria sagged wearily once more against the seat and Michael took hold of her hand and squeezed it.

As they reached the harbour, the sun was rising, at first just a tiny red ball in the sky, but as they alighted, Michael could already start to feel the beginning of the heat that was to come. The sea journey from St. Elizabeth to the port of Mordeena was short and Michael decided to stay on deck and watched as the shoreline of St. Elizabeth receded, the white houses glowing pink in the early morning sun. He wondered where Vonryn and Nadia had gone. He'd meant to make arrangements to see them again, but with the commotion at the airport he'd forgotten. The sea was clear, in places light turquoise, but where it was deeper it changed to jade and as the yacht scudded through the waters, Michael watched as shoals of tiny fish followed them, obviously hoping for any leftover food that would be flung overboard. In front of him he saw a small island and felt disappointment creep over him. He'd thought that Innisver would have been much larger. Luke appeared on deck carrying two cups of coffee and explained that the island they were passing was called Morwen. There were only a few villages on the island and the centre was a nature reserve.

Michael gratefully sipped the cup of coffee and he and Luke stood quietly and soon a dark shape ahead of them began to materialise into the island of Innisver. As they came nearer, he could see the small white villages and numerous domed churches that dotted the shoreline. The narrow, dusty roads twisted and turned upwards until they disappeared into the wooded hillsides. As they disembarked, Michael noticed that his grandmother had recovered and that the colour was back in her cheeks, but he still made sure that she took his arm as they walked to the waiting car that was to take them to Innisver Castle.

Michael looked around with interest as the car wound its way steadily upwards through narrow streets of whitewashed houses. Colourful lines of washing were strung at first floor level between the houses and these fluttered slightly in the early morning breeze. Shutters of all colours of the rainbow were flung open wide to air the houses and cool the rooms. It wasn't long before the houses and narrow streets were left behind and the road widened into an avenue that cut straight through open grassland. Jacaranda trees that edged the long avenue were in full bloom, their pale purple flowers contrasting with the azure blue of the sky. At the end of the Avenue stood an impressive building. To purists it would have seemed a nightmare, with its different architectural designs incorporated into one façade.

Michael looked at his grandmother enquiringly as the car entered through ornamental gates built into an archway in one corner of the building. Ria shook her head.

"I'm sorry to disappoint you Michael, but that building houses various Government offices and Innisver Police headquarters."

Once through the opening the car had to turn left, as facing them across a vast sloping shaded lawn and to the left and right of them were other impressive edifices.

"The building behind you is a museum and picture gallery and the one facing us are apartments for use by Government officials. The large building across the lawn houses more government offices.

Once again the car made a sharp turn, only this time to the right and again there was another tree lined large square with buildings on both sides, but no building in front of them, only a very high thick stone wall.

"Behind us," Ria said, "is the seat of government, like your Houses of Parliament only smaller and to your front are the state rooms and more offices. The state rooms are only used for visiting dignitaries, but at certain times of the year they are open to the public."

The car slowed down as it came to the centre of the wall and two armed guards pressed a button and two massive gates swung open to allow them to pass. The first sight of Innisver Castle was a big disappointment to Michael; he had expected something more ornate. As the days went by, however, he came to appreciate that there was beauty in its simplicity. It was a complete misnomer and anything less like a castle Michael couldn't imagine. It was a long two-storey house of stone and as usual in the islands painted white. The roof overhung verandahs that extended the whole of the front and rear. The austere structure was softened by the different varieties of bougainvillea that tumbled riotously over the verandah, adding a welcome splash of colour to the whitened stone. For many years, Ria had explained, the original fortified house had stood alone in an elevated position, surrounded on three sides by open grasslands that sloped down towards the sea. It was an ideal place to defend against any enemies. To the south the original small settlement of Mordeen had sprung up and over the centuries had grown to such an extent that it was now the capital of Innisver. Gradually other grander buildings had surrounded the original castle.

Inside the massive front door was a large, marbled floored hall, which continued upwards through the two floors to the roof. The central marble staircase divided halfway up to the first floor and a balcony extended around three sides of the hall giving access to the various rooms off it. Again there was no ostentatious show of wealth.

"I'm off to have a shower and lie down," Luke said kissing his mother on the cheek. "You really ought to do the same, you look weary."

"Don't worry about me, Luke. I'm home now and everything is going to be fine. Lena is going to make me a nice cup of tea and I'm going to sit out on the lawn and relax. You show Michael to his room. I've put him next to you in his mother's old room." She looked kindly at her grandson. "I never thought I'd live to see this day, but I have and I'm very happy." She patted Michael on his arm.

As they came to where the stairs divided, Michael noticed some oil paintings on the wall in front of him.

"Turn to your left, Michael," Luke said. "Grandfather will no doubt take great delight in explaining to you about your long dead ancestors." A corridor divided the upper floor in two and Luke flung open the third door down the passageway. He walked straight across the room and flung open the shutters that enclosed the French windows.

"Let's have some light in here. It shouldn't get too hot yet. The sea isn't far away and usually there's a slight breeze at this time of day. I'm afraid there isn't any air conditioning, but there are fans in the ceiling. The geography of the room is simple. The first door on your left as you came in is a walk in wardrobe, and the second door is the bathroom."

Michael followed his uncle to the window and looked out. "Which direction is the sea?"

"In front of you and to both sides. The castle, the old port of Mordeena, which we just drove through, and the capital city Mordeen, are all built on a peninsular. Ahead of you at the end of the garden are the cathedral and various houses belonging to it. Beyond that there is open grassland stretching for about a quarter of a mile and then you reach cliffs, with a beautiful sandy beach at the bottom. The strong can walk down a winding path to it, but there is a lift for the less able bodied."

"I heard the row you and grandfather had by the car," Michael said. "Will you stay long?"

Luke shook his head. "A few days only. I don't want to antagonise him too much. As you gathered he's still very angry with me. Anyway before I take up my position as Archbishop, I have to return to Leil for a couple of months to wind matters up there and to say goodbye to all the friends I've made. My invitation still stands for you and Kathryn to visit me there."

Michael moved out onto the verandah and leant over the railings. Below was an informal garden enclosed with the cathedral at the far end and other buildings at each side. Apart from a large stained glass window set high in the cathedral wall, none of the other buildings that enclosed the gardens had windows and complete privacy was ensured. Most of the large garden was laid to lawn with a much tougher grass than in the UK and there were shrubs and climbing plants giving bright splashes of colour. Michael noticed with interest that a swimming pool was immediately beneath them and as the sun rose steadily in the sky, the cool blue water seemed to beckon him.

"Would it be all right if I had a swim?" Michael asked.

Luke looked surprised. "Of course it would. You don't have to ask. Father may be an egotistical manipulator, but you're his grandson and whilst you're here you must treat this place as your home. Robert will be bringing up your cases in a few minutes, so if I were you, I'd get my bathing trunks out and have a swim. You don't have to go back into the house to get to the pool. If you look at the far ends of the verandah there are stone steps leading down to the garden."

~*~

The days passed quickly. There were meetings to attend, tours of the island and nearly every evening there were official functions to go to. It was obvious that Drystan was enjoying introducing Michael to all and sundry as his grandson. It hadn't been apparent in the UK how important a man Drystan Pendenny was. The informality in which they travelled and the lack of pomp and ceremony hadn't prepared Michael for the fact that the Larn of Pendenny was in reality 'King'. He'd known his grandfather was very wealthy, but thought that the title Larn would be something equivalent to a Duke. The daily papers were full of Michael's visit and the fact that Vonryn was adopted. Speculation was rife in the journalists' reports that Michael was being groomed to take the office of Vaga. He read these articles one morning to his grandmother as they breakfasted by the side of the pool. A feeling of excitement was creeping over him, although deep down he knew it was only a dream and that it would never come true but still a little voice nagged him that possibly it might. He did wonder about his grandmother's silence and thought she might have been pleased for him, but he failed to notice the tight-lipped expression she wore whenever he read out those articles to her. He had been ten days on the island and still hadn't telephoned Kathryn. Each morning he had arisen with good intentions, but every day was so full of appointments that he never got around to it. In the end, it was his grandmother who dialled the number and made him speak to his fiancée to find out what day and flight she would be on. Kathryn was very cool with him on the telephone, which slightly surprised him, but when he mentioned the fact to his grandmother, she said that she wasn't at all surprised. If her fiancée had gone ten days before phoning, she would have been furious, not cool, and would have told Michael so in no uncertain terms.

"I know grandmother," Michael said sheepishly. "I deserve that. I should have made time to phone before. I got wrapped up in everything here. It isn't that I love Kathryn any the less, because I don't. I'll make her understand when she arrives. Did you know that she's travelling to St. Elizabeth with mother and father? They've managed to find other tenants for the house on the Isle of Wight and father will be taking up his position as Governor General next week. They're going to have a reception at Government House and naturally we're all invited. I don't think Luke will be able to make it as he's back in Leil."

Ria watched Michael bound off. Sometimes he was like a young puppy. He still had a lot of growing up to do. With a bit of luck Kathryn would be there for him. She was more mature in many ways than Michael, but Ria knew that at heart Michael was a good young man. He needed a responsible post on the islands, not the one of Vaga that Drystan had in mind, but something else. She'd have to figure out what, and then the hardest part would be she'd have to persuade her husband.

~*~

Michael arrived at the airport just as Kathryn was collecting her luggage off the carousel. As he went to kiss her on the lips, she turned her head deliberately so that his kiss landed on her cheek.

"I'm in the dog house then," he said as he picked up the cases.

There was no smile on her face as Kathryn looked at her fiancé.

"What do you expect," she replied. "No phone call for ten days, just complete and utter silence. I thought your grandfather had finally brainwashed you into dumping me and that you were too much of a coward to tell me."

"He'll never separate us. I promise you that. Come on Kathryn trust me. I'm sorry I never telephoned, but I seem to have been caught up in a whirlwind here and the days just merged into one another. You're here now and I want us to enjoy ourselves."

"I suppose you're right and I do so want to enjoy our holiday together, but I'm convinced that your grandfather will try and separate us one way or another."

"Never," said Michael firmly. "How are my parents?" He asked as they made their way to the exit.

Kathryn smiled for the first time since she'd arrived.

"They're fine. They've been really kind to me. I like them both very much and I think they like me. Your mother confided in me that since they've decided to come home, as she put it, they couldn't be happier."

"Yes, something seems to have happened in their marriage." He stopped talking as he manoeuvred the car through Mordeena's narrow streets, concentrating on remembering the way. His grandfather had offered to send a chauffeured car to collect Kathryn, but Michael had declined the offer and Ria had backed him in his decision.

"It's strange," he said. "I can never remember them quarrelling when I was young, but they were always terribly polite to one another. Even to a child it didn't seem completely natural, but I think I've found out a secret from their past."

Kathryn didn't look surprised. "I suppose most parents have things they don't tell their children. Did you discover it here?"

"No." Michael shook his head. "The day you left, I went up the attic to get some more suitcases and I found a photograph album that I thought my grandparents would like to see, so I packed it and then completely forgot all about it until yesterday evening. The stitching was coming undone down one side and I thought I'd get it repaired before I gave it back to my mother. Tucked inside the gap were two old snapshots, one of my mother at a wedding and one of a very young baby."

"A lot of people have photos of themselves at weddings and of babies," Kathryn replied. "Perhaps they got between the cover by mistake."

"There was no mistake. The leather stitching would have had

154

to be unpicked and then re-stitched. There was no way the photos could have got there any other way."

"Strange," Kathryn mused. "Why would your mother, or someone else want to hide two snapshots?"

"I want you to help me get to the bottom of it."

"Do you think we ought to Michael? Your mother must have had a reason for hiding them. Perhaps it was an elopement and the bride was your mother's friend and they had to keep it secret for a while. She probably hid them there and then forgot about them."

"I haven't made myself clear, Kathryn. My mother wasn't a guest at the wedding, she was the bride and the bridegroom wasn't my father. As to who the baby was I don't know. It isn't me, I'm positive of that. Anyway, we're nearly at Innisver Castle now. We'll talk more about it later on."

As they left the narrow streets, Kathryn gasped in delight as she had her first glimpse of the avenue of Jacaranda trees.

"They're so beautiful," she said.

Michael by this time was used to the sight of them and could be blasé about their beauty. "They're past their best now. You should have seen them when I arrived."

It wasn't long before he was parking the car outside the Castle and one of the servants hurried out to take the cases inside and another took the car keys from Michael preparatory to putting the car in the garage. Michael led Kathryn through the hall and library to the patio where he was sure he would find his grandmother. He was right; Ria was there seated by the side of the swimming pool. She was looking through the photograph album that Michael had brought with him. She smiled at the sight of Kathryn and putting the album down she got up and kissed her on both cheeks.

"You're here at last. I'm so pleased. Come and sit down Kathryn and have some iced tea. Lena has just made some. Michael said he'd be bringing you straight here so we thought you'd be arriving about now."

Kathryn flicked the pages of the album whilst she drank her tea. She noticed where the old leather stitching had broken.

"You left the album in the library last night Michael," Ria said. "I hope you don't mind me looking through it."

"Of course not. That's the reason I packed it. I wanted you and grandfather to see how I looked when I was small."

Ria produced a brown paper bag from under the table. "I got Lena to get some new leather from the market to re-stitch the cover. I was just going to make a start on it when you arrived, but I want to consult cook about lunch, so I'll do it later on. After Kathryn has finished her tea, show her which room she's sleeping in Michael. Lunch will be at one o'clock prompt. Your grandfather has a meeting at two o'clock and you know how he is for punctuality."

Michael waited until his grandmother had gone back inside and then he inserted his finger between the cover feeling for the photographs.

"They've gone," he said.

"Could they have fallen out?" Kathryn asked.

"It's a possibility. Perhaps I didn't push them back in far enough. I'll ask grandmother later on if she's seen them."

"Do you think they were important?"

"No," Michael shrugged. "I think I was reading too much into them. No one would be interested in two old photos. Come on," Michael pulled Kathryn out of her chair. "I'll show you your room and if you're not too tired come down and have a swim."

Half way up the staircase, they stopped to look at the oil paintings.

"These are my illustrious ancestors," Michael explained. "Grandfather did tell me who was who, but I've forgotten." They turned to the right and continued making their way up the stairs. As they reached the door of Kathryn's bedroom, Michael paused. "I've been thinking those photographs couldn't have dropped out."

"I thought you said they weren't important."

A worried frown creased Michael's forehead. "I don't know. I've got a funny feeling about this. If my mother was married before, why didn't she tell me? In this day and age a previous marriage is nothing. I'm beginning to wonder if my father knows, and who is the baby? It's no good, I can't let it rest. There are too many unanswered questions. Mother wouldn't have hidden them for no reason. I've got to find out the truth."

Kathryn put her hand on his arm. "I'll help you if I can, but don't forget Michael, this is your mother's secret. We can't betray her. Your mother and father were so happy when I left them today. I wouldn't want to be the one to spoil things. If we find the photographs, we'll stitch them inside the album and if we are able to find out the truth, we must keep it to ourselves."

Michael turned to look at Kathryn. "I do love you Kathryn. I know I haven't behaved very well to you lately and I've no excuse really."

"I hope you love me and I want to believe you, but you make it very hard sometimes, but returning to the question of the photographs, I'm sure you're worrying over nothing."

"I do hope you're right," he said, but it was obvious from the tone of his voice that he wasn't convinced.

Chapter 14

July

Dear Mum and Dad,

I'm finally on my way to the Islands. I don't think I ever believed I'd get there, especially since Michael went back with his grandparents. I spoke to Michael the other night and he seems to be having a great time. It's worrying me slightly as from the way he was talking things seem to be going to his head. It has come out that Vonryn was unofficially adopted and he has issued a statement that unless the Islands' Council votes unanimously for him to be the next Vaga, he will stand down. The next meeting isn't scheduled for six months and Michael said there has been talk of calling an emergency meeting and representatives of the British Islands will be present as well. I'm sure that Drystan wants Michael to be Vaga as he is the only male relative left who is eligible and hasn't refused the position. I think he has started grooming him for the role already.

I'm so sorry for Nadia. As I told you the other night on the phone, Vonryn has broken off their engagement. She is heartbroken, and I've had her on the telephone a few evenings sobbing her heart out to me. I pointed out that they could still get married, but she said that Vonryn has told her that he wouldn't let her give up everything for him. It would mean exile and straitened circumstances. It wouldn't worry me being poor, but Nadia has always had money, so unless her father continued her allowance, she'd find it hard. I won't see her as I hoped. She has gone to the USA on business in place of her father, who supposedly isn't too well at the moment. I've a feeling he will make a swift recovery once Nadia has left on the plane and that he just wants to get her out of the country for a while. As you can imagine the islands' newspapers are full of the fact that Vonryn was adopted and are speculating as to his real parents. It must be a terrible time for him, and although I didn't get to know him well on the Isle of Wight, he seemed a kind and genuine person. The last time Nadia spoke to me, she said that Vonryn was living like a recluse on Zerrebar, hardly speaking to anyone, just spending the days riding his horse and swimming. Since their conversation when he broke off their engagement he has refused to speak to her and she has to rely on news of him from the Vaga.

To be truthful, I don't think that Michael and I will be engaged for much longer. I didn't hear anything from him for ten days, and then I think it was Ria who nagged him into phoning me. I spoke to Ria on the telephone the next morning and she urged me to arrange my holiday as soon as possible. This wasn't difficult to do, as after the promotion night in April, Head Office is very interested in the potential of the Islands as a new and exciting travel destination. Although I'll officially be on holiday, Head Office has asked me to try and find time to look into this.

I don't know if I told you, but I'm travelling as far as Lorentia with Michael's parents. As you know I've always liked Michael's father, but now I've got to know his mother better we get on very well. They'll only make a fleeting visit back to the Isle of Wight to sort out the tenancy of the house. I know Michael said they were like gypsies, but sometimes even gypsies stay longer in a place than they did in the Isle of Wight.

To go back to Michael and myself, I think that he has fallen completely under Drystan's spell, and I don't know if things can ever be the same between us again. I'll just have to see what happens during this holiday. Perhaps I was in too much of a rush to get engaged.

The captain has just announced that we're starting the descent so I'll finish this letter later. If you remember, I'm having to change to a smaller plane for the short flight to Innisver where Michael will meet me....

...I'm finishing this letter in my bedroom at Innisver Castle. Doesn't it sound grand? Actually it's not really a castle at all. It's a very large house set down in the middle of a maze of shady squares and impressive buildings. The road from the airport through the port of Mordeena was via very narrow winding streets, almost impossible for two cars to pass, but they manage it somehow. Most buildings are painted white with different coloured shutters on the windows. You'd love the flowers, they're everywhere - a riot of colour tumbling down white washed walls.

The castle inside is lovely, cool marble floors throughout and wide roofed verandahs on the first floor with steps at each end down to the garden. My bedroom is the opposite end of the house from Michael. It's a lovely large room with French windows opening out onto the verandah and overlooking the garden and swimming pool. Even though the garden is surrounded by buildings, the garden and house aren't overlooked. From what Ria said during lunch, the house was here first, and the other buildings grew up around it as the port of Mordeena and Mordeen expanded. In those days, it was also a form of protection to Innisver Castle and also in this climate they shade the garden. It was a condition of building that no windows, apart from a stained glass one in the cathedral, should face inwards so it is quite private. Apart from the cathedral at the bottom end of the garden, I haven't found out yet what the other buildings surrounding the castle are.

I think living here could be quite claustrophobic. Everything is done for you, even my cases were unpacked and my clothes put away. Also there are about three gates to go through before you reach the outer squares and each gate is guarded. You can't just get up and decide to go for a walk. It's a lovely way to live for a while, but I don't know whether I'd like it on a permanent basis.

I was sunbathing by the side of the pool this afternoon when Lena (Ria's maid) told me that there was a phone call for me. Michael and his grandfather had gone to a meeting and Ria was having a siesta. It was my boss and the only way he could have obtained this number was through Michael's grandfather. He told me that head office had arranged for me to take some tourists on

160

a five-day tour of the islands. I'm to leave Mordeen in two days time, spend one night with Ruth and then leave with the tourists. To say I was annoyed is the understatement of the year. I tried to argue that I was on holiday, and that although I didn't mind making enquiries as to future tours, I didn't see why I should take a party of tourists around the islands. He was very apologetic, but pointed out that it was out of his hands. Head Office had made the decision. It was up to me but if I could pull it off it would earn me brownie points. I know you'll think I'm paranoid; first it was Michael's mother I thought had it in for me and now Michael's grandfather. Honestly, the only person with enough clout to arrange everything so quickly has got to be his grandfather. No wonder he was so nice to me at lunch earlier today. He knew I wouldn't be his houseguest for very long. I'd cooled down slightly by dinner and I plucked up courage to ask Drystan if he had helped expedite matters so that a tour could go ahead. He was quite shameless in admitting it, saying that he was only trying to help me. Michael, I'm pleased to say, was annoyed with his grandfather as well, especially as I shall have to miss the reception to welcome his father as the new Governor General. I hoped he would tell his grandfather that it was impossible for me to go but not him, he let his grandfather convince him that it was all for the good of my career and didn't say a word. We had an awful row afterwards and I told him just what I thought of his manipulative grandfather. I gave him the ring back and told him that it was obvious he was going to have to choose between his grandfather and me. I didn't want to do it but if you were here with me you'd understand. It's such a silly reason for breaking up. I've heard of couples finishing for other reasons, but never because the grandfather came between them. Michael pleaded with me to take the ring back, but I said that it was best if we both thought things through carefully for a while. I told Ria what had happened and said that I wasn't going to stay two days but wanted to leave first thing tomorrow morning. I told her that if a flight couldn't be arranged, then I'd prefer to stay in a hotel. She was very upset, but she understood and said that even if an inter island flight couldn't be arranged the ferries travelled frequently. I'm sorry to end this letter on a sad note, and I don't want you to worry about me. I'll survive. I'm not holding my breath that Michael and I will patch things up and if we don't I'll do this tour and then I'm coming straight home. To be honest, I can't wait to see you all again. Drystan Pendenny has made it clear that I don't belong here.

Miss you all.
Kathryn
xxxxxx

Chapter 15

Ruth drove Kathryn and Vonryn to the harbour, but as there was no sign of the mini bus containing the tourists, they adjourned to a nearby cafe to await their arrival. Although still early morning, the cafe was bustling with people. There were the commuters snatching a quick cup of coffee before their workday started, and the men who worked in the harbour, loading and unloading the ferries, enjoying a hearty English breakfast, a legacy of years of British rule. The air was heavy with the smell of frying bacon and sausages. They barely had time to drink their coffees before the tourists arrived. Ruth bade Kathryn and Vonryn a fond farewell, but she also heaved a sigh of relief as she watched them shepherd their charges aboard the ferry.

After waving goodbye to them, Ruth returned to her car and drove slowly home. The last few weeks had been a nightmare. Firstly she'd had a hysterical Nadia on the telephone at all hours of the day and night. She was grateful when Nadia's father had packed her off to America until the whole business of Vonryn's parentage had been settled once and for all. Secondly she'd then had Vonryn turning up on her doorstep. She couldn't say that he'd been a difficult houseguest. He hadn't asked for anything, but had seemed content to mope around doing nothing. She'd been busy trying to find something to occupy his time when the third and most unwelcome interruption had come. This was an unexpected phone call from Drystan Pendenny demanding that she make arrangements for a package tour around the islands for five couples. Ruth had been momentarily silenced by the audacity of the man, but all her protestations to the effect that she led a busy lifestyle as an MP fell on deaf ears. She had never met Drystan Pendenny, but knew enough about him to know that he could be a bitter foe if crossed. She'd known she was being cowardly, but with independence coming nearer she felt she had to acquiesce to his demands. She had ventured to ask why her and not any one of his numerous acquaintances. She then discovered that the main reason he'd chosen her was because she knew Nadia and the work she'd been doing to promote tourism. She remembered the one sided conversation with clarity.

"I'm sending you a fax with the dates and destinations and a choice of hotels. All you have to do," he'd continued, "Is to pick out five couples from the tourists staying in Lorentia, see which ones can extend their stay for an extra five or six days and then cancel their flights home and arrange for new flights. Tell them everything is free and any extra expenses incurred due to rearranging their flights will be paid for personally by me. All they have to do is fill in a questionnaire at the end of the holiday."

Ten minutes after the telephone call, the fax had come through. She'd been furious with the man and decided she'd take a shower and prepare some lunch for herself and Vonryn before looking at it. When she went to call Vonryn to tell him that lunch was ready, she found him reading the fax.

"I'll sort this out for you Ruth," he'd said. "It will give me something to do and to say thank you for putting up with me in my bad mood, also this tourist idea was very dear to Nadia's heart. She had very definite ideas about the way things should move forward. It shouldn't be too difficult; there aren't that many hotels to choose from. Let's hope they're not fully booked, otherwise we may have to arrange accommodation in private houses."

Vonryn had then asked the same question that had bothered Ruth. Why was Drystan Pendenny getting involved? At the time, that had been something she hadn't understood either. Wanting to promote tourism was one thing, but to deal with it himself was quite another. Drystan Pendenny had enough underlings so that all he had to do was give orders. Ruth hadn't long to wait before the reason for Drystan's involvement became crystal clear. Later that day, Ria had telephoned telling her that Kathryn was to escort the tour around the islands and would Ruth mind having her for a houseguest for a few days. Vonryn had volunteered to sleep on a camp bed in the small dormer bedroom and Kathryn moved into the guest room. The house seemed to be bulging at the seams and Ruth realised how used she'd become over the years to living on her own. Having to arrange the tour, however, had brought Vonryn out of his gloom and when he showed her the final itinerary, it amazed Ruth how efficiently he'd gone about it.

Ruth had been so engrossed in thinking about the events of the past few weeks that it took her by surprise to realise how close to home she was. After garaging her car, she unlocked her front door and as she entered, felt the silence surround her. I'm getting anti social, she thought, but it was good to reclaim her solitude.

That night she was to attend the reception to welcome Richard Vandrell as the new Governor General of Lorentia and Sarena. Once she'd discovered that the old Governor General, Gregory Rollins, wasn't able to attend, she'd been looking forward to going. The last meeting with Gregory when he'd accused her of being in a conspiracy with the Vaga and she'd refused his proposal of marriage had been traumatic for both of them.

She'd purchased a new dress for the reception; a midnight blue creation made of fine material and cut in a severe style, which suited her best. She was thankful that over the years she hadn't put on weight, as the flimsy material would show every extra pound of flesh. She removed the dress from the wardrobe and held it up against herself. Yes, she thought, it had been a wise choice. She felt young again and knew that it was because she was hoping that Luke Pendenny would be there. Surely he would come to his brother-in-law's reception. All the front pages of the newspapers had been taken up with speculation about Vonryn and who his real parents were, but tucked away in a small corner, she'd read with interest that the new Archbishop of Mordeen was to be Luke Pendenny. Her heart had missed a beat on reading that item. After all these years, he was leaving Leil. She wandered out onto the terrace and leaning her arms on the balustrade she looked across the clear blue waters of the bay to the Governor's mansion. Why was he leaving after all these years she wondered? Perhaps tonight she would have answers to questions that had troubled her for a long time.

If Ruth had used her binoculars she would have been able to see Drystan Pendenny sitting on the terrace of the Governor's mansion and watching as preparations went on around him for the reception that evening. He was quietly satisfied. He'd seen Kathryn off, for the time being anyway. She wouldn't be there tonight even though she'd been invited. Michael was still sulking, but Drystan was sure that he'd come round eventually. He shut his eyes and dreamt of the day when his grandson, Michael, would be Vaga of all the Islands and of a wedding in Mordeen Cathedral between Michael and Nadia. He disregarded the fact that both were in love with other people. He held the view that in such marriages, love was a bonus that came after the ceremony if you were lucky, and if you weren't, you just got on with your life. There was a small disquieting thought at the back of his mind and that concerned the two photographs he'd discovered tucked away between the covers of Michael's photograph album. He'd been quietly glancing through it, enjoying seeing old family snaps of Michael's childhood, when he'd noticed the stitching needed re-doing. He'd been about to ring for a servant to take the album for repair, when something made him look between the covers. It had been a perfect hiding place for the photos he'd managed to prise out with the aid of one of his wife's knitting needles. He'd looked in horror at the wedding photograph, for although the bride wasn't dressed in white, there could be no doubt it was a wedding. He'd recognised the church instantly. He'd visited his son Luke there once to try and persuade him to return to Mordeen, but without success. His younger son, Justin and his daughter-in-law Leah were in the photograph, standing each side of the happy couple, but it was the identity of the bride and groom that nearly gave him a heart attack. His daughter, Ilona, and Morgan Draymer were the bride and groom. There had been no doubt in Drystan's mind who had married them and who was behind the camera, his other

166

son Luke. His first instinct had been to call his wife and demand an explanation, but as she wasn't in the photo, he'd wondered if she'd known about the wedding. Perhaps Ilona hadn't wanted to tell her mother until afterwards, and then Morgan Draymer had been killed in the car crash that many had blamed Drystan for, so there had been no need. The other photograph of a newborn baby had set his mind racing. He compared it with photographs of Michael taken when he was a baby, and was positive that it wasn't him. Why would Ilona keep a photograph of someone else's child hidden away? Commonsense had told him that she wouldn't. Quietly he'd had copies of the photographs made and set his team of investigators on to searching the records. He'd returned the photographs to their original hiding place, never realising that Michael had already discovered their loss.

Ria watched her husband from the balcony window. He was a meddling old fool, she thought, and would lose everything if he wasn't careful. Although Michael was sulking about Kathryn going on the tour, he still wasn't ready to stand up and defy his grandfather, the relationship was too new and still in the honeymoon stage. Ria was so overjoyed at having a daughter and grandson nearby that she was torn as to whether she should interfere, not that she'd come up with any worthwhile plan. She decided that she would join her husband and try and talk some sense into him. When she arrived on the terrace, Drystan was finishing a telephone conversation. He replaced the mobile phone on the table and looked intently at his wife.

"I think it's time we talked," he said seriously.

Ria sat down opposite her husband. Her heart had started to beat faster; she didn't like the sound of his words. She poured herself a drink of fresh orange juice and sat there quietly waiting for her husband to speak first.

Drystan picked up the brown envelope that lay on the table and slid it across to her. "Open it and tell me what you think of the contents."

Ria could see that Drystan was watching her intently and she knew that whatever was inside the envelope, she had to show no emotion whatsoever. Her hands trembled slightly as she picked it up. Her husband was watching her face for her reaction, so she prayed earnestly that he hadn't noticed the tremor in her hands.

She took a quick glance at the photographs and her hand shot to her mouth. Where had he found these? "My God," she said. "It's Ilona and Morgan Draymer." She cast a sly glance at her husband. She noticed that his whole body had relaxed, and she thanked God, for it seemed that Drystan was satisfied with her reaction.

He reached across the table and took her hand in his. "You'll never know how glad I am that you weren't in the photograph. I don't know what I'd have done if you'd betrayed me as well."

Ria felt a pang of guilt, but then stifled it sharply. After all these years, she wasn't prepared to confess that although she hadn't been there, she'd known all about the wedding.

"It seems," he continued, "That despite everything I said they went ahead and got married. That part of it doesn't bother me. Morgan died shortly afterwards, but did he get Ilona pregnant, and if so where is the child." His features once again took on a suspicious look and he swiftly released Ria's hand. "Are you sure you knew absolutely nothing about this wedding?"

Ria mustered all the acting skills she possessed and looked innocently at her husband. "You don't think for one minute they would have told me, do you?"

Drystan grunted. "Maybe not, but I'll get the truth out of Leah tonight."

The surprised look on Ria's face was genuine. "I didn't think she'd been invited. Justin said they were on the point of separating."

"I took it upon myself to invite her, and if she knows which side her bread is buttered, she'll tell me what I want to know."

"I'm sure she will," Ria agreed, wondering what time Justin was due to arrive. She'd have to get him to speak to Leah first before Drystan did.

"That's it!" Drystan thumped his fist on the table with such a force that the table shook. "I know how they did it."

Ria kept silent and waited for Drystan to elaborate.

He got to his feet and started pacing. "My agent couldn't find any record of a marriage that would tie in with the period when I threw Morgan out of Innisver Castle and the date of his death. The only strange occurrence at that time was when a batch of marriage certificates for the district of Leil had been destroyed accidentally." He stopped pacing and to Ria's relief sat down abruptly. A smile lit up his face and he picked up the telephone and quickly tapped out a number. "Damn, it's engaged. Never mind, I'll try again in a few minutes. I'll get the proof of the marriage from the church records there, the birth will be more difficult, unless Leah can help me."

"I'm still not clear how they did it."

"Quite simply. You see the marriage and the birth had to be recorded in their true names. Hallam Draymer had a hand in this; it couldn't have been done otherwise. Out of the five marriage certificates that were accidentally destroyed and reported to the Registry, I'm convinced if we search the church registers, we'll find that only four of their entries will be blank, the fifth one will be the one I'm looking for. It was foolproof, no one bothers to go to out of the way churches looking for their ancestors anymore, everything is on computer."

"It could have been discovered at any time," Ria objected.

"A million to one chance. When Ilona married, Leil was a very tiny fishing village. People were born there and tended to spend the whole of their lives in one place. They knew all about the lives and families of their ancestors, so they would have no need to search the registers."

Drystan looked triumphant as he re-dialled. This time the line wasn't engaged and as he started to bark instructions down the line, Ria got up and walked slowly away, her heart was very heavy. Everything was going to come out in the open now. She was positive of that fact, but would the truth bring down both the Draymer and Pendenny families with it. Perhaps the ordinary people of the islands wouldn't forgive the deception. Drystan's single mindedness over the question of who should succeed the Vaga and his search for the truth of

Vonryn's parentage could bring their whole world crashing down around their ears.

~*~

Leah took one final look at herself in the hotel bedroom mirror before leaving the room. Her hair and makeup were immaculate, and she decided the salon's exorbitant price had been well worth it. She took the lift to the ground floor and head held high slowly made her way through the foyer to the waiting car. Her dark gold dress shimmered and rustled as she walked and a satisfied half smile crept across her face as she noticed the admiring glances thrown her way. Once inside the car, however, her bravado left her and she started to feel nervous. It was all well and good to be brave when hundreds of miles separated her from her dangerous father-in-law, but now she was on his territory, even though it was still technically British soil. She almost tapped the screen that separated her from the driver to tell him to turn around and take her back to the hotel, but decided against doing that. There was to be no escape.

The Governor's Mansion was within walking distance of the hotel, and as the car rounded the corner, the familiar cream coloured stone building could be seen on the brow of a hill overlooking the south side of the bay. As the journey was so short, she didn't have time to think of happier days when she'd lived there with her father when he was Governor General. She wondered momentarily if her brother Richard found it strange to be living there again and taking over from where their father had left off.

It was a beautiful, balmy night, the sky not black but a navy blue that shimmered with diamond like stars that surrounded a large full moon. The whole building was ablaze with light and Leah thought that under different circumstances she would have been able to enjoy herself. As soon as she entered the hallway, she saw Justin, her soon to be ex-husband. He bent down and kissed her cheek, but at the same time took her elbow in a vice like grip.

"I want a word with you Leah," he whispered in her ear. "If you don't want a scene, don't struggle. It would look most undignified and you might tear your new dress."

He propelled her to a side room and shut the door firmly behind them, standing with his back to it and cutting off her retreat.

"Well," she said defiantly. "You can't keep me here all night. Your father has commanded my presence."

"Oh, I know that, and I'm going to tell you exactly what to say."

"The truth frightens you then," Leah felt that she was gaining the upper hand.

"No it doesn't frighten me. You can tell him everything you know, with one omission."

"And that is?"

"My mother's name is to be kept out of it. Do you understand?"

"And what if I don't?"

"You won't get any maintenance from me ever."

Leah laughed. "Your father will see I'm well provided for, and failing that I'll take you to court."

"My dear girl, my father can't live for ever and I wouldn't believe his promises. He has a bad habit of forgetting he ever made them. Once you've told him all he needs to know, he'll expect you to leave the islands. Also he adores my mother and I wouldn't like to be the one who tells him she went behind his back and betrayed him."

Leah was silent. She knew Justin was right. She couldn't afford to place her trust in Drystan Pendenny.

"If I agree to your terms, what then?" she asked.

"I'll make sure you have enough money to live a comfortable life in England but not here. Of course you may already have ruined everything by talking to the Press."

Leah suddenly felt frightened.

"How could that ruin everything?"

"You've opened a can of worms and the people may decide they'd prefer a republic." Justin shrugged his shoulders. "I may be joining you in England my dear. You might even have to soil

171

your hands and look for work to help keep me."

Leah recoiled in horror. "You're joking."

"I wish I were Leah, I wish I were. If we're to salvage anything, the Vaga and my father are going to have to work together for once in their lives. Will you keep my mother's name out of it? Luckily she wasn't involved that much so it shouldn't be difficult. Whatever action she took, say I did it."

Leah was a realist and knew when she was beaten. Suddenly she felt frightened at the prospect of a lonely future ahead.

"Yes, I'll do it," she said quietly.

"I think you've made the right decision," he said. As he went to open the door, she caught hold of his arm.

"I'm so sorry Justin. You know I've always loved you, and that's why I blackmailed you into marrying me. All I ever wanted was for us to live a normal life and be happy."

He gently removed her hand from his sleeve.

"It's too late. Do you know something Leah, I loved you and fully intended to ask you to marry me, but no, your jealousy of Ilona and your blackmail killed any feelings I once had for you."

Tears welled up in Leah's eyes and she didn't see him leave the room, but heard the sound of the door as he shut it quietly behind him. She remained there alone for a few minutes to compose herself, checking in her hand mirror that her mascara hadn't run. Taking a deep breath she followed Justin out of the room to where her brother and sister-in-law were waiting to greet their guests.

Ilona kissed her sister-in-law lightly on the cheek.

"I'm so glad you could come," she said insincerely, trying not to let any animosity she felt for her show.

Leah smiled sardonically. "Always the perfect hostess. Pity you didn't think fit to send me an invitation. You both know I'm only here because your father commanded me to attend."

Ilona kept a rigid smile on her face and turned just in time to see the Vaga and Vonryn's parents approaching. Richard ushered Leah firmly through the doorway to where Drystan and Ria were seated and beckoning a waiter, took a glass of wine from the tray and placed it in front of his sister. She proceeded to gulp it down in one go, much to Richard's dismay. Damn and blast his sister, he thought as he returned to Ilona's side. Why did she take such a delight in stirring things? He was just in time to greet Hallam Draymer and flashlights popped as the few journalists that had been allowed inside took a photograph. Richard hoped fervently that they hadn't overheard Leah's remarks. There was enough adverse publicity in the Press about them already, and many people at the reception that night were quite capable of making mischief. He was under no illusions as to that. Many ambitious men and women were fighting for a role in the new independent islands, and some of them would be quite happy to see both the Draymer and Pendenny families brought down.

Ilona looked at Vonryn's mother with interest. This was Morgan Draymer's earlier love and the one he might have committed adultery with. She wasn't at all as Ilona had imagined her. Barbara Santella was a short, slightly overweight, middle-aged woman, with short, thick, iron grey hair that had been cut and styled to show off her features to their best advantage. She was immaculately groomed, wearing a black silk jacket and long matching skirt. Her hands betrayed her nervousness and she clutched her small evening bag as though at any moment someone might snatch it away from her. She seemed ill at ease and smiled timidly at Ilona as they shook hands. Making sure that her husband and the Vaga were talking to Richard, Barbara whispered to Ilona.

"I must see you tonight."

Ilona looked more intently at the woman in front of her and noticed the black rings under her eyes, which spoke of sleepless nights. It was obvious that Barbara Santella was under a lot of strain. Ilona moved slightly away from Richard.

"Is it about Vonryn?" she asked.

Barbara nodded. Ilona thought quickly. It wasn't going to be easy, but she would have to find time to talk to Barbara.

"Keep an eye on me throughout the evening. I'll try and slip out onto the terrace and you can follow me."

As the Vaga and the Santellas made their way into the ballroom,

Richard came and stood by his wife.

"What were you two whispering about?" He said.

"It was about Vonryn," she replied. "I'm going to try and meet her on the terrace later on in the evening. Try and cover for me. Do you think it looked suspicious or that anyone overheard us?"

"I noticed, but I don't think anyone else did. I was closest to you and I don't know what was said. As for it being suspicious what is more natural than you chatting to a guest."

Richard gently nudged Ilona to warn her not to say anymore as a new group of guests was arriving, one of whom was Ruth Graham.

After greeting Richard and Ilona and making the customary polite exchanges, Ruth made her way into the ballroom. The room was immense and covered the whole length of one side of the building. Down one wall, shuttered French windows had been flung open and the air was heavy with the scent of flowers that wafted in on the gentle evening breeze. The windows led to a paved terrace that overlooked the harbour. A six-piece orchestra was on a raised dais at the far end of the room and above the murmur of voices, the strains of a popular melody drifted her way, the name of which completely eluded her. She accepted a glass of wine from the white-coated waiter and went to stand by one of the windows. Lights twinkled from the hill on the other side of the water, where her own house stood. She glanced across to the doorway where Richard and Ilona were still greeting their guests. There was something strangely familiar about Ilona, and Ruth wondered if they'd ever met, although she couldn't think where. Probably it was Ilona's likeness to her brother Luke that had triggered off Ruth's feelings of having met her before. She searched amongst the faces of the people in the room for Luke, but there was no sign of him. However, it was still early and he might arrive later in the evening. Sipping her drink slowly she looked around hoping to see a familiar face. A group of her fellow MPs and their wives were at the far end of the room, and as she made her way through the other guests, she caught a glimpse of Michael standing out on the terrace. He looked so forlorn that on an impulse she decided to join him. He glanced up as she approached.

"I suppose you've come to tell me off for the way I've treated Kathryn."

Ruth shook her head.

"It's not for me to interfere. You've got to sort things out between you."

Michael leant over the balustrade. "I didn't want her to break off our engagement, but I didn't want to hurt my grandfather either. I know he wanted us to split up, but not because he didn't like Kathryn."

"She knows that. She doesn't dislike him either." Ruth crossed her fingers at this white lie. It wasn't really a lie for Kathryn had told her that her feelings for Drystan were akin to hatred and there was a big difference between dislike and hate. "It's just that she feels you're completely under his thumb since you've arrived here."

Michael smiled ironically. "She told me that and many more home truths just before she threw the ring back at me. I suppose I was seduced by the power he had. The money didn't make a lot of difference. I've never been poor, so I was used to the trappings of wealth, but power was something else. He wants me to be Vaga, did you know?"

"I guessed," Ruth replied. "It seemed obvious what he was up to just by reading the newspapers. It won't work you know."

Michael sighed deeply. "No I know it won't, but for a short time I kidded myself. Perhaps if I'd been raised here I would have been accepted." He straightened up and took hold of Ruth's elbow. "Let me escort you back to the ballroom and then I'm going to look for grandfather and tell him that I'm going to find a law firm in Lorentia or one of the other islands that will offer me a job."

"If you're serious about what you've just said, there's a vacancy in my office here in St. Elizabeth. This is confidential Michael, but I don't intend to stand as an MP again. I'm reverting from a silent partner to a working one and we're thinking of opening an office in Innisver, which they want me to run."

Michael's face lit up. "That's wonderful. I promise you I won't let you down. I'll go and phone Kathryn straight away. I'll tell her I love her and beg her to come back to me." Ruth laughed to herself at the impetuosity of youth.

"Slow down. I'll put a good word in for you, but the post isn't guaranteed. You will have to make a good impression on my partners."

"I will."

"Another thing Michael, tell Kathryn your plans straightaway by all means, but don't say anything to your grandfather tonight, not in the middle of your father's reception. You mustn't spoil this evening for them, and try not to be too hard on your grandfather. I think if you go about things the right way you could still remain friends."

"You're right about not telling him tonight," Michael agreed. "I'll do it first thing tomorrow morning, but I'm going to phone Kathryn and I'd like to see her so we could talk over things face to face."

He was silent for a moment. "I haven't got her itinerary. Did she leave it with you?"

"I know it off by heart. Telephone her tonight at the Swallow Hotel in Mordeen and tell her you'll see her in Leil on Friday. It's only a few days off. They'll be on the last leg of the tour by then and perhaps you could persuade your Uncle Luke to stay a few days and you could travel back with him."

"Luke's not coming," Michael said matter of factly, oblivious to the look of dismay that crept across Ruth's face. "You're right again of course, Kathryn is working so I mustn't interrupt that. I'll just speak to her tonight and tell her I'll see her in Leil at the end of the week."

Ruth's heart had sunk at Michael's first words, so Luke wasn't coming after all.

"I was hoping to see your uncle here this evening," she said casually. "We knew each other many years ago in Leil. Why isn't he coming?"

"His parishioners are organising a farewell dinner in his honour and after all these years he didn't want to let them down. My parents understood."

Ruth made a quick decision. "I'm coming to Leil with you," she said. "Leave everything to me. I'll make the necessary arrangements. All you need to do is speak to Kathryn and put things right between you."

It did flash through Michael's mind that it was strange Ruth should want to visit Leil to see his uncle, but he shrugged the thought aside. It was none of his business.

They made their way back into the ballroom and Michael went to fetch Ruth some food. They found a small table and both sat there silently deep in their own thoughts. It was Michael who broke the silence.

"Did Kathryn tell you about the photographs that went missing?" he asked.

Ruth had just taken a bite of a vol-au-vent and couldn't answer, but she nodded.

"It was strange," he continued, "but when I went to pack the album, I found they'd been returned."

"Are you sure they hadn't just slipped further down and you didn't notice?"

"No, they were taken all right and I hate to say it but it could only have been either of my grandparents who took them."

"Have you told your mother?"

"If they hadn't been returned, I would have, but now I don't know what to do. I unpacked this morning and placed the album upstairs here in the attics. I suppose Kathryn told you that the photographs were of my mother and a baby."

"No she didn't tell me that. She said she had a feeling they might be very personal and thought it better not to say too much."

"The one photograph was of a very young baby and the other was of a wedding, my mother was the bride, but my father wasn't the groom."

Suddenly Ruth knew where she'd seen Ilona before. Her thoughts took her back to the day she'd returned to Leil to see

177

Luke and she'd seen a small wedding party. Ilona had been the bride, but Michael was correct, Richard hadn't been the groom, of that she was sure.

"I think I can solve the mystery of the bridal photograph," she said. "But you'll have to be patient until we get to Leil. I think the Church there will hold the secret."

Michael started to say something, but Ruth stopped him. "I'm not going to say another word until we're in Leil. I'm going over to see my friends now, but I'll telephone you tomorrow or the next day with our travel arrangements."

As she made her way across the room, Michael called after her.

"There's dancing later, save one for me."

Ruth turned and smiled. "You'd better make it a slow one then. I'm too old for those fast ones you youngsters do."

~*~

It was late in the evening before Ilona was able to get away to the terrace for her rendezvous with Barbara. She was glad to escape the heat of the ballroom. Even though all the windows had remained open and the ceiling fans were whirling, the ballroom had become stuffy. Some of the guests, who knew of the absence of air conditioning, had brought fans with them and Ilona thought that air conditioning would be top priority in the list of things needed to be done to modernise the Governor General's residence, but doubted if they'd be there long enough to have it installed. After a few duty dances with different partners, she whispered to Richard that she wouldn't be long and waiting for the next dance to start, she slipped out on to the terrace, hoping that no one had spotted her. The night air was warm and no clouds obscured the moon that rode high, a golden yellow ball in a black sequined sky. She took a deep breath and waited for Barbara to join her. The evening so far had been successful. Many of the older statesmen and their wives remembered Richard when he had lived there with his father and were able to reminisce about the good old days. The younger generation had also been welcoming and they had both been kept busy mingling and talking to various groups. Mainly the talk was about independence and the future of the islands and which was the best way forward. There were fears that the Islands would be too small to survive on their own without the backing of the Mother country. Ilona had noticed that the older people were slightly wary of the changes that were to come and quite a few were fearful that a peaceful transition would be impossible. Amongst the younger generation, however, there was an air of excitement. Ilona was slightly surprised to hear her usually reticent husband allaying the older people's fears and making salient points about the Islands' future. Yes, she thought, he'd definitely done his homework. It was obvious from the confident way he talked that he'd made a point of bringing himself up to date on all pertinent matters, and his memory for names and faces seemed infallible.

Out of the corner of her eye, she saw Barbara emerge from a window further along the terrace and she beckoned to her to follow her around the corner of the house, where Ilona knew there was a tiled seat.

"If people come out onto the terrace for a breath of fresh air, they won't see us here, and also if we talk quietly no one should be able to eavesdrop."

"I want you to know the truth about what happened all those years ago," Barbara said quickly.

"I know Vonryn is Morgan's son," Ilona replied. "When he and Nadia came to stay with us in England, he looked so much like Morgan and then when he removed his sunglasses and I saw his yellow eyes, I was never in any doubt as to whose son he was. Oh Richard tried to fob me off saying that the yellow eyes are probably a hidden gene that resurfaced through your husband, but I never really believed that."

"You're right, he is Morgan's son," Barbara's voice was so low that Ilona had to strain to catch her words.

"And yours," Ilona said scornfully. "Oh I know Morgan only married me because his father told him too. Then he carried on his affair with you. Didn't your husband mind when you foisted your lover's bastard on him, or did you let him believe Vonryn was his?"

"That's not true." For the first time Barbara looked long and hard at Ilona and Ilona was the first to look away. "Morgan loved you Ilona. He had eyes for no one else once he'd met you." Barbara paused and sighed deeply. "Out of all this business, do you know what hurts the most?" It was a rhetorical question and Barbara didn't wait for an answer. "Vonryn believes the same ridiculous thing as you. He thinks I was unfaithful to his father. He even left without saying goodbye to his stepbrother and sister. They were terribly upset. They adore Vonryn and because of the ten years difference in their ages they've always looked up to him."

Ilona smiled. So Morgan had loved her and not Barbara after all. "Hallam told me that he'd look after my son. If I'd been thinking straight, I would have realised that he would want to watch him grow up, especially with Morgan dead."

"That wasn't the only reason. Naturally he wanted to see his grandson grow into a man, but he had it all planned that Vonryn would be his heir and Vaga."

"And by virtue of Vincent's blood ties to Hallam he could be of course," Ilona interrupted. "The cunning old devil. He's as bad, if not worse, than my father. He could have protected me and I could have kept my son. We could have told the truth, but it was obvious he didn't want it that way. He wanted my son all to himself."

"Why didn't you keep Vonryn? Hallam never said."

"I was young, frightened and desperately unhappy after Morgan's accident. I suppose I did what I'd always done and took the easy way out. I'd never rebelled against anyone until I fell in love with Morgan and when he died, nothing seemed to matter. Why did you agree to take another woman's son?"

"For similar reasons to yours. You never said no to the Vaga for one thing, but the most important reason was that I'd just suffered a miscarriage and the doctors weren't sure if I'd ever have children. They were wrong of course as I had the twins ten years later, but at the time I didn't know that. Once I saw Vonryn and knew whose son he was, I didn't really need persuading. I loved his father and I used to pretend that he was really mine and Morgan's. Do you hate me for all the years I had with him and you didn't?"

Ilona looked surprised. "Why should I? It may have been a stupid decision, but I was after all the one who agreed to give him away. I should thank you and Vincent for taking such good care of him all these years."

"I wish I could get my hands on whoever leaked this to the Press," Barbara clenched her fist and her eyes blazed with anger. "I want to hurt them as much as they've hurt Vonryn." She laughed sheepishly at her outburst and at the look of amazement on Ilona's face. "I probably wouldn't do anything, I'm not the type," she ended lamely.

"If you really wanted to do anything, I wouldn't stop you. I know who told the Press. You needn't look any further than the ballroom. It was my sister-in-law, Leah."

Barbara looked incredulous. "Why would she want to hurt Vonryn?"

"Vonryn didn't enter into it as far as she was concerned. I was the prime target. It's obvious she didn't know the whole truth that I was his mother, otherwise she'd have told them. She must have swallowed the story that my son had died. I've given up wondering why she hates me and my family so much. We were good friends once; at least I thought we were. I know that she's a desperately unhappy woman, but enough of Leah and her problems. I think it's time we took control of the situation."

"Whatever you say Ilona, but what can you do?"

Ilona sighed. It was apparent that Barbara, after her uncharacteristic flash of anger, was back to her meek self, and whatever was decided wouldn't be a joint decision. Whatever did Morgan see in her, flashed through Ilona's mind. She pushed the thought away. She mustn't antagonise Barbara in any way. A friendly Barbara would be like putty in her hands. She would make a decision and then cajole or bully Barbara into accepting it.

"One thing puzzles me, did you adopt Vonryn legally?" Ilona asked.

"No," Barbara shook her head. "Hallam said there was no need."

"How did he get a passport without his Birth Certificate? He would have had to have one to visit us in the UK with Nadia."

"I never thought about it before. It wasn't the first time he'd been abroad so he must have had one," Barbara said. "I remember now. Vonryn wanted to go to America when he was about sixteen and Hallam arranged everything. Someone from the passport office came to the island."

Ilona stood up. "We'd better get back to the reception," she said. "You go in first and I'll follow shortly. My first instinct is to tell Vonryn the truth. The Press will probe and probe and eventually will discover some details. It's better if we make a statement first, than have half-truths floating around. That could do more damage than the truth. I can't do anything whilst Vonryn and Kathryn are taking tourists around the islands, but I'll meet them in Leil and tell him then. It must be his decision in the end if we go public. He's going to hate me for giving him away and I don't know what Michael will think of me either."

A look of alarm came over Barbara's face.

"Are you going to inform your father and Hallam?"

"Eventually, but not until I've told Vonryn. It will then give me great pleasure to telephone them and tell them what I've done."

"Hallam will blame me."

"No, he won't. He'll realise that Leah started it all and by that time she'll be back in the UK so it won't matter. The only reason she's here tonight is so my father can blackmail her into telling the truth as she knows it."

They walked together to the corner of the building and Ilona peered cautiously around.

"It's all clear," she giggled. "We're like two naughty school girls who are trying to sneak back into school after an evening out."

Impulsively, Barbara kissed Ilona on the cheek and hurriedly made her way along the terrace. Ilona watched until she'd disappeared into the ballroom. She sighed deeply and stood for a few minutes watching the lights from the fishing boats twinkling and dancing on the waves. She wasn't looking forward to the next few days. A cool breeze had sprung up and suddenly she shivered. It was time to return to the ballroom. Before she could make a move, she saw to her horror her father and Leah come out onto the terrace. There was now no alternative but to wait, and for the first time in her life she intended to eavesdrop. She prayed that they wouldn't come around the corner, but luckily they only moved as far as the balustrade.

"You decided to accept my invitation then," Drystan said, speaking in a low voice and Ilona had to strain to catch his words.

"What alternative did I have?" Leah's voice sounded subdued. "What exactly do you want to know?"

"Did my daughter marry Morgan Draymer, and did she bear him a child?"

"Yes to both questions. Luke married them in Leil and she gave birth to a boy?" Leah turned to go back into the building. "Is it all right if I return to the reception now?"

Drystan caught hold of her elbow. "No, I haven't finished with you yet. Where's the child?"

"He died."

There was silence for a few seconds and Ilona breathed a sigh of relief. Leah still believed that her son had died.

"Have you proof of the death?" Drystan barked.

"None whatsoever. Now if you don't mind, I've told you all I know, so if you'd kindly take your hand off me, I'll go inside."

Drystan smiled. He didn't like Leah, but she had spirit.

"One final question and then you can go where you like. Did my wife know about any of this?"

"Of course not. She would have told you if she had."

Even to Ilona's ears, Leah's lie sounded convincing. She was glad Leah had kept her mother out of the web of deceit, but she couldn't understand why.

The smell of cigar smoke assailed her nostrils. Her father must have decided to have one of his rare cigars, and she knew he wouldn't go back inside until he'd finishing smoking it. Some homecoming this was turning out to be. Whilst her father puffed away, Ilona wondered if her return to the islands was to be a short one. All those years wasted in exile and now she was going to put it all in jeopardy, not only for herself, but for both the Draymer and Pendenny families. There was no doubt in her mind that neither Hallam Draymer nor her father would survive long away from their beloved islands, but it was too late now and the best thing would be to confess everything, first to Vonryn and then, if he agreed, to the people.

Chapter 16

August

Dear Mum and Dad,

You'll be glad to know that Michael and I are engaged again. Michael phoned me on the first evening I started the tour. I was in my room at the hotel in Mordeen getting ready for bed, when there was a knock on the door. It was the girl from reception to say that there was a phone call for me and as the bedrooms didn't have phones, I had to take it at the desk in the hotel foyer. Luckily, I'd only just slipped my dress off, so it didn't take me long to get dressed again and go downstairs. He told me that he was phoning from the party given for his father on becoming Governor. As you know I was invited, but because of this tour wasn't able to attend. He told me that he wanted to meet me when I arrived in Leil so that we could talk things through. I agreed to meet him there, but warned him that the itinerary had been changed, because the ferry we were taking from Envetta to Leil only called there for two hours before going on to the next port of call at St.Cecilia. It had been decided that instead of the tourists touring the island by bus, we would only stop for lunch at Leil before re-boarding the ferry. I went to bed feeling much happier than I had in days.

The next morning, however, just as we were leaving, he phoned me again saying that something urgent had come up and that he wouldn't be able to make it to Leil after all, but that he'd explain later. I was so annoyed with him that I put the phone down. I was still in the foyer, making sure that no one had left anything behind and had handed in their keys before we boarded the bus, when he phoned back. Of course, everyone had seen me slam the phone down and they were all very interested, although they tried to pretend they weren't, so I decided it was easier to listen to him than to make a scene. He pleaded with me to hear him out. He begged me to trust him and he also told me that Ruth was arranging for him to start work in a Solicitors' office in St. Elizabeth and that for the time being he would be living with his parents in the Governor's Mansion and not staying in Mordeen with his grandfather. He wants me to give in my notice when I go home, which under my Contract of Employment is twelve weeks. I hope you're pleased for me. I know you think he has behaved badly, but deep down I can see how it happened. The only problem is that Michael still has my ring. If you remember, I told you I gave it back to him, or to be honest, threw it back at him. It's too valuable to entrust to the post, but Michael said that Ruth is going to Leil to see Luke and she'll bring it with her. I'm being nosy, but I'm curious to know why she's meeting Luke. Perhaps after all these years, they'll get back together. It would be lovely if they could.

Now that my personal life has been sorted out, I must tell you about this tour Vonryn and I are doing. I can't remember if I told you that Vonryn is helping me. Thank goodness there are only five couples. I've never done this sort of thing before, nor Vonryn come to that, and I don't think I could have coped with a large busload. When the few times we've been on coach holidays, I never appreciated the tour rep enough. There are four married couples, three of them in your age group and the fourth couple who are quite young. We think they are on their honeymoon, but they're trying to act as if they've been married for years. The other couple is a pair of retired schoolteachers, both spinsters. They're very nice, but they treat both myself and Vonryn as if we were still in school. So far there haven't been any complaints, and as they're not paying for anything, I really don't see how they can complain, but it is important that they tell us truthfully what they think. Both Vonryn and I impressed that on them the first day we met when we were having coffee on the boat that was taking us from Lorentia to Innisver.

As the sailing distance between the islands isn't long, there is plenty of time left when we land each day to settle the people in their hotel, and after lunch offer them a short tour of part of the island in a mini bus, or if they wish they can rest in the hotel grounds by the pool or on the beach. After the tour we all have dinner and get a good nights sleep and then leave the following morning on the boat to the next island. I'm enclosing a rough sketch of the islands and names of the places where we're staying.

All the guests decided to go on the tour of Innisver and it was so strange to drive up the same avenue towards Innisver Castle. They all found the sight of the avenue of Jacaranda trees in bloom delightful, as I had done when I saw them for the first time. I accompanied them into the cathedral and other places of interest around the castle and Vonryn was able to fill them in on the history of the places they were visiting. Of course, we weren't able to see the castle itself as it is tucked away in the middle of the other buildings. I was glad that Michael wasn't in Mordeen. We hadn't made up our quarrel at that time and I wouldn't have wanted to bump into him.

Apart from visiting the capital Mordeen, we went on a short tour of part of the island. It took us quite a while as once away from the capital, the roads narrowed and twisted and turned in all directions. Vonryn had arranged for us to stop for refreshments at a vineyard up in the hills. It was a pretty area and from the terrace, where they served us wine or cups of tea if you preferred, you had a good view over the one side of the island. As well as the vines, Vonryn said that this area was mainly for fruit growing. Mr Roberts, one of the tourists, engaged Vonryn in a long discussion on the way back to the hotel about the economy of the islands. I didn't take a lot of notice as Mrs Roberts was showing me photographs of her numerous grandchildren. I gathered that the islands are a good place to invest your money and that there are several tax free ports, and of course big cruise liners call in at the outer shores and the passengers spend quite a bit of money when they come ashore. Unfortunately, as I've told you before the central straits aren't suitable for big liners, and that is why they want to develop something different in the way of tourism in this

187

area.

Vonryn and I breathed a sigh of relief when they'd all gone to bed, taking their questionnaires with them. We did have slight panic earlier on. Mr Johnson went out for a breath of air and to see if he could find an English newspaper before dinner. Both Vonryn and I told him that if he found one, it would be days old, but he insisted, so we let him go. He managed to get himself lost in the narrow winding streets of Mordeen and didn't arrive back until two hours later. His wife took it quite calmly and said that he had a terrible sense of direction. She ate her dinner and didn't seem in the least bit worried. I'm sure if it had been Dad that had gone missing, you wouldn't have been able to tuck into a three-course meal. You'd have been out searching for him. He'd called in a few bars to ask for directions. Luckily he had a rough sketch map of where the hotel was which Vonryn had drawn for him. In one bar the people there had taken pity on him and given him a free drink.

The majority of the hotels we're using aren't geared up for the wants of foreign tourists, they mainly cater for local people or visitors from the other islands, but so far they've done remarkably well. English though is widely spoken to varying degrees as it is taught in all the schools.

The next morning we set sail (metaphorically as the ship has an engine) straight after breakfast for Quan Tomay. It didn't take us long to reach the capital of Christenbech. It was a lovely old city, very narrow stepped streets, no vehicular access, so it was pleasant to wander and look at the shops. Vonryn pointed out the island of Zerrebar, the home of the Vaga. Twice a day the island can be reached by a causeway and there is only a limited period for access this way. The tide was just going out when we were there and it was a strange sight. The tide doesn't just ebb away from the island leaving one side of it exposed, but the waves separate and it's like in the Bible when Moses commanded the Red Sea to part. Our group didn't realise that the island Vonryn was talking about had been his home until very recently. After about two hours in Christenbech we crossed the bay in another boat to the port of Erda, and then our mini bus took us across the island to our hotel in Saint Thomas, where we had a late lunch. The rest of the day was free for people to do what they wanted. Most of them, myself included, opted for a swim in the sea and a lazy afternoon on the beach.

I'm writing this in a quiet corner of the boat as we travel to Envetta. Vonryn has taken the tourists for coffee and I'd better join them, so I'll finish this letter later on today or tomorrow.

Chapter 17

It had been late afternoon when Luke saw the stranger for the first time. There was something about the man that didn't ring true. Not many tourists were seen at that time of day in the village. The tourists who did come were ones with their own boats seeking a secluded beach. After mooring their craft in the small harbour, they sometimes strolled around the village, bought lunch in the bar outside which Luke was now sitting, and then were content to lie on the long white sandy beach that lay to the north of the village, and which was only a short stroll from the harbour. As there was no hotel in Leil, no one stayed overnight unless it was in their own boats or with friends or relations. Luke was drinking a glass of wine and waiting for his old friend and adversary, Paul Karna, to arrive for their evening game of chess. Paul was the Mayor of Leil and had been ever since Luke's arrival in the village. Each village, no matter how small, had a mayor and over the years, opponents had stood against Paul in the elections every five years, but so far no one had managed to oust him from his position. Luke wasn't sure whether it was fear, corruption, bribery or affection for the man that kept people voting for him, and early on had decided not to delve too deeply into the matter.

Paul was a few years older than Luke and theirs was a love hate relationship. They had crossed swords on many occasions over religion and politics, and sometimes these discussions had turned into acrimonious rows, when Luke had to remind himself that he was a man of God and should always be the first to extend the hand of friendship.

Whilst he waited for his friend, Luke thought back over the years he'd been in Leil. He was sad they were coming to an end, but in some ways excited. His work here was finished and had been many years ago if truth were told. He was ready now to return to a more sophisticated way of life. He recalled the day he'd left home and arrived in Leil. The sun had just risen above the horizon as Justin had driven him through the gates of Innisver Castle in the old car he'd borrowed from his valet. Justin's own sports car was once again in for repair. He was too fond of driving quickly through the narrow streets and bumping into walls. Thankfully that was all he'd ever bumped into. The car spent more time in the repair garage than it did in Justin's. That morning, after a gentle reminder from Luke that this car was only borrowed and was his valet's pride and joy, Justin had driven with extreme caution and had manoeuvred it deftly through the maze of alleys that led to the port of Mordeena. At that hour in the morning, the streets had been deserted and only a solitary dog wandered through the empty market square, looking for anything edible that had been left behind the day before by the traders. It had been a short drive to the harbour and the brothers had kept their goodbyes short. Luke knew how hard it had been for Justin to accept the fact that his brother was now a priest. They had both reached a turning point and their lives from then on were going to be so different.

Before Luke embarked they'd shaken hands as politely as if they'd been strangers. Justin hadn't even waited for the ferry to leave. He'd sensed that Luke's heart and soul had long since left Innisver Castle and that all his thoughts were centred around a cluster of small whitewashed houses in the fishing village of Leil, situated on the southernmost tip of Sarena, one of the British islands.

The first friends he'd made when he'd arrived in Leil had been Paul and his wife Teresa. They'd accepted him as their parish priest; Father Luke Denny. He'd dropped the first part of his name and no one knew that his father was Drystan Pendenny. Eventually he'd told Paul and Teresa of his true identity, and they'd kept faith and not revealed his secret to anyone else.

He smiled to himself as he recalled the young eager priest

he'd been, trying in the first few months to do too much and not getting anything done. Another friend in the village when he arrived had been Father John Carey, the retiring priest. He'd postponed his retirement for a few months and stayed on to help him settle in although at the time Luke couldn't wait for him to leave so that he could run the church his way. It was only years later that Luke realised how much he'd learnt through spending that time with Father John.

Paul and Teresa were newly weds when Luke had arrived in Leil. He'd shared their joy on the birth of each of their three sons, but as the boys grew into men, they'd become restless and wanted more than the village could offer. He'd joined in Paul and Teresa's distress when two of them had emigrated, one to the UK and one to Australia. It was after witnessing Teresa's tears on the departure of the second son that Luke had decided to use his money and influence to aid the village. The fishermen had started a co-operative and had opened a small refrigeration unit on the outskirts of the village, where fish could be frozen and then delivered in special refrigerated vans to various restaurants and hotels that were springing up on the north of Sarena and on Lorentia. Father John before him had tried to help bright pupils in the school, but without money behind him he'd only been able to help one or two by applying for grants. Luke had resources, and he picked up where Father John had left off and encouraged bright pupils to study hard and go to University. He had many a tussle with his conscience over this, because he knew that the majority of them would never return to the village or the old way of life. His next plan to help the village had come about by accident. He'd been on one of his rare visits to see his parents, and he'd told his mother about his plans for the village and it was she who remembered drinking wine that had been made by Drystan's eccentric Uncle Solomon. It had never been marketed as the family had thought it beneath their dignity to do such a thing, but Ria remembered drinking it and said that it was an exceptionally fine wine. They'd ploughed steadfastly through Solomon Pendenny's notebooks until they'd found the recipe they'd been seeking. The recipe, however, had been a great disappointment, for it was a commonplace one using berries from the Zarin tree. There had been a footnote, but this had been written in pencil and had faded over the years and was virtually impossible to read. All they had been able to decipher was that for every pint, a handful of something had to be added to the mixture. Luke remembered his frustration at the time, for without that mystery ingredient, there would be no point in making the wine. The berries of the Zarin tree grew in such abundance that even the poorest villagers made wine from them.

Over dinner that evening, Luke had told his father about the recipe and the futile attempts he'd made to read the footnote. Drystan hadn't said anything, but Luke had noticed that a self-satisfied smile had lit up his father's face when he'd thought his son and wife weren't looking.

"That's a portrait of your great uncle Solomon on the wall behind you," Drystan had said when they'd finished dinner and were sipping their post prandial brandies.

Luke recalled how he'd taken his brandy glass and walked over to take a closer look at his ancestor. Solomon had been painted out of doors seated beneath a Zarin tree. In a dish by his side there were a few killun fruits, a small round hard fruit that was mainly left on the bushes for the birds and animals to eat, although it could be made into jam. He remembered wondering why anyone would want to have a dish of inedible fruits by their side, when the solution had dawned on him. Luke had turned to his father who merely nodded. Armed with this recipe, Luke had returned to the village, and after experimenting with the proportion of each ingredient, had been able to produce a fine wine. Soon the demand for this wine far exceeded its output and the recipe was a closely guarded secret known to only a few people. Just in case an accident should befall the people who knew it, Luke had placed a copy in a bank vault in Mordeen. If the recipe were lost for a second time, it was unlikely that a connection would be made between the painting of his Uncle and the wine. Luke came back from his reverie to see Paul coming towards him.

"Teresa says you're to have dinner with us tonight," he said as he heaved his large frame onto the flimsy chair that must have been stronger than it looked, for so far it had never collapsed. "I took the liberty of telling Angelina. I hope you don't mind."

"Of course, I don't. I want to see as much of you and Teresa as I can until I leave next week. All the village has been so kind, the party the other night and the presents they gave me, which I know some of them could ill afford."

"I signed the deed for the land adjacent to mine this morning," Paul said, as he poured himself a glass of wine. "Next spring Simon and his wife and family will be coming home from Britain to help us run it. We will have two sons here then. Teresa's cup of happiness would be full if only Peter would return also."

"I'm only sorry I won't be here to help his wife settle in."

"Paul looked puzzled. "I don't understand. To live here is like living in paradise."

Luke shook his head; everything was so simple to Paul.

"She'll need help. It will be a big culture shock for her, the way of life, the language.

Everything will be different to what she has been accustomed to. To start with Paul, you must see to it that they have a place of their own to live in before they arrive. Your other son, Adam, has built his own place now and I'm sure he wouldn't mind helping you build a small bungalow."

A worried expression flitted across Paul's face. "I see what you mean. We were so thrilled he was returning home, that Teresa and I couldn't think of anything else. If she doesn't settle, then Simon won't, and if he leaves Leil again, Teresa will never recover. There is an old dwelling on the land I've just bought, and perhaps Adam and I can do it up for them."

"Don't worry too much. Just don't expect her to behave as Teresa's generation did. Even your native born daughter-in-law behaves in a more modern manner. Make allowances that's all. Was she brought up in a city?"

"No. Her father had a small farm. Simon was working on a big farm nearby."

"That's something at least. She will be used to village life, which

I don't suppose is that much different here."

The two men sat in companionable silence in the pleasant warmth of early evening. They moved their chess pieces across the board, both conscious of the fact that there were only a few of these evenings left to them. Luke hated to leave his friend, but the excitement of Simon's homecoming would alleviate the parting of two old friends. Eventually Paul called checkmate and Luke was about to suggest another game, when a shadow fell across the board. It was the stranger. He was of average height, with a dark swarthy skin and wavy black hair that had been flattened with grease in a futile attempt to make it lie flat. His eyes were hidden behind sunglasses, although the strength of the sun's rays had lost their brightness. Everything about him spoke money, from his casual, but expensive clothes, to the designer glasses.

"May I join you Father?" He asked. His voice was deep and accentless. "I have a slight problem and I hope you can help me."

At the sound of a stranger's voice, Luke's dogs, who had been lying quietly under the table, raised their heads and looked warily at the man. Luke spoke softly to them and with one final appraisal of the stranger, they once again rested their heads on their paws and slept.

Luke motioned for the man to sit down. "Anything I can do, I will."

"It's a simple problem really. I've missed the last bus out and as there's no hotel, I was wondering if you knew of any suitable lodgings for one night. I was looking around your church and completely lost track of time."

"You're most welcome to stay with me in the presbytery. There is plenty of room."

"That's very kind of you, if you are sure it won't be too much trouble. My name is Marcus Trevant by the way."

Luke introduced himself and Paul and the three men shook hands.

"I'm going out this evening for dinner, but I'm sure my housekeeper could fix you a snack before she goes home." Luke kicked Paul under the table. He hoped that Paul would realise that the kick meant he wasn't to invite the man to join them for dinner. Paul felt the kick, and not knowing what it was for, decided the best thing to do was to keep silent.

"A snack would be most welcome. I had a large lunch here earlier on."

Paul offered Marcus a glass of wine and beckoned to the owner to fetch another glass.

"What made you come to Leil, and more especially why by public transport, the buses are very infrequent in these parts?" he asked.

"I'm researching my family tree and that's the reason I got so engrossed and forgot the time. I had a few days to spare and thought I'd visit Leil for myself. I'm staying in the island capital of St. Cecilia and intended driving down for the day, but when my hire car developed a fault, I decided to visit Leil by bus. I persuaded the man you'd left in charge of the church to let me have a look at the church records. I hope you don't mind?" he turned to Luke.

"Of course not, they are public records after all, but why come all this way, when you could have looked them up in the records office on computer."

"I started that way of course," Marcus turned to thank the owner of the bar for the glass and Paul filled it to the brim. "It was an impulse really. I wanted to see the village and church and feel the ambience of the place. To get in touch with my roots if you like," Marcus looked a little embarrassed at this speech and Luke tried to refrain from smiling.

"I see," he said. "You noticed of course that one book is missing."

Marcus nodded. "Yes, I was very disappointed. It covered the years I wanted to see, but as you said it's all on computer, and at least I've visited the church. What happened to the other book?" he asked.

"It got damaged by fire," Luke replied. Paul looked bemused. He was trying to think when there'd been a fire in the church, but couldn't. Luke hoped God would understand his white lie. The book had been damaged by fire, but only slightly. He himself had put a match to it in one corner, snuffing out the flames before they got a hold. The book, wrapped in polythene, lay under a stone beneath the altar. Luke had worked hard one evening doing this. Knowing the nosiness of the villagers, he'd told them that he was relaying some of the stones in the nave that had sunk over the years, and as a cover for his story he'd been obliged to do this as well.

Luke groaned suddenly. "I've just remembered, computerisation of the records started after the fire so you've reached a dead end there as well."

Marcus shrugged his shoulders. "It doesn't matter. It would have been nice to find out but it wasn't that important."

The clock on the church struck the hour and Paul downed his wine in one gulp. "We'd better go," he said. "Teresa doesn't like being kept waiting for dinner." He turned to Marcus. "I'm only sorry we haven't more time to chat. I know most of the family histories of the villagers and I'm sure I could have helped you."

Marcus smiled, "Yes it is a shame, but I have to leave tomorrow, pressure of business you know."

As Luke stood up, the dogs crawled out from under the table and the three men walked to the Presbytery. Luke introduced Marcus to his housekeeper and took him to the room where he would be spending the night. As Angelina would be leaving after she'd prepared a snack for Marcus, Luke told him to help himself to wine and showed him where he kept the television.

"If you should want to go out for a walk, you'll have to wait outside until I return home, as I don't have a spare key." Luke said as he was leaving.

Marcus intimated that he'd be perfectly happy to sit and watch television until Luke's return.

It was only a short walk to Paul's house, through lanes that smelt of rosemary and wild thyme. Paul looked thoughtful as they left the presbytery.

"I've racked my brains and I can't think of any family by that name who lived in the village."

"You won't Paul. It was all a big bluff."

197

"I know you're a man of God Luke, but aren't you a bit trusting then, to leave a complete stranger in your house and one you don't trust at that. You should have left the dogs there."

"It will give him plenty of time to search it," Luke replied enigmatically. "Anyway it was obvious the dogs didn't take to him so they'd have only got in his way, even maybe prevented him from doing what he came for."

"You're speaking in riddles Luke."

"I know. I think I'd better tell you the whole story. It doesn't matter now, because I think it's going to come out in the open shortly, but until it does, please don't tell anyone else, not even Teresa."

Paul listened in silence as Luke told him about Ilona's marriage to Morgan Draymer and of the subsequent birth of their son Vonryn.

"I understand what you're saying Luke, but it's obvious that your father knows the truth already, so why send a man down here. It all seems pointless to me."

"There's a huge difference between suspecting and being able to prove it. Once he holds the proof, he can decide what to do, make it public or destroy the evidence. I hope Marcus didn't find the hiding place in the church."

"Of course he didn't find anything," Paul said, unlatching the garden gate, and bending to pat two brown and white dogs of indiscriminate parentage that greeted him excitedly. "If he'd found anything there, he wouldn't have missed the last bus. There wouldn't have been any reason for him to do so."

Luke smiled. "You're right of course and I don't believe he came by bus. He probably has some sort of transport waiting for him somewhere. That was a ploy so he could stay the night. He knew there were no lodgings here and that a priest wouldn't refuse him refuge. It was a bonus that I was going out." Luke wrinkled his nose and sniffed appreciatively. "That smell coming from the kitchen is delicious. Do you think Teresa would mind if I didn't rush home afterwards? I must give Marcus the opportunity to search thoroughly."

~*~

As Angelina, the housekeeper, lived out, Luke normally prepared his own breakfast. Usually he breakfasted on fruit and cereals, but the following morning he decided he would give Marcus a good send off, and cooked bacon and eggs for them both. He deftly lifted the fried eggs out of the pan and placed them with the bacon and grilled tomatoes on the two plates he'd left warming in the oven. Luke smiled to himself; Marcus didn't seem to have much of an appetite, yet he seemed to be the type of man who would enjoy his food. It was obvious that Marcus had failed in his mission to find proof of Ilona's marriage. He couldn't resist saying to Marcus that he was sorry his search for his ancestors hadn't been successful. Marcus didn't reply and Luke felt an unchristian sense of satisfaction knowing how much Marcus must be dreading telling Drystan of his failure. He was relieved when the eleven o'clock bus left the village and his unwelcome guest had finally departed. He wondered whether to meet the bus when it returned later in the day and ask the bus driver if Marcus had travelled all the way to St. Cecilia, but in the end decided against it. What did it matter if Marcus had a car in the next village, the important thing was that he'd gone.

He walked slowly back to the presbytery deep in thought. The sun was hot and a few beads of perspiration trickled down his forehead. It would be nice, he thought, if he could wander around in shorts, but didn't think the people of the village would like it. It was selfish of him, he knew, but he didn't want to think about Vonryn or the Islands' independence. He wanted to savour his last few days in Leil in peace. As he approached the church he noticed a woman sitting on the low stonewall that surrounded the churchyard. Her head was turned away from Luke, but on hearing footsteps, she stood up and to Luke's surprise he saw it was Ruth Graham. For a few seconds, they stared at one another and then Luke found he was holding her closely, but who had made the first move he could never remember.

"I'm so pleased to see you Ruth, but I must admit you're the last person I expected to see. When you didn't reply to my note, I thought you didn't want to meet me."

"I left Christenbech straight after the meeting, so by the time your note reached me at home, it was too late." She didn't say that Gregory Rollins had delivered the note, but let Luke assume that the hotel had forwarded it on to her. "I thought I'd see you at the reception to welcome Richard, but of course you were having a party of your own."

Realising they were out in the road, and at any moment someone from the village could pass, he let his arms drop and released Ruth from his embrace. "We can't talk here," he said. "We need somewhere private." They walked slowly through the churchyard until they reached a wooden door that led into the Presbytery garden. The door was set into a high brick wall and creaked slightly as Luke opened it. "I've been meaning to oil these hinges for some time."

He stood aside so that Ruth could enter first. She looked around her and memories came flooding back. Nothing had changed she thought. It was as though she had stepped back in time, except she wasn't a young girl any longer. As they walked up the garden path a smell of cooking wafted out to meet them.

"It smells as if Angelina is cooking her famous chicken stew, that is if she is still with you after all these years."

"Oh she's still with me, somewhat greyer and fatter than when you knew her, but she doesn't trust anyone else to take care of me."

He opened the fly screen door. "Angelina," he called. "Look who has come to visit you?"

Angelina turned from the stove and looked at Ruth. She brushed back a piece of hair that had flopped down over her forehead. It was obvious that she didn't recognise the elegant woman who stood before her. She wiped her hands on her apron and proffered a now clean hand to Ruth in formal greeting.

"Lina," Ruth said. "Please make cream tart for me. You know it's my favourite."

As recognition swept over Angelina's features, all formality was forgotten and she threw her arms around Ruth and clasped her so tightly against her bosom that Ruth thought she would suffocate.

"Why did you stay away so long? Why didn't you write more? How long are you staying?" A torrent of words flowed from Angelina's mouth.

"If you'll let me breathe, I'll answer your questions, but first do you think I could have something cool to drink."

Angelina released Ruth and started to hustle them out of her kitchen. "I'm forgetting my manners," she said. "Go and sit on the terrace the both of you. Lunch is ready and just before you came in I put a bottle of wine out there in an ice bucket." A worried expression came over her face and she looked at Ruth's linen suit. "I hope I didn't mark it when I hugged you."

"You didn't, but I wouldn't care if you had. It's washable."

The table on the terrace was only laid with one place setting, but Angelina soon rectified that. An overhead trellis, covered in bougainvillea, screened them from the increasing heat of the mid day sun. During the simple meal of sardine salad and small new potatoes, cooked in their skins and then sprinkled with sea salt, neither Ruth nor Luke spoke much, and the little they did say was confined to everyday matters. After eating, they sat contentedly drinking sweet black coffee, and in the distance, they could hear Angelina singing to herself as she washed the dishes. Ruth stood up and waited for Luke to finish his coffee and then carried the cups out to the kitchen. She picked up a tea towel and started to wipe the dishes.

"I see he hasn't bought you a dishwasher yet?"

"What do I want with one of them things? I don't live in anymore, and Father Luke doesn't entertain a lot these days."

Ruth was surprised. "When did you move out?" she asked.

"About a month ago. I'm not getting any younger and I don't know if I could put up with a new priest, so when I heard Father Luke was leaving, I was terribly worried. There aren't any places to rent in the village at the moment, so I thought George and me could go and live with my sister in St. Cecilia for the time being and then maybe get a flat there, but George didn't want to go, and to tell the truth I'd miss the village."

Ruth remembered George, Angelina's husband very well. He was a small wiry man and Angelina even in her younger days would have made two of him, but he had a will of iron and what George wanted, George usually got. It was sad that they'd never been able to have children, because Angelina would have made a good mother, as it was she was a surrogate mother and now grandmother to many of the children in Leil."

"So you managed to get a flat here then?"

"It's not a flat," Angelina said with great dignity. "It's a small house. It's down by the harbour. One of those small cottages up on the cliff, with lovely long gardens, where we can grow our own vegetables and there's room for George to keep his chickens. When the old man who lived there died, his children wouldn't rent it to anyone. They've all moved away from the village so they wanted to sell it. It was Father Luke's going away present to us." She looked around guiltily. "I'm not supposed to tell anyone that. Father Luke says that when people ask, I'm to say I saved up for it, but no one will believe me. How could George and me have saved such a sum of money? Anyway I promised faithfully I wouldn't tell."

Trying not to smile Ruth wondered how long Angelina would keep the secret. All the village would know as soon as Luke left Leil, Ruth was sure of that. Angelina wouldn't be able to keep quiet any longer.

"I'm going to miss him terribly." Tears welled up in the corner of Angelina's eyes and she used the corner of her apron to wipe them away.

"I know you will," Ruth said and put a comforting arm around the housekeeper's shoulders.

"Could I stay with you tonight, Angelina? I know there's plenty of room here, but you know what the people in the village are like. They wouldn't approve."

"No, my house is too small, but you can stay the night here. Don't worry about gossip in the village; I'll make sure they know that I'm spending the night here as well. George won't mind. If I'm not there, he'll be able to stay out as late as he likes playing cards and drinking with his friends. I'll go upstairs straight away and prepare the rooms. It will be like old times having you here." She paused and looked pleadingly at Ruth. "Before you leave, it would be nice if we could have a long chat. You could tell me all about what you've been up to and why you've never come back to see us."

"I'd love that," Ruth said simply, patting her hand. "I did return once, but only for a few hours."

Angelina looked at her long and hard. "I understand more than you think. Don't forget I'm not that much older than you and I had eyes to see what your feelings were for him."

Ruth looked at the short fat housekeeper before her and realised with surprise that Angelina was only about fifteen years older than her and Luke. She'd always seemed so much older.

"It was easier to stay away. I thought I could forget him and I did up to a point."

"You never married?"

"No. I never met anyone else I wanted to make a lifetime commitment to, so I buried myself in work."

"What I could never understand though was why he let you go." Angelina continued. "After you left he was desolate. It never made sense, at least not to me. You shouldn't be here helping me with the dishes; you should be out in the garden chatting to Father Luke. We can chat later on. I'll go and prepare the bedrooms and before I go I'll leave this chicken stew in the oven on a very low light. Don't forget about it. As you're here, I won't come back until this evening. I'll leave you to see to his tea."

Ruth promised faithfully not to forget the stew and kissed Angelina affectionately on the cheek before returning to the garden and Luke. She was dreading it, but the time had come for them to talk of the past and hopefully put it behind them. The question she most wanted answered was - did they have any sort of future together?

"The coffee's still hot if you'd like another cup Ruth, or I could open a bottle of wine.

"No, coffee will be fine." Ruth returned to the kitchen and

fetched two coffee cups and then they sat in silence until they heard Angelina shutting the front door.

"I suppose Angelina has made a bed up for you and she'll be staying the night?"

"How did you know that I'd be staying?"

He laughed and the years seemed to drop away from him and he was the young priest she remembered.

"I took it for granted. I felt the things we had to say to one another shouldn't be hurried. If you'd said you'd be rushing back, I'd have tried to persuade you not to."

"I could have been staying with Angelina. I understand she doesn't live in any more."

"No. When I told her I was leaving, I could see she was worried about a new priest coming and her and George getting older, so I decided to buy a property for them. With the pension they'll be having from me, they'll manage just fine. It's a nice little cottage, but it's too small to accommodate you as well. There's no hotel in Leil as yet, although Paul has plans to build a small one eventually, so the logical place for you to sleep was here. Angelina has very strict moral guidelines so I knew she would be staying as well. Does that answer your question?"

"Why did you want to see me?"

"I wanted to tell you I was leaving Leil, and after seeing you in that meeting, I felt I owed you an explanation. You were the last person I expected to see."

"It was quite a shock to me too," Ruth replied. "I never connected Father Luke with Drystan Pendenny. After the meeting, my emotions were so confused that I had a mad impulse to hire a boat and follow you to Zerrebar. Nadia pointed out that if I'd tried to land I would have been arrested."

Ruth bent down and reached into her handbag and pulled out a small parcel.

"Will you give this to Kathryn tomorrow? I take it you know they're stopping here."

"Yes to both questions. They're all having lunch at the tavern. A new extension has been built at the rear as there is quite a lot of trade in the day time." He handled the package thoughtfully. "This feels like it might be a ring box. Is the engagement on again and if so why isn't Michael here himself to give Kathryn it back."

"I don't know. One minute he was full of coming with me and then the next thing I know is he's changed his mind, but apparently they are still engaged."

"Do you think my father had a hand in changing his mind?" Luke asked.

"I don't think so, but to be honest I don't really know. As soon as Michael said he wouldn't be travelling with me, I caught the next ferry, hired a car in St. Cecilia and here I am."

Ruth then went on to explain about the photographs that Michael had found, and how they'd disappeared when Michael was staying in Innisver Castle, but then mysteriously had reappeared.

"I see," Luke said, but didn't elaborate. No wonder Marcus had turned up in Leil, he thought. It was obvious his father had seen the photographs and now wanted proof.

"Did you see the photographs?" he asked casually.

Ruth shook her head.

"No, but when I met Ilona in the reception, I couldn't help feeling that we'd met somewhere before, and then it came to me. I'd seen her here that day I returned to tell you I'd got my degree. You'd just married a couple and Ilona was the bride, but Richard wasn't the bridegroom. Are you going to tell me the truth now?"

"Yes." Then for the second time in two days he spoke of Ilona's marriage and the subsequent birth of Vonryn. He didn't ask Ruth to keep quiet, he just knew she would.

"Is that the reason you've stayed here all these years?"

Luke didn't reply for a minute.

"I don't honestly know. I always intended to stay here for a good while if the people wanted me, but maybe not as long as I have done."

"I thought you loved me," Ruth sounded bitter, "But you made it quite obvious then that you couldn't wait to get rid of me."

"It wasn't as simple or as straightforward as that. I cared for you very deeply, but I'd just conducted a secret wedding ceremony.

I knew my father didn't want Ilona to marry Morgan, but I went ahead and did it. I loved you enough to let you go. I thought it would only be for a short time, but then Morgan got killed and things got more complicated and I had to stay here, but apart from losing you, I didn't really mind. You see I've never had much ambition, unlike my father, and I was happy. I could have asked you to come back here and share my life, but what sort of career could you have had in Leil? It wasn't meant to be, the timing was all wrong and I wasn't ready to leave."

"Because of Ilona and her secret?" Ruth said, unable to keep the bitterness out of her voice.

"Never think that. You can't blame Ilona. She never asked me to stay. It was my decision. I thought at the time I was doing the right thing. Answer me truthfully, Ruth. Have you ever felt you'd missed out by not marrying and having a family?"

"I've never thought about it," she replied.

"You've just given me your answer. I don't believe that there is only one woman for one man or vice versa. Throughout our lives we meet other people with whom we could fall in love and have a good relationship. I wouldn't believe you if you said that you'd never been attracted to anyone else. Think about it."

"I've been attracted many times, but not enough to make a lifelong commitment."

Luke stood up suddenly. "Let's take a stroll to the beach. I've time before I hear confession."

Ruth followed him down the garden. Luke had given her quite a few things to think about. They walked silently through the winding streets of the village, and across the square. Inquisitive eyes looked at her, but there was no recognition on their faces. Had she changed that much, she wondered. She wanted to shout out and say, I'm Ruth Graham, I was born here. I'm not an outsider, I'm one of you, but suddenly it struck her. She was an outsider, and from the first day she'd left, only one thing would have brought her back to Leil, and that would have been if Luke had asked her.

They sat in companionable silence on the sea wall, watching the sunlight dancing on the waves and the small brightly coloured boats bobbing up and down in the sea.

"You were right," she said suddenly. "I never felt I'd missed out on a family. I've been too busy enjoying my career in the law and then in politics, although I'm not standing as an MP again. Apart from Michael and my partners, you're the only person I've told. I had to tell Michael, because I've arranged for him to have an interview for a job with my old law firm in St. Elizabeth. He has a good chance of getting it and not because of who he is."

"Why are you giving up politics now? I would have thought that after independence it would have been an exciting time."

"It will be exciting, but I'm getting older and I feel I'd like more time for myself."

"Will you retire completely?"

Ruth looked horrified, "I'm not ready for that yet. I'll go back to being a working partner with my old firm. That's one of the reasons I wanted to speak to you. My partners are thinking of opening a new office in Mordeen. Both Stephen and Hugh are married and they don't want to relocate. If Michael had more experience he could work there, but as he hasn't, I'm the obvious choice. I have no ties, apart from loyalty to my housekeeper, who has been with me for many years, but I'm confident she'll be happy to come with me. I know she originally came from Innisver and still has a large family there. I feel I owe my partners a favour, as they were quite happy to take over my workload whilst I was off being an MP. I'd heard on the grapevine that you were leaving Leil and moving back to Mordeen and," she broke off abruptly.

"You weren't sure what my reaction would be to your move there," Luke finished off her sentence. He stared out to sea, his face impassive and Ruth was unable to read his thoughts.

She stood up abruptly.

"I can see you hate the thought of me living in the same town as you, so I'll suggest we open an office somewhere else."

She felt her eyes filling up with tears and didn't want Luke to see them. After all these years, she'd hoped for so much from this meeting. Then she felt a hand on her wrist, pulling her down on to the wall, and she turned to look at him.

His face was wreathed in smiles. "It will be wonderful," he said. "When I saw you again at the meeting, I knew I'd made a huge mistake all those years ago, and now fate is offering us a chance to start again. We'll take things slowly and see what happens, if that's all right with you."

Ruth smiled back at him. "We might be sick to death of the sight of each other in a couple of months."

"I don't think so, but we'll worry about that if and when it happens."

They walked happily back to the village, and Luke tucked her arm through his. As they neared the square, she tried to remove her arm, but he stopped her.

"What will the villagers say?" She remonstrated.

"I don't care. Let's give them something to talk about. Angelina will put them straight eventually. Don't worry."

Chapter 18

.... I never did get around to finishing this letter yesterday evening. There was entertainment laid on in the hotel, just folk dancing, but by the time it finished, I was ready to go to bed. You can't say we're doing much each day, but it is surprising how tiring all this moving around from one place to another is, and of course you're living out of a suitcase which doesn't help. As I said the entertainment was only a local folk dancing group, but everyone enjoyed themselves. The folk dancers dragged some of our party on to the floor to dance with them. It was hilarious, as none of us knew the steps.

After breakfast we were once again on the move, this time to Nereda, which is the capital of Envetta. I'm enclosing a few postcards of the islands we've visited and you'll see how different Envetta is from the others. There is a coastal plain around the island, which I gather is quite fertile, but the centre is heavily wooded and mountainous and the summit is above the tree line. There are no roads from one side of the island to the other, only mountain tracks and during certain months of the year these can be dangerous. The island boasts one main highway, which runs all the way through the plains around the island. Envetta gets the most rain of all of the islands because of its position and high mountains. Of course Mr Roberts wanted to know why, and Vonryn wasn't around at that moment, but luckily he'd left me some notes about Envetta and I was able to look it up for Mr Roberts. If I ever do another tour, I'll have to do some homework and have certain facts at my fingertips. It doesn't give a good impression if I have to look up everything. The majority of people are content to look at beautiful scenery and have a swim and sunbathe, but you'll always get the ones who want to know the ins and outs about a place.

To get up into the mountains you have to make a tortuous ascent along narrow tracks by cog railway. It looked very old and ramshackle. How they ever built it is a mystery to me, but they did. We were all very quiet travelling upwards in to the clouds. I think we all had visions of something going wrong, but the man in charge assured us that the railway was perfectly safe. He was a jovial fat man, who told us that he augmented his income from farming by working on the railway three days a week. When he laughed his whole body shook. It was quite unnerving.

We travelled upwards at a leisurely pace, through dense avenues of trees that clung tenaciously to the hillsides, marvelling at the sight of brightly coloured birds. Every now and again there'd be an open space between the trees, and provided the clouds had drifted away, we'd get some spectacular views over the Neran Straits to Quan Tomay.

We eventually arrived at our destination where the terrain levelled out into a small plain before rising once more above the tree line. Only experienced mountaineers travelled any further up the mountain, which still had a sprinkling of snow on its peak. It wasn't cold, but there was a freshness in the air which after the humidity of the coastal belt was refreshing. We were to stay the night in the small hotel there. Vonryn told us that a section of it belonged to the Vaga and used to be the summer home of the Royal family. Occasionally it is still used by the Vaga, but not exclusively, and for most of the summer it is given over to tourists. Usually the people who stay here are ones who are interested in either the geology of the region or the flora and fauna, or the type who want to really get away from everything. I don't think I should like to stay too long. It is much too quiet, although the hotel itself is very comfortable and there is a small heated indoor swimming pool to the rear.

After lunch, Vonryn took us on a short guided walk. Envetta is the island where Philip had his accident, but Vonryn knows his way around so he didn't take us anywhere dangerous. He showed us small walk-in mines where Envis stones used to be cut from the rocks. Commercial mining had never been that big an enterprise, but now that scientists have found a way to make synthetic stones, most mining has stopped. There was a small museum in the hotel showing some small stones of all different hues set into different pieces of jewellery, and alongside there were similar pieces set with synthetic stones. The synthetic stones seemed duller in comparison with the real ones, but they were still very beautiful, and once separated from their genuine neighbours, it would take an expert to tell the difference. I told Vonryn about the stone I'd seen in the vault in London. He said it was very rare and a perfect example of an Envis stone, and remarked that it was strange that such a stone should be in the possession of Michael's parents. I remembered that Richard had told us in his talk that all Envis stones belonged to the Vaga and that only members of the immediate family of the Vaga had the right to wear one. I made a note to ask Michael about it next time we met, that is if we don't quarrel first. We did find some semi precious stones, very small but very pretty in the stream nearby. The heavy rains sometimes dislodged the tinier stones from their rock homes. We all enjoyed ourselves, but our arms got rather wet and cold. Mr Carter, the one we think is on honeymoon, spent ages poking about in the stream, and we had to nearly drag him away with us, as we didn't want him to get lost. Back at the hotel, our small bags of stones had to be weighed and if we wished we could buy them. I could see Mr Carter in deep consultation with Vonryn. He kept looking over his shoulder and looked very shifty. I wondered what on earth it was all about, but Vonryn said he'd been asking where he could get the stones polished and mounted as a present for his wife. Attached to the hotel is a small workshop that specialises in such a thing and the three of us went along to see for ourselves. I'd asked Mrs Roberts to keep Mrs Carter occupied for a while. It would be a shame to spoil her husband's surprise.

There was a father and son working there, and once again they only did this on a part time basis. The older man showed us some wonderful designs for brooches, necklaces and bracelets that could incorporate the smallest of stones and bring out their best. Dependent on what price you wanted to pay, you could have them set in various metals. I was only sorry I hadn't collected enough to have something made for you Mum, but in the end I bought you a lovely pair of earrings that were on sale there. Mr Carter decided on a cross and, believe it or not, it would be forwarded to our hotel in St Elizabeth before the Carters returned home, how is that for service for you.

We were all quite tired when we returned to the hotel, and after dinner, most people retired to bed early. Vonryn and I did stay downstairs talking for a while. He still doesn't know what he is going to do once this tour ends, but at least he is doing something and not sitting around moping. I did try to broach the subject of Nadia, but he refused to discuss it, saying that it was better for them both if they married others. I said that he couldn't believe Nadia would put money before him, and he said no, he knew she wouldn't but he was frightened that one day in the future she might regret the sacrifice.

The next morning, for the first time in my stay in the islands, I awoke to a cloudy morning. I opened the bedroom curtains and couldn't see any further than the balcony. During the night a dense mist had descended. By the time we'd eaten breakfast, the heavens had opened and it was as if I was back home in Wales. It was tipping down with rain. The five couples seemed shell shocked. They didn't have an umbrella or mackintosh between them. The hotel must have been used to this sort of weather, because they kindly supplied us with huge umbrellas as we made our way to the small buggies that were to take us to the railway. This time we were descending to the other side of the island, to a small village called Lorand. We would then catch another ferry for Leil where Michael's uncle is the priest. We've had quite a bit of feedback from the tourists. They are enjoying the short tour, but the majority are fed up with catching different ferries each day. They would prefer to be based on board a ship or stay on one island and have the choice of doing tours or lazing on the beaches. To make it viable to use a ship, we'd have to have more people on the tour.

You couldn't have an empty ship, albeit a small ship, waiting each night just to act as a floating hotel for a handful of people. It is definitely something to consider though.

It had stopped raining by the time we boarded the railway, although all we could see above and below us were fluffy white cotton wool clouds. Everything seemed unreal. Suddenly there was a break in the clouds overhead and a small sliver of blue sky appeared. As we descended, the clouds drifted away and we could see the coastal plain and a beautiful green lake shimmering in the sun. Vonryn said it was Lake Iris. As we descended, steam was rising from the ground as the hot sun dried out everything and then over the mountain behind us the most beautiful rainbow appeared in the sky. We all gasped at the clarity and purity of the colours. Vonryn said that a legend had arisen that when the rainbow made a circle the islands would once again be reunited as one country. I can't see that ever happening, can you?

I hope you can read my writing. I'm scribbling away like mad. If I don't get this posted today from Leil, I'll probably be home in Bath before you get it. We're having lunch in Leil, but as it won't be ready for a while, Vonryn has taken our party to see the church. Apart from some local dishes on the menu, our lot were thrilled to see that if they wished they could have a full English breakfast or fish and chips for lunch. As we're off the beaten track for tourists, we were quite surprised, but on speaking to the proprietor it transpired that he'd spent some time in England and knowing that we were coming, he thought the tourists would appreciate it. After lunch we'll board the same ferry again and travel around the island to the capital, St. Cecilia, where we spend the night. It's a pity we can't see more of this island, but the ferry only stays a couple of hours here loading and unloading and picking up inter island passengers. After breakfast tomorrow it's only a short ferry ride across to the island of Lorentia and after a tour of that island we arrive back in St. Elizabeth, our starting point. I don't know whether I'll stay with Ruth for a couple of days, but I think I've imposed on her long enough, so I'll probably fly straight home.

See you soon.
Love,
Kathryn
xxxxx

P.S. Vonryn came back from the church and he had my engagement ring. I knew Michael was arranging for Ruth to bring it. As I said earlier, I'm dying to know why she wanted to see Luke. Vonryn asked me if I'd mind going on alone with the tourists to St. Cecilia. By all accounts Ilona had flown in to the island that morning and was on her way to Leil. She and Luke had urgent business to discuss with Vonryn. I told him that I didn't mind going on alone and that we'd meet up later in the evening at the hotel. I didn't ask him how he'd be getting there, but presumably Luke or Ilona will arrange something.

Chapter 19

It was nearing one o'clock before Ilona and Richard bade farewell to their departing guests, and thankfully retired to their private quarters. Michael was already there, sprawled in a chair in the corner of the room, his legs dangling over the arm. He was watching a video, but when his parents entered the room, he pressed the remote control and switched off the tape. "I've made coffee for all of us," he said. "I expect you could do with it."

Ilona slipped off her high-heeled shoes and sank into one of the large pale green brocade settees that stood each side of a huge tiled coffee table. The coolness of the marble floor brought relief to her weary feet. She looked around the room with pleasure. In the forthcoming months, this would be the place where she could retreat from the social niceties expected of the Governor General's wife and relax and be herself. There were only a few pieces of furniture in the room that had travelled from England with them, one of them being a bookcase and bureau, somewhat scratched in places through their constant moves. The high ceilings and walls were all painted white, and as she accepted a cup of coffee from her husband, she contemplated which of their few paintings would bring some colour into the room. Tomorrow, she decided, she would unpack her collection of miniature houses and display them on the glass shelves each side of the fireplace. The fireplace served no useful purpose in that climate; it was merely a focal point. Sometimes the evenings could get a little chilly and then the electric fire that was inset into the fireplace could be turned on. The double French windows opened out onto a balcony that commanded a good view of the bay. The lightweight curtains fluttering slightly in the night breeze were also white with a delicate floral design that matched the pale green of the furniture. Before settling down on the settee opposite his wife, Richard shut the windows, foiling the efforts of a large moth that, attracted by the light, was trying to gain entry.

"You look tired," he said.

"I'm just glad that it's over. How do you think it went?"

"Very well. Quite a number of people remembered my father and seemed genuinely pleased at my appointment."

Ilona yawned. "I'd forgotten how tiring it is to make polite conversation with people you don't know. Also I've been trying to remember their names and faces, so that next time we meet, I'll be able to address them by name without any prompting."

Michael laughed. "Your memory is shocking at the best of times. You'll never manage it."

Ilona joined in laughing, "I know, but at least I try."

"You're in a good mood Michael," Richard remarked. "It's nice to see you smiling and not moping around after Kathryn." Ilona glared at her husband.

"It's all right mother. I won't go all moody on you. Ruth has said there's a job going with her old law firm here in St. Elizabeth and she'll put in a good word for me."

"Darling, that's wonderful news. Your father and I are so pleased for you."

"The best news, however," Michael continued, "Is that I telephoned Kathryn tonight. The engagement is back on and I'm meeting her in Leil on Friday to give her back the ring and to talk about our future together. Ruth is travelling with me to see Luke."

Michael failed to notice the look that passed between his parents.

"Where are your grandparents Michael?" Ilona asked.

"They came upstairs as soon as the Vaga and Vonryn's parents left for their yacht. Grandmother said to me earlier that she would have liked to have come up sooner, but that grandfather wouldn't budge until the Vaga had left. They're safely tucked up in bed by now I should think." Michael raised his legs off the arm of the chair and stood up. "I'm going to bed as well."

"No Michael, don't go yet, I've something to tell you." Ilona turned to her husband, who was sitting opposite. "It has to be done Richard. Vonryn should have been the first to know, but nothing but the truth will stop Michael from going to Leil on Friday."

"Yes you're right." Richard turned to his son. "Come and sit down here on the settee and please don't interrupt, no matter how much you want to. Let your mother tell the story first and then we'll try and answer any questions you might have afterwards."

Michael seated himself next to his father. "This sounds serious," he said.

After making Michael promise that he wouldn't breathe a word of what she was about to tell him to anyone, and that included Kathryn, she told him the whole story, of her marriage to Morgan, his death, the birth of a son and then the traumatic decision to give the baby up to the Vaga for adoption.

"So that's what the photographs were about. No wonder you kept them hidden," Michael said triumphantly.

"What photographs?" Ilona and Richard asked in unison.

"Hidden in the cover of that photograph album I took to show grandfather and grandmother. I didn't think you'd mind, and when the photos fell out, I didn't know what to make of them. I was going to ask you next time I saw you, but after the quarrel with Kathryn and her breaking off our engagement, I forgot all about it."

"Did you put the photos back in their hiding place?" Ilona asked sharply.

"Yes, I thought I better had, but then a funny thing happened, they disappeared for a few days. I don't know where they went, but then suddenly they returned as if by magic."

"Now we know why my father was ferreting around trying to find out things. It was he who removed the photographs."

"You've omitted to tell me one important fact. Do you know where my half brother is and have you seen him?" Michael was intrigued.

"Yes, I discovered the truth tonight, although both your father and I have suspected it for a few weeks, but we needed to have it confirmed. Your half brother is Vonryn Santella."

Michael whistled. "Oh dear, that has put the cat amongst the pigeons. They say old sins cast long shadows. Wait until the Press gets hold of this. Does Aunt Leah know?"

"No, Leah doesn't know. She was told that the baby had died and I discovered tonight that she still believes it. I must say Michael," Ilona continued, "You're taking this very well. I dreaded telling you."

Michael crossed over and sat by his mother. He put his arm around her shoulders. "What's the point of me being angry or upset? You're going to have to tell your other son the truth aren't you?" Ilona nodded her head. "Vonryn may not take it as well as I've done. There's one thing I don't understand, why couldn't you have confided in grandfather, he's not the ogre you make him out to be. He wouldn't have harmed a tiny baby just so his favourite son could be Vaga. I'll never believe that of him."

Ilona patted her son's hand. "You're probably right. I wasn't thinking straight at the time. He would never have hurt the baby, probably had him adopted, so things would have been just the same as now. I think the real reason I listened to Hallam was because he'd lost his only son and in my heart I knew that even though he wouldn't keep the baby himself, he'd still keep an eye out for his only grandson."

Michael stood up and kissed his mother on the forehead. "Why don't you want me to go to Leil on Friday?"

"I'm going there myself," Ilona replied. "I'm going to meet Vonryn and tell him the truth."

"I see. That settles it then. I won't go to Leil, but if the pair of you can come up with a convincing story for Kathryn why I can't go, I'd be grateful. It's more than likely she'll break off the engagement again."

Ilona didn't know whether to laugh or cry as she watched the back of her departing son. He could be so aggravating at times, but tonight she'd seen for the first time a more mature Michael and liked what she'd seen.

~*~

Ilona's parents, accompanied by Justin, left for home the following morning, and she was then able to make her plans to visit Luke without the fear of being overheard. She'd half expected Drystan to confront her with the facts he'd learnt from Leah the night before, but apart from him giving her some penetrating looks over the breakfast table, he'd remained silent, which in its way was more sinister. Before they left she'd managed to take Justin to one side and tell him what she intended to do. The only comment her brother made was to say that he'd better stick around with his parents until she broke the news to them.

"I'd be grateful if you would," she said. "I'll telephone as soon as I can after I've spoken to Vonryn." Michael had managed to get Kathryn to trust him for the time being, but Ilona could see he was unhappy about his promise not to tell her. She tried to talk about it as he drove her to the airport on the following Friday morning.

"Things will work out, so don't worry. You said she's handing in her notice when she returns, so obviously she is willing to trust you."

Michael grunted, but made no reply, as he steered the car through the narrow roads leading to the airport.

"Take the job you've been offered and show Kathryn that you can be independent of your grandfather without falling out with him, and I'm positive everything will be fine."

Michael made to turn the car into the airport car park, but she stopped him.

"Don't park the car, just drop me off outside the departure lounge."

"Are you sure? I was going to wait with you until your flight was called."

"I'm positive. I'll have a cup of coffee and the time will soon pass. Anyway I'll be on the nine o'clock flight tonight, so arrange it with your father who's coming to meet me."

~*~

219

The small plane took off for the short flight to St. Cecilia. It flew over Lorentia until it neared the town of Selar and then it was only a short ride over the Brenin Straits until the plane started to descend. Because they were flying low, Ilona could see the tiny, whitewashed villages below her, isolated by groves of citrus trees and vineyards. She collected the hire car that was waiting at the airport and drove from the north of Sarena to Leil in the south. She'd only ever visited this island once before and that was the day she'd married Morgan and then they'd arrived by motorboat. The roads were narrow and poorly signposted, so she drove carefully, not wishing to lose her way. Finding Leil in the end had been no problem, but she'd had to ask a few of the villagers how to find the Presbytery. She couldn't understand the strange looks she was getting, but later when she told her brother, he laughed and said it was because she was the second strange woman in two days who'd come seeking him. As she turned the corner to the Presbytery, she saw a car parked outside. It was the same model and colour as hers, obviously a hire car. Then she saw Luke and Ruth Graham come out through the garden gate. Ilona, not wishing to intrude, waited until she saw the car pull away, and turned her head as Ruth drove past, but it was obvious that Ruth hadn't seen her. She looked radiantly happy and Ilona forgot about her meeting with Vonryn to wonder about Ruth and Luke's relationship. She couldn't help teasing her brother.

"Who was the other strange woman who came seeking you?" she asked innocently.

"Anybody I know? Only I thought I saw Ruth Graham leaving."

She bent down to hold out her hand for Luke's dogs to sniff, so her brother couldn't see the mischievous grin on her face.

"You know it was. I'd hoped you'd get here before she left. I know you met at the reception because Ruth told me, but I'd have liked you two to get to know one another better."

Ilona tucked her arm into Luke's. So that's the way the land lies, she thought.

"There's plenty of time for me to get to know Ruth once this mess is sorted out, but as you said I did chat to her for a few minutes the other night. She seems very nice and I'll be eternally grateful to her for helping Michael get a job. Did she tell you?"

"Yes she did." Luke ushered his sister through the large front door, leaving the dogs outside in the garden. "Would you like a drink, or are you hungry? Angelina left something in the fridge that can be heated in the microwave."

"I couldn't face food at the moment. My stomach is churning with the thought of telling Vonryn, but I'd love a small glass of wine."

Luke opened a door on the left hand side of the hall.

"Make yourself comfortable in the study and I'll get the wine and glasses."

Ilona looked around the room with interest. Although shabby, the study was a pleasant and airy room. There was a large shuttered window that overlooked the garden. It was obviously a working study, for the large desk in the corner had a computer sitting on it and there were papers and open books strewn around on any available surface. One whole wall was devoted entirely to bookshelves and on studying the titles; Ilona saw that they ranged from theological works to thrillers.

Luke came in carrying a tray and looked around desperately for an empty space on which to deposit it.

Ilona stepped forward. "Let me take the tray whilst you shift your papers. I would have tidied up for you, but I didn't want to touch anything. It looks a mess, but it may be that you know exactly where everything is."

Luke looked shamefaced. "I don't actually," he said and started gathering everything up into a pile. He opened a cavernous drawer in the bottom of the desk and pushed the whole lot into it.

"I don't allow Angelina in here to tidy very often. She tends to throw out bits of papers that I need. I keep the room tidy myself."

Ilona raised her eyebrows. "I'm not saying a word. You'll have to sort it out before you leave here. Couldn't we have talked to Vonryn somewhere else in the house?"

"No. I picked this room because it has a double door and the Presbytery is open house to all comers wandering in and out. If I lock the front door, they'll wonder what on earth is going on. I don't want our conversation to be overheard."

"I see. When are you expecting Vonryn?"

"He shouldn't be long. He brought the tourists to see the church and they've gone back to the inn to have lunch. He won't go on the ship with Kathryn and the others, but will return here. We'll get him back to St. Cecilia in time for dinner this evening, or at least that's what I promised him."

"That won't be any problem. I'm booked on the nine o'clock flight myself tonight, so I'll drive him to St. Cecilia, that is if he'll let me after what I'm going to tell him."

~*~

Vonryn smiled and chatted to the tourists over lunch, but his thoughts were elsewhere. He toyed with the idea of not going back to the Presbytery, but his curiosity was aroused. He couldn't think why Ilona wanted to see him. Surely the Vaga wouldn't have asked her to talk to him. He strolled leisurely through the deserted streets of the village. Most of the people were inside taking a siesta from the fierce heat. As the perspiration formed on his brow and started to drip into his eyes, he wished that he were on the ferry with the rest of the party. At least once away from the shore, there would have been sea breezes to alleviate the heat. As he opened the garden gate, Luke's dogs came rushing towards him, barking wildly. He stood perfectly still and let them have a good sniff at his legs. The barking stopped and their tails started to wag and Vonryn surmised that they remembered him from his morning visit. Vonryn was just about to raise his hand to knock on the large iron doorknocker, when Luke opened the door. He'd heard the dogs barking and realised that Vonryn had arrived. He ushered his nephew into the study where Ilona was waiting. She was standing by the window, her back towards the door, but turned as they entered the room. She walked towards Vonryn and extended her hand in greeting.

"It's very nice to see you again Vonryn. I hope you enjoyed

your stay with us in the UK?"

"Yes, I did, very much, but I don't think you asked me here to discuss that."

"No, of course not. It's just that I'm not sure where to start."

Luke motioned Vonryn to sit on one of the shabby, but comfortable leather armchairs. He poured himself and Vonryn a glass of wine, but Ilona shook her head. "I daren't have any more. I've got to drive back to St. Cecilia."

Luke turned to his sister. "Shall I tell him?"

Ilona smiled gratefully at her brother, but shook her head.

"No. It's my place to do it, not yours." She looked straight at Vonryn and said bluntly, "I know who your real parents are."

Vonryn shrugged his shoulders.

"If that's the only reason you've asked me here, you might as well know you're wasting your time. I know my mother had an affair with Morgan Draymer."

"How do you know? Did she tell you?" Ilona asked.

"No she didn't, but she didn't deny it either."

Morgan was your father, but your mother didn't have an affair," Ilona paused and then took a deep breath. "I'm your mother," she blurted out.

Vonryn was on the point of taking a sip of wine, but at Ilona's words, he tilted the glass and seemed unaware of the fact that wine was trickling down his shirt.

There was a box of tissues on the desk, and Luke took the glass out of Vonryn's hand and gave him the tissues to mop up the spillage.

"Good job it was white and not red wine."

Vonryn put the tissues down and stood up, his face was ashen under his tan. "I don't believe you. How can you both be so cruel? You know my whole world is crashing down around my ears and you drag me away from the tour to tell me a pack of lies. I think it would be better if I leave now. I understand there will be a bus leaving for St. Cecilia shortly."

"Sit down Vonryn," Luke spoke sharply. "The time for half truths and lies has long since gone. Half of the journalists are seeking the truth, not to mention my father and his team of investigators, so before they start printing their versions, we thought it was time you knew the whole story. I can produce the relevant marriage and birth certificates, although if you want to see them today, I'll have to do a bit of digging in the church first," he added wryly.

"Birth and marriage certificates don't prove that I'm Ilona's son. They only prove that she married Morgan and had a son by him, but that son could be anywhere."

Luke started to say something, but Ilona put her hand on his arm to stop him.

"Vonryn's right, Luke. The certificates don't really prove that. When you visited us in the Isle of Wight, I knew you were Morgan's son, you looked so much like him and the colour of your eyes confirmed it. I had to know if Barbara had had an affair with Morgan, so last night at the party, I confronted her and she told me the truth."

Vonryn sat down again and, with a dazed expression on his face, listened as Ilona told him about her secret marriage to Morgan Draymer against her father's wishes. She spoke about the tragic car accident that had killed Morgan before they'd had time to confront Drystan with a fait accompli, and after that there didn't seem much point in telling anyone about the marriage, until to her horror she'd found out that she was pregnant.

"I didn't know what to do. I was in such a state of despair. I convinced myself that my father would harm you once you'd been born, or spirit you away so I'd never see you again. I turned to the Vaga for support, believing that he'd help me, but instead he brainwashed me into giving you up. I thought he'd be proud to tell the country about the marriage and the fact that I was carrying his grandson, but he didn't. Instead he sent me to the summer retreat in Envetta and I spent the rest of my pregnancy there."

Ilona's voice started to falter as she recalled her lonely exile.

"Did your father ever find out?" Vonryn asked.

"Not then, no. He thought I was sulking because he wouldn't let me marry Morgan and then when Morgan died, my mother convinced him that a trip overseas would help me get over things. It wasn't at all like my father to believe what he was told, but I think he was so relieved that I couldn't marry Morgan he was careless. It's only very recently that he started to get suspicious. Michael took an old photograph album from home. It was one nobody had looked at in years. It never crossed my mind that Michael would go rummaging around in the attic and take it to show his grandparents. I had a photograph of my wedding and of you as a newborn baby hidden in the cover. The stitching came loose and unfortunately father found them, at least we believe he did, otherwise why would he be ferreting around trying to find out things. He even invited Leah to the party the other night in order to question her, but luckily she believes you were stillborn."

"Why did you let me be adopted?" Vonryn's eyes flashed. "Surely Hallam would have let you keep me, and I don't believe for a minute that Drystan would have harmed me just so James could be the next Vaga."

Ilona thought for a few minutes. "In hindsight, I'm convinced my father wouldn't have harmed you, but you would have disappeared, I don't doubt that. Some desperate young couple looking for a baby to adopt and then they would be given a marvellous opportunity to emigrate. I would never have seen you again."

"You didn't see anything of me anyway, and you didn't know where I was, so what difference did it make."

"What you say is true, but I believed that Hallam would watch over you, as he did. He had you raised by a relative and groomed you to take over as Vaga, which was yours by right."

"It still doesn't answer my question as to why Hallam couldn't tell the world that I was his grandson."

"I really don't know, you'll have to ask him. Drystan and Hallam have always loved playing games against one another, first one wins then the other. I think Hallam enjoyed all the years of watching you growing up and knowing that you were Morgan's son, when my father thought there wasn't an heir."

Vonryn once more got up and turned politely to Ilona and Luke.

His voice was cold as he spoke.

"You've convinced me of the truth, and I suppose I should be grateful. At the moment, I don't know what I feel. I do, however, need time alone to come to terms with what you've said and to think about what is the best thing to do for myself and also for the Islands."

Ilona too rose from her chair and went to touch Vonryn, but he stepped back and she shrank from the look on his face.

"Can't you see Vonryn? I was young and frightened. The man I married against my father's wishes had just been killed, and then I found I was pregnant. I didn't know what to do. You may hate me, but I've always loved you. The day they came to take you away was the worst day of my life, the pain was unbearable. Will you ever forgive me?"

"I really don't know."

Vonryn nodded his head to them both and made to leave the room.

"How will you get back to St. Cecilia?" Luke asked.

"I'll get the bus."

Luke looked at his watch. "I'm afraid you've missed it and the next one won't be for two hours. Look Vonryn, be sensible, Ilona is going back there, let her take you in the car."

"I'd sooner walk."

"Now you're being childish. I know you've had a shock and I know you need time to be alone to gather your thoughts, so if you want to go for a walk somewhere, I'll telephone my friend Paul to see if he or one of his men can be outside the Presbytery in an hour and run you back. Will you agree to that?"

"Yes. Thank you Luke. I know I'm behaving childishly, but I can't seem to help it at the moment." Vonryn turned to Ilona. "Barbara will always be my mother. She may not have actually given birth to me, but she was there when I needed her. I'll try and understand why you gave me up. You see I do know how manipulative both the Vaga and your father can be. If you don't mind Luke, I'll go and stroll around the village for a while."

Ilona waited until she heard the door slam before she collapsed into her brother's arms. Even though he was a priest, he could find no words of comfort to offer his sister. It was probably the remnants of British rule, but his first thought was to make a cup of tea and get Ilona to drink it. He then had three phone calls to make, the first one was easy, to ask Paul if someone could run Vonryn to St. Cecilia, but the other two wouldn't be so easy. Ilona protested weakly that she should be the one to break the news of what she'd done to the Vaga and Drystan, but Luke overruled her. He prayed fervently that Justin would pick up the telephone. He'd always been a little afraid of his father.

Chapter 20

PPS. I couldn't find a letterbox in Leil so I wasn't able to post this letter. The receptionist at the hotel where we're staying assured me that if I get it posted in the box in the hotel lobby by nine o'clock tomorrow morning, it will be collected at 9.30. As I hadn't sealed the envelope, I've got time to add some more news.

This is the last night of the tour and I can't tell you how glad I am, although I've still got to collect all the questionnaires from our party and make out a report. Everyone is having a farewell drink in the bar and chatting about their experiences, but already you can sense that they're distancing themselves from one another. The usual exchange of addresses is taking place and I often wonder how many people do keep in touch once a holiday is over. Mr Carter is worrying that the cross he ordered won't be in St. Elizabeth tomorrow, but Vonryn told him not to worry, and that it would be waiting for him, and said that even if it wasn't, he'd personally make sure it was forwarded on.

Vonryn arrived back from Leil in a foul mood. I thought it was because he'd had to catch the local bus back, which would have meant driving slowly around country roads to out of the way villages, stopping all the time and sharing your space with livestock. A bus ride here is quite an experience I can tell you. It wasn't that, however, because Vonryn said he'd had a lift from Luke's friend and the reason he was late was because he'd gone for a drink in St. Cecilia and completely forgotten the time. There was barely time for him to have a quick shower before dinner was served. He didn't volunteer any information about what Ilona and Luke wanted, and I didn't like to ask, although I was dying to know.

After dinner, I went back to my room to get my camera to take a few photographs and who should I see as I got out of the lift but Ilona. She seemed taken aback to see me, although she must have known that we were staying in the Sarena Hotel, as Michael had the itinerary. I think she was hoping to avoid us for some reason. We exchanged pleasantries and she kissed me, saying that she was delighted the engagement was back on and that she'd telephone me when I got back home. Michael had told her that I was handing in my notice and she seemed genuinely pleased, but I could sense there was something else on her mind. I asked her if she wanted to join us downstairs, but she refused. By a strange coincidence, her room was a few doors down from mine and we walked along the corridor together. As I was putting the key in the lock, she asked me not to tell Vonryn that she was staying the night here. She said that she had intended to catch the nine o'clock flight back to St. Elizabeth, but she just couldn't face the thought of it, and had booked another flight for ten o'clock the following morning. I suggested that she forget about the flight and catch the ferry with us, but she smiled grimly and said that that wouldn't be wise under the circumstances. Something is going on, but I don't know what. Whatever it is, it's causing a lot of pain to quite a few people. The strain showing on the faces of Ilona and Vonryn is proof of that.

I'm definitely not going to write another word tonight. See you soon.

Kathryn

Chapter 21

Whilst she waited in Kennedy airport for the first of the flights on her journey to St. Elizabeth, Nadia thought about the cryptic phone call she'd received from Vonryn. He'd warned her that reporters would be waiting at St. Elizabeth and told her what to say. The business for her father in the USA had been conducted swiftly and efficiently. She hadn't worried about her father's health, as she'd soon realised it was a ploy to get her away from Vonryn. In between the numerous boardroom meetings and the invitations to business lunches and formal dinners, she'd been too immersed in work to dwell on her own unhappiness. At the end of each long day, she'd fallen asleep as soon as her head touched the pillow. She was ashamed now of her hysterical phone calls to Ruth and had bought her a gift as a way of saying thank you for being such a good listener. The only reason she'd agreed to make the trip in place of her father was to distance herself from the Islands and get things into perspective. There'd been a few moments in the heavy workload when she'd pondered what her future would be like without Vonryn, or with him but without her wealth and status. Deep down she knew she really wanted the status quo, but until his phone call that had seemed an impossible dream.

After speaking to Vonryn, Nadia was impatient to get home. In between the various flights and the waiting at different airports as she changed to yet again a smaller plane, there'd been time to reflect and puzzle over what had happened to make a marriage between them possible. A two-hour delay had been announced before her last and shortest flight. With the knowledge that journalists and photographers would be waiting, she'd used the delay to repair her make up and brush her long black hair until it shone and then skillfully fastened it into a chignon. She was thankful that the clothes she'd chosen for the flight were crease resistant, and before leaving the ladies' cloakroom, took a critical look at herself in the mirror and decided ruefully that under the circumstances it was the best she could do.

A crowd of journalists and photographers were indeed waiting as she went through customs. She didn't feel threatened by them, because behind the journalists she could see her father, flanked by two bodyguards. The flash bulbs almost blinded her, but she smiled radiantly and it was obvious to everyone that she was happy.

"Is the engagement still on?" One reporter asked, pushing in front of the others and sticking a mike in front of her face.

Nadia flashed her ring at him.

"It was never off." She omitted to mention that at the start of the crisis they'd both forgotten about the ring and Nadia had continued to wear it.

"What stone is it?" A woman's voice asked. "It's a pink sapphire," Nadia replied sweetly, ignoring the groans of the male journalists, who felt they had more important questions to ask. They elbowed the female journalist aside and flung questions at Nadia.

"When's the wedding?"

"What about Vonryn's real parents? Do you know who they are?"

"Are you going straight home to St. Helena?"

Nadia raised her hand to silence them. "Gentlemen please, you're confusing me with your rapid fire questions. I'm not used to it." God, she thought, I nearly said little ole me. I must sound like Scarlett O'Hara from *Gone with the Wind*. Still, if it got the reporters off her back, so what. "The wedding will be very soon, but no date has been set."

"Why have you brought the wedding forward? Have you any special reason?"

"Yes, we have a special reason."

There was silence. Everyone else wanting to ask the obvious question, but not quite knowing how to phrase it.

Nadia read their thoughts and giggled. "No, I'm not pregnant. I know that's what all of you were thinking." Suddenly she was serious. "We decided to bring the wedding forward so that next year everything will be focused on independence and what it will mean to the islands."

This is easy, she thought, as she parried questions and answers with them. She even flirted a little with some of them. The men in turn looked at the radiant young woman in front of them and they too thought how easy it was to obtain the answers they wanted from her. For one fleeting second, Nadia's dark blue eyes met those of the woman reporter, who now stood isolated at the rear. She clapped her hands silently at Nadia's performance, for she'd soon realised that her male colleagues had absolutely nothing new to give to their editors, apart from the fact that the wedding was still on.

Nadia edged forward and the two bodyguards moved swiftly to stand each side of her. "I'm very tired after my long journey, but I'm sure we'll be meeting many times in the future." Nadia greeted her father fondly and they walked swiftly out to the waiting limousine, the guards preventing the journalists from following them. She sank thankfully into the soft upholstery.

"What is going on?" She asked her father. As they made their way through the darkened streets of St. Elizabeth to where Drystan Pendenny's yacht was moored, Stephen Laridon made sure that the window between them and the men in front was closed before telling his daughter about the developments of the last few days.

"I can't believe it. Ilona is his mother! Why Kathryn and I will be sisters-in-law," she exclaimed delightedly.

"Yes, well I think there are more important matters to discuss than that," her father said drily.

"I know," Nadia squeezed his hand. "But it's so good to be home, at least back in the islands, if not St. Helena. What happens next?"

"We'll spend tonight on Drystan's yacht and cross over to Mordeen after breakfast tomorrow morning. The whole Pendenny clan is meeting the following day to discuss what to tell the people.

They are supposedly all coming for Luke's induction the same as us. The Vaga is also attending, and for the first time in centuries the Vaga will set foot on Innisver soil and be the guest of the Pendenny family. A press release was given out to the effect that the Draymer and Pendenny families are coming together in a gesture of peace and reconciliation to mark the coming of independence from the British. Luke's first duty after his induction as Bishop in the cathedral will be to offer a special prayer that this will continue into the next century."

"How was the news received by the public?"

"From polls taken, it seems the majority of people think it is a good idea, but of course the Press keep raising the question of the Vaga's successor and Vonryn's parentage."

"I see," Nadia said and fell silent. Her high spirits in the airport had evaporated and she felt despondent. Things weren't as clear-cut as she'd imagined.

~*~

It was past 10 o'clock the following morning before Nadia and her father arrived in Mordeen. A few cotton wool balls of cloud played hide and seek with the sun, but already the temperature was rising and soon it would become uncomfortable. Nadia, as so many before her, was disappointed when she saw Innisver Castle for the first time.

"I thought it would be bigger." Nadia remarked as the car pulled up at the main door. "It doesn't even look like a castle."

Stephen laughed. "What were you expecting, something on the lines of Windsor?"

"Something slightly grander than this, especially after all those wonderful buildings we've just driven past."

"Don't be such a snob. This is their home. The grander state apartments are separate, as I pointed out to you. Look there's Ria waiting to welcome us," and he added sarcastically. "She's managed to open the door herself, without an army of servants to help her."

"All right. I'm a snob," Nadia smiled at her father affectionately.

Ria kissed Stephen and his daughter and showed them into the large comfortable lounge which was situated at the rear of the castle. There were two sets of French windows, both of which were open to let in any stray breeze. There were fans on the ceiling, but these hadn't been switched on.

"I'm afraid we don't have air conditioning," Ria apologised. "Drystan can't abide it. He says it's too noisy and gives him headaches." If only this was a normal family gathering Ria thought. Innisver Castle, although not large, was an empty and lonely place and now for the first time in years, it would be full. Perhaps, she thought, if the meeting goes well, we can all enjoy one another's company afterwards and attend the cathedral together as one big happy family. She sighed deeply, knowing that her dreams were unrealistic, but at least even if they were quarrelling, they'd all be together again under one roof. Stephen heard the sigh and was just about to say something when Vonryn bounded in. His eyes lit up at the sight of Nadia, but he shook his future father-in-law's hand before kissing Nadia resoundly on the lips. He caught hold of her hand and started to pull her gently in the direction of the door.

"Come on, I'll show you to your room. Carlos will take the bags up as soon as he's put the car away."

Nadia hesitated and looked at Ria for approval. She desperately wanted to be alone with Vonryn, but good manners dictated that she shouldn't rush away.

Ria smiled fondly at Nadia and her newly acquired grandson.

"I was going to offer Nadia something to drink, but I'm sure she'd rather be in your company. You two have a lot to talk about so off you go. Don't forget though, lunch is at one o'clock so be on time. Drystan is a stickler for punctuality."

Stephen waited until the door closed and he could hear their footsteps moving away, before he turned to Ria.

"Right," he said. "Now, tell me how Drystan is."

"Not very good. His mood swings are so rapid you can't keep

pace with them. I wanted to call a doctor to give him a sedative, but he wouldn't hear of it."

"It's to be expected, I suppose."

"One minute he's raging at Hallam for not telling him all these years, then he's delighted that his grandson will be Vaga. Of course, he wishes that it were James, Philip or Michael and not Morgan's son. Surprisingly, Justin has been a tower of strength. He issued a press release and persuaded James and his family to come over for the induction, but primarily so he could attend the meeting."

"Why did he have to persuade him? I thought he would have wanted to be here to talk over what to do."

"We put a blackout on speaking over the telephone about this matter, and as James and his family weren't coming for Luke's induction and could see no reason for changing their plans, Justin had to resort to telling a few white lies to get them here. In the end he told James that Drystan wasn't well and that the whole family had better visit. It was only a white lie, because if Drystan doesn't calm down, he's well on the way to a heart attack."

"You must be really worried about him."

"I'm concerned about his health and the future of both our families. Also Drystan tends to forget that there are servants around who have eyes and ears. Obviously, with all the extra guests staying I need more help, but it's such a strain watching every word you utter. We don't want the truth to leak out to the Press until we're ready."

"Was James aware of the truth all along?"

"No, the first he knew about it was when they all arrived last night. It was quite a shock to him. He'd no idea that Ilona had married Morgan. You see although they were all good friends when they were small children, once they grew older James always seemed to be on the fringe of everything. They probably grew apart because James spent most of his school holidays with his maternal grandparents in the UK.

Did you know Susan, James' mother?" Ria asked.

Stephen shook his head. "I've seen photographs of her and the oil painting that's hanging in the hall here. She was very beautiful."

"Yes she was. In the beginning that oil painting was a bone of contention between Drystan and me. I didn't want it hanging there, but in the end I could see that it wouldn't have been fair to James to remove it. Even though she was dead, I felt I couldn't compete. She had classical features and long natural blonde hair and the complexion that went with it, although she had to be extra careful and avoid the sun."

"It was a tragedy that she died so young. If I remember rightly it was a boating accident."

"Yes, gossip says that they'd had one of their usual violent rows that morning. She missed London society and was bored with life on the islands. She craved change and excitement. James doesn't take after her at all in that respect. He is very conventional. By all accounts, she'd told Drystan that she was leaving him for a man she'd met whilst she was on holiday in England. Knowing Drystan you can understand how angry that would have made him. He could dispense with people, but they mustn't leave him. I understand she got in her car, drove like a mad woman to where her speed boat was moored and the rest is history."

They'd been so engrossed in their conversation that neither Ria nor Stephen realised that someone had entered the room. James and his father were standing on the threshold. Ria's hand flew to her mouth, as it was obvious from the expression on James's face that he'd heard every word.

"Oh James, I'm so sorry. I never meant for you to find out and not in this way."

"I should think not," Drystan said angrily. "You knew I never wanted him to know about his mother."

"Father, please don't upset yourself unnecessarily. It doesn't bother me in the least."

Both Ria and Drystan ignored him and years of pent up emotions spilled out of Ria.

"I'm sorry, I forgot. Susan's reputation still has to be protected." Ria snapped at her husband. "It didn't matter that I loved you all

236

these years and gave you three fine children. Oh no, Susan's son had to be Vaga not one of mine."

"He was the eldest."

"Yes and if he'd wanted the position, I wouldn't have minded, but you knew he didn't want it. The real reason was that you always loved him more than our children, simply because he was Susan's son." Ria looked scornfully at her husband.

"Until Morgan died you could only dream about it happening, but when the dream became reality your cup of happiness was full."

Drystan looked aghast at his wife's words.

"I never wanted Morgan dead and no matter what people say, I had no hand in his death."

All the fire suddenly went out of Ria and she buried her head in her hands.

"No, I know that," she mumbled.

James crossed the room and sat next to his stepmother. He put his arm around her shoulders.

"You mustn't upset yourself either mother," he said. "I suppose I've got to tell you now, but I've known the truth for years. I saw a bureau similar to my mother's in an antique shop in St. Elizabeth. I was curious to know if it was valuable so I went inside. The dealer asked me if I knew about the secret drawer. I had to confess that I didn't, so he showed me how to access it. It was so cunningly concealed you'd never find it in a million years. I was at university at the time and couldn't wait to come home to look. Unfortunately, I found more than I'd bargained for. Inside was a bundle of letters from the man she was running away to England with. He was waiting for her in St. Elizabeth."

He turned to his father. "I didn't realise you knew, so I thought the best thing to do was burn them and that's what I did."

Ria was amazed. "All this time and you kept it to yourself. You're a good man James."

"All I remember about my mother is a vague impression of a woman in evening clothes, smelling of gardenias, kissing me goodnight. As far as I was concerned Ria was my real mother."

Ria's eyes filled with tears. "Thank you James for saying that."

Drystan looked down at his wife and Ria noticed with relief that a little of the old autocratic infuriating man was back, and not the feeble shadow of himself that he'd been recently.

"Enough of this sentimental nonsense," he barked, but his smile belied his words.

"You, Ria are a stupid woman. I loved Susan, but we were never right for one another. If we'd been any other couple, we would have gone our separate ways earlier. She probably would have been much happier living in England, and once I'd cooled down, I would have made her a generous settlement, but it wasn't to be. What you and I had was something completely different, something that has lasted. All these years you've been jealous of a ghost and I never once realised it." Drystan paused as if ashamed of showing his feelings and then asked suddenly. "Where's Hallam?"

"Sitting in the arbour at the end of the garden, as far away from you as possible," Ria said smiling at her husband. Yes, Drystan was right, she thought, she had been stupid all these years being jealous of a dead woman. "Why do you want Hallam?" she asked suspiciously.

"I've got to talk to him, without arguing if possible. We need to put our heads together and carefully plan an exercise in damage limitation."

Stephen gratefully accepted the whisky and soda that James handed him. He felt acute embarrassment at the emotional scene he'd just witnessed, although it was obvious that neither Ria nor James seemed disconcerted.

"Will they manage to come up with something?" he asked.

"They may be old men," Ria said, "but they're still the craftiest two I've ever met. If they can't no one can. We must just hope and pray that they can pull this family back from the brink of disaster."

~*~

Nadia followed Vonryn up the wide marble staircase, stopping every now and again to admire the portraits.

"I suppose these are your illustrious ancestors?"

"Presumably, but don't ask me their names. I didn't know we were related until a short while ago. Remember I'd never stepped on Innisver soil until recently, let alone been in the castle. When they reached the landing half way up the staircase, Vonryn turned right. They climbed the remaining stairs then bypassed a few closed doors in the corridor before he flung open one at the far end.

"This is your room," he said. "But before we go in, I'll show you a short cut to the library. He pointed to a door at the end of the corridor. "If you go through there it leads to a staircase which will bring you out near the library. I'm afraid your room is one of the smaller ones, but the place is bulging at the seams this weekend as you can imagine. Normally Drystan and Ria rattle around the place like two peas in a pod."

"It's a lovely room," Nadia said, opening the curtains and letting the sunlight stream inside. She looked around at her surroundings and noticed that there were two other doors in the room. She opened each in turn and peered inside. "I don't know how you can call it small. There's a walk in wardrobe and a bathroom."

"There's a nice bed too." Vonryn crept up behind her and kissed her neck. "We could test it out." He turned her to face him and started to kiss her passionately, his hands caressing her body. Nadia felt herself responding to his touch and didn't try to stop him when he started to unzip her dress. They were brought back to earth by a tap on the door.

"Damn!" Vonryn pulled Nadia's zip up. "That's Carlos with your cases. I forgot about that. I'd better let him in."

Carlos deposited the cases saying that a maid would be up presently to unpack. Nadia looked at Vonryn, a slightly puzzled expression on her face.

"What's wrong?" he asked.

"You seem different somehow. I've never known you behave so impulsively before."

Vonryn grinned wickedly.

"We've had many a passionate session before today."

"I'm not denying it, but before you were always in control. You never did anything without careful consideration. When I went to the UK for months, you accepted it as though I was just going for a short break. Sometimes I felt ours was going to be a marriage of convenience."

"It was never that, surely you knew." Vonryn's handsome face was suddenly serious. "I'm sorry if you felt that way. I never realised. I suppose I did take everything for granted once we'd got engaged. Our wedding plans were in place and your time in the UK was for the good of the islands, so I accepted it, but that didn't mean I liked being apart from you. These past few weeks though have shown me how much I could have lost and could still lose. We're not out of the woods yet."

"I realise that, but my time in New York showed me one thing and that was I want our marriage to go ahead, whether we're able to live here or in exile."

"It may not come to that, but if it does, we'll talk again because I'd want you to be absolutely sure in your own mind before you did anything drastic." He looked at his watch. "Let's go and have a swim. We've got plenty of time before lunch. I'll meet you by the pool in five minutes. We can talk about the wedding afterwards."

He turned as he got to the door and blew her a kiss. "Oh, I forgot, you can reach the pool from up here. Just go out on the balcony and there's steps down to the garden. You can't miss them."

Nadia undid the smallest of her two cases and rummaged around until she found her bikini. She liked to swim every day if possible, but hadn't found the time whilst in America. The sun was at its zenith when she stepped out on to the balcony, and the tiled floor was uncomfortably hot to her bare feet. As Vonryn had said, the outside staircase was quite visible; there was one at each end of the balcony. The water looked cool and inviting and she slipped into its blue depths gratefully. It was a large pool and she'd already swum a few lengths when Vonryn joined her, diving

240

in at the deep end, not very gracefully.

"That was nearly a belly flop," she called out.

"Diving's not my strong point," he shouted back. "Race you to the end."

Although Nadia had a head start, they still touched the handrail together. She climbed the steps and placing a towel on one of the loungers, she stretched out on it under the shade of one of the large umbrellas.

"Are my eyes deceiving me, or are your grandfathers talking to one another?" Nadia asked.

Vonryn shaded his eyes and looked towards the far end of the garden.

"Good heavens, you're right, and they're not even shouting at one another." Vonryn stretched out on the lounger beside Nadia. "Forget about them and their silly feud for a minute. I know I said we'd forget about if we had to live in exile until it was forced on us, but are you sure you'd want to go ahead with the wedding if that happened?"

Nadia looked at Vonryn thoughtfully. "If you'd asked me that a few weeks ago, I would have said no, and to be completely honest with you, I would prefer things to stay as they are. This is all I've ever known."

"I see," Vonryn's voice was cold.

Nadia reached out and placed her hand on his. "You haven't let me finish, so don't go all sulky on me. I'm determined to go ahead with the wedding. I'd rather live in exile with you than here without you."

Vonryn's face was wreathed in smiles.

"I hoped you'd say that. Now all we've got to do is decide on a date to get married. I should think four weeks next Saturday would be ideal. We'll get married in the cathedral here and Luke can marry us."

Nadia opened her mouth to protest about the way that Vonryn was making all the decisions, but then changed her mind.

"Can I tell the Vaga and Drystan what we've decided?"

In answer to his question, Nadia leant across and kissed him.

~*~

Ria had her wish that evening for, apart from Ilona and Richard, all her family gathered together in the dining room to eat a delicious meal. Hallam and Drystan ate in silence and took no part in the general conversation. Even if servants hadn't been present, no one would have dared to ask what they'd discussed in the garden earlier. Ria would have loved to eavesdrop on their conversation, but she was content that the evening was going well and it seemed as though there weren't going to be any arguments.

The following morning Ilona and Richard arrived just a few minutes before the meeting was due to start. It was held in the dining room, but now the large table was set out for a formal meeting and not a pleasant meal. Ilona looked pale and haggard and the sunlight streaking through the windows highlighted the deep shadows beneath her eyes. Ria rushed over to her daughter and flung her arms around her. After one fleeting glance at his daughter, Drystan averted his eyes. Vonryn stood up and walked over to Ilona and taking her arm led her to an empty chair at the far end of the table away from her father.

"Now that I've had time to think, I'm glad you told me the truth," he said quietly. The others were all at the far end of the room and were engrossed in their own conversations. "I won't say that I'm not hurt because that would be a lie, and perhaps in time I'll be able to accept what happened."

Ilona smiled wanly. "I can understand how betrayed you must feel."

"Yes, I do feel betrayed, but, at the moment, the good of the islands must come first. By the way my mother, I mean Barbara, sends her best wishes," he said.

"She is your mother Vonryn. You were right first time. She was there for you and I wasn't."

Normally Hallam Draymer took the chair at the Islands' Council meetings, but this one was different in a few ways, one of which being that it wasn't held in Christenbech. He remained seated by the window silently gazing out at the garden."

Drystan stood up and rapped on the table with his knuckles and waited whilst they all took their seats.

"Hallam and I have agreed that I should chair this meeting. We're all here today to decide what to do for the best. Should we tell the truth and if so how can we put it over so that we all come out of this intact?" He looked at the others expectantly.

"I think you're expecting the impossible," Justin replied. "We could just announce the date of Vonryn's wedding and say that you've agreed to him being the next Vaga and that all the rumours are malicious lies."

Vonryn shook his head. "That won't work. It's now common knowledge that my father was in America when I was conceived, so unless my mother admits to adultery with Morgan, I have no right by birth to be Vaga."

His grandfather started to interrupt, but Vonryn put his hand up to stop him. "I know what you're going to say. Although I was never legally adopted, Vincent and Barbara acted as my parents until I was of age and that is as good as a legal adoption in the eyes of our law. I don't think the people will accept it grandfather. Maybe if there hadn't been all this quarrelling they might have, but it's too late now. There is one point on which I want to make myself clear and that is, there is no way will I allow my mother to admit adultery when it never happened."

There was silence in the room as they all realised the implications of what Vonryn had said, and waited for Drystan to reply.

"We anticipated you'd say that, and Justin your idea won't work for the reasons Vonryn gave. Yesterday, after Hallam and I talked in the garden, we telephoned the Prime Minister and First Ministers of all the Islands and said that we'd tell them the truth on their undertaking not to reveal it to anyone else until we said. They all agreed to this and consequently they all have full knowledge of the facts."

"I thought you said we couldn't talk on the telephone," Michael interrupted. "I wanted to explain to Kathryn what was going on."

"There wasn't any risk involved, all their lines are scrambled. Anyway as we'd decided that the only way forward is to tell the truth, it wasn't quite so important. The only point to discuss is when to tell it and how."

"You're the limit father," James sounded angry, which was unusual for him. "You drag me and my family over here to this meeting and now I find our journey was unnecessary as you and the Vaga have already come to a decision."

"I'm sorry James," the Vaga spoke for the first time. "We genuinely wanted your help initially as your father and I have been at loggerheads for so many years that no one thought we could talk sensibly to one another." He smiled. "It's amazing after all these years of feuding that we find we quite like one another."

"If only you'd found that out years ago, we wouldn't be in this mess now," Justin exclaimed. "Still better late than never, I suppose. You'd better tell us just what you propose to do."

The Vaga glanced at Drystan for confirmation as to whether he should continue speaking. Drystan gave a slight nod of his head.

"Tomorrow, we'll announce the date of the wedding. I understand from Vonryn that it is to be here in the cathedral in four weeks time. We will also tell the people that as a result of our feuding Vonryn was placed out for adoption on the death of his father."

"How did the Ministers react?" Richard asked.

"Surprised naturally," Drystan answered his son-in-law. "The Ministers of our islands, that is Innisver, Quan Tomay and Envetta, felt that it wouldn't make any difference. They think that the majority of the people will be relieved that the feud is finally over and that a descendant of both families will eventually rule over them. The Prime Minister of the British Islands wasn't so sure. A large number of the populace on those islands are apprehensive about independence anyway and many of them are genuinely worried about what will happen after the handover. As you know," he continued, "our aim was to have one Parliament, but even without this problem of the succession, I can see it was highly unlikely that that would have happened initially. It was too much too soon. There is to be a status quo with regard to the various parliaments, but the British Islands' Prime Minister felt that the people might be happy to form an alliance with the other islands and acknowledge the Vaga as head of state. He suggested a referendum on that point might be the way forward. Hallam and I agreed with him over that. It isn't what we dreamed about all these years, but an alliance is better that nothing."

Hallam cleared his throat and Drystan looked at him enquiringly.

"Have I missed anything?" he asked.

"No nothing, but there is something else I intend to announce tomorrow. I couldn't sleep last night wondering if there was anything else I could do to make up for all the pain I've caused over the years."

"We've caused," Drystan interrupted and smiled as he saw the amazement written on the faces of the people around the table.

"I'm abdicating."

There was a stunned silence in the room at Hallam's statement. "I've prepared my speech and hope to broadcast it tomorrow to all the islands. I shall take the title Larn of Zerrebar and Vonryn will become Vaga straight away. The wedding and the crowning ceremonies in each island will help to take people's minds off everything else, and I think the people of Lorentia and Sarena would be more prepared to accept a new younger Vaga as head of state, one whose descendants could eventually rule over all the islands." Hallam reached into his jacket pocket and pulled out a small ring box. He pushed it across the table to Nadia.

"I had this made especially for you. I want to ask you if you'll wear this as your engagement ring."

Vonryn opened his mouth to object, but Nadia shook her head to stop him. Hallam turned to his grandson. "I know you gave Nadia a beautiful ring when you got engaged, but traditionally the wife of the Vaga should wear an Envis stone as a token of their betrothal. There is no need to discard the other ring, Nadia can wear it on her other hand."

"It's up to Nadia," Vonryn said. "I have no objection."

Nadia transferred the pink sapphire to her right hand and opened the ring box. She gasped. "It's beautiful."

She put the ring on her engagement finger and held her hand aloft for the others to see. A pure Envis stone had been set into a filigree setting of white gold, and as a shaft of sunlight alighted on the stone, all the colours of the rainbow danced before their eyes.

Justin gave a low whistle.

"I've heard it all now. I think I could do with a drink, and not water," he added as Luke pushed the jug across the table to him. "I take it this meeting is closed."

Drystan nodded. "Yes, it is, and I think it's time we all adjourn to the lounge and have a drink, although it is very early in the day."

As they started to leave the room, Drystan raised his hand. "Two things I forgot to mention. The first is that Hallam and I took another unilateral decision yesterday that this was to be the last meeting of the Islands' Council in its present form. A new, more democratic one, will take its place with some elected members sitting on it."

"And the second?" Ria spoke for the first time during the meeting.

"The second really only applies to Michael. Until tomorrow's announcement, there must still be a blackout on telephone calls. Are you happy with that Michael? Once everything is made public you must telephone Kathryn and put matters right with her."

Michael nodded. What harm would another day make, he thought. He and Kathryn had the rest of their lives to be together.

Nadia barely heard his words, as she was wondering how on earth she was going to plan a wedding in four short weeks, even with the army of helpers she could call upon. It was only later in her room that she remembered the phone call she'd made the previous evening to Kathryn. She dismissed the niggling worry; Kathryn hadn't been in so she hadn't said much, only left a short message with her new flat mate. Surely that wouldn't cause any problems.

Ria sat in the lounge, a bemused look on her face, surely the one glass of sherry she'd drunk couldn't have gone to her head. She wasn't sure how many people would be staying for lunch, but

Marjorie in her usual practical way, had said she would discuss the luncheon menu with Cook. Visions of many more happy gatherings such as this filled her thoughts, although being a realist, she didn't expect Drystan to change his nature overnight, but he was trying. He was even now talking to Ilona in the corner of the room and she saw her only daughter touch her father's arm and reach up and kiss him on the cheek. All the family were staying over for Luke's induction, and then she had two weddings to look forward to. It was turning out to be a perfect day and she prayed that nothing would spoil things in the coming months.

Chapter 22

Dear Mum,

I tried to telephone you a couple of times yesterday evening, and when I couldn't get through, I phoned Tom. It was only after there was no reply from his house that I started to get worried. I had visions of one or other of the family lying in hospital. Eventually, I calmed down and commonsense told me that someone would have let me know if anything bad had happened. In the event I telephoned Cassie next door and she said that you'd all gone away on a weekend break to Blackpool.

I only wanted to tell you that my engagement is off once again. This time it is for good. Yes, I know you've heard it all before, but Michael is marrying Nadia. He didn't even have the guts to tell me himself, but let Nadia do it. I don't think it will be on the news about their marriage. The Tomayon islands don't mean anything to people living over here, but as independence is being given to the British islands shortly, you never know. I hope not. It's one thing being dumped, but to have it announced on television will be the last straw. I was out when Nadia telephoned with the news that she was getting married within the month, but Lucy, my new flat mate took a message and left me a note. I was a little surprised that the marriage was taking place so quickly as Vonryn and Nadia's wedding had been planned for next year. I knew before the papers got hold of the fact that there was some doubt as to who Vonryn's parents were, but I thought that perhaps everything had been sorted out and that they didn't want to wait any longer. As I read on though I had quite a shock. Although the message was cryptic, one thing stood out and that was Nadia's insistence I be told her future mother-in-law's name was Ilona. Michael is Ilona's only son so how many daughters-in-law can she have? Unfortunately, I couldn't question Lucy about the phone call as she'd left to go on a course before I got home, but I doubt if she could have told me anything more. I always knew that Drystan would eventually get his own way and split us up. Michael just isn't strong enough to stand up to him, at least not at the moment, in a few years maybe. I know Michael doesn't love Nadia, nor she him, so it's a marriage of convenience. I hope they'll both be very happy. It's obvious that Michael isn't going to phone me so I'm thinking of ringing him and giving him a piece of my mind. As Lucy's away, I've unplugged the phone until I decide what do to.

I'm being very selfish moaning on about myself. I intend to get myself sorted out and get on with the rest of my life - to hell with Michael and his family. I do hope you all enjoy your break and that the weather keeps fine, it makes all the difference. I expect the kids will have a whale of a time trying out all the rides. I'm not sure if you'll be too early to see the lights. I don't know what date they switch them on.

I've got to make up my mind what I'm going to do about my job. As you know, I gave in my notice. I can't decide whether I should just leave without saying anything to anybody, but the truth will eventually come out and then I'll feel a right fool and I'll be out of work as well. Jobs aren't that easy to come by these days, so I must think things through carefully. Luckily the post hasn't been advertised yet. The advert has been drafted ready for insertion in various newspapers and for placing in the Job Centre. I was going to see to it first thing next week. I think I'll have to swallow my pride and tell my boss what has happened and rescind my notice. He said he was sorry to lose me so I expect he'll give me my job back. I'm lucky I found out now before it was offered to anyone else. It would definitely be too late then. I'm also going to ask for a transfer. I'd love to come back to Cardiff, then I could live at home for a while, that is if you want me to. I'm in need of maternal TLC at the moment. Hopefully I'll keep my job and then wait for a vacancy back home. I expect something will turn up. I can't say I'm happy living down here at the moment, but I'll survive.

I'll speak to you in a couple of days and you can tell me all about your weekend break.

Love,
Kathryn
xxxxx

Chapter 23

Kathryn threw on her coat and slammed the door of the flat behind her. No way was she going to sit indoors and mope - what she needed was company and she'd find that at the Exiles' Club. On the way she posted the letter to her mother. As she entered the club she took a deep breath and squared her shoulders. If they knew about her broken engagement, so what, she had to face people sometime. To her surprise the club was almost deserted for a Saturday evening and there was no one there she knew. I'll have one drink and then go home she thought as she waited for the barman to get her a gin and tonic.

"Where is everyone tonight?" she asked.

"A coach load have gone to London and as for the rest..." he shrugged his shoulders. "I might as well close up early," he said morosely.

Feeling conspicuous that she was on her own, she took a sip of her drink wondering whether to stay at the bar or sit at a table. The barman didn't seem inclined to talk for he'd wandered off to the far end of the bar and was reading something.

"There's a turn up for the book," he said suddenly coming back towards Kathryn and waving a piece of A4 paper in her face. "Have you seen the newsletter that was faxed through earlier this evening?"

Kathryn shook her head and took the newsletter from him. This was something that was regularly faxed through from the islands so that exiles could keep up with events back home. Kathryn found a table and started to glance idly through the letter. Much of it was taken up with the forthcoming handover of the British islands and she skipped that part but her hands started to shake when she read the last paragraph. The Vaga was abdicating in place of his grandson Vonryn. It revealed the fact that Ilona had been secretly married to Morgan Draymer and that Vonryn was their son. No reason was given for the clandestine marriage but everyone in the islands knew of the feud between the Draymer and the Pendenny families so could draw their own conclusions. The untimely death of Morgan Draymer was mentioned and the fact that Ilona had on her remarriage opted to spend her life away from the Islands.

Kathryn finished her drink in about ten seconds flat, grabbed her coat and rushed from the club. How stupid she'd been. The cryptic message was clear now. Nadia was going to be her sister-in-law or half sister-in-law; if there was such a thing. She wanted to speak to Michael and hear his voice. He must never find out she doubted him and would have to warn her mother not to reveal the contents of her letter. On reaching home she rescued the phone from the waste bin, where she'd flung it in a fury after unplugging it but to her horror it was broken.

"Hell!" she said out loud. "I'm in a right mess. I can't make or receive phone calls." She knew her mobile couldn't be used for calls to the islands so, as in all times of crisis, she made a cup of tea and pondered her next move. Phoning from the phone box at the end of the road was not on, even if it hadn't been vandalised and was in working order. She needed to speak to Michael from the privacy of her own home. Then she remembered the young couple who'd moved into the downstairs flat. They'd seemed friendly enough on the few occasions they'd bumped into one another in the shared hallway. Praying that they were in, she tentatively knocked on their door. They were just on their way out but when Kathryn explained the position, omitting the fact that she'd flung the phone into the waste bin, they'd offered to lend her the one from their bedroom until she was able to buy a new one.

Kathryn eventually tracked Michael down at the Governor's Mansion. He seemed relieved to hear her voice.

"I've been trying to get hold of you all evening," he said. "When

Nadia told me about the message she'd left, I was worried what you might be thinking. It had to be vague because until the official notice was issued only a handful of people knew what was happening. Knowing you, I thought you'd probably get hold the wrong end of the stick and think grandfather had talked me into marrying Nadia."

"No such thought crossed my mind," Kathryn lied glibly, fingers crossed that Michael would never find out.

"That's all right then. You know you're the only woman for me."

"Why did you want to get hold of me? Was it important?" Kathryn asked.

"Important! That's the understatement of the year. The Vaga has abdicated in favour of Vonryn who's really his grandson. Once the news was leaked that Vonryn wasn't Barbara and Vincent's son, the Vaga knew he had to do something because that fact barred Vonryn from the line of succession."

Michael sounded so excited that Kathryn didn't have the heart to tell him about the Club's newsletter.

"My mother married Morgan Draymer secretly years ago and Vonryn's their son, so I've got a half-brother. If only we could have been brought up together," he added wistfully.

"What's the reaction to the abdication?"

"Too soon to say. The news only broke earlier today. In an ideal world the islands would unite under one government and one ruler but some people are using the scandal for their own ends and to try and stop this happening. People on the British islands are wary about independence and a little frightened that there might be bloodshed."

"Can you see that happening?" Kathryn enquired. "My mother will be worried to death and I'll never hear the end of it; her baby daughter living in a war zone."

"Talks are ongoing as to the way forward. There'll be the usual petty squabbles but if people see their lives aren't going to change for the worse, I think the majority will accept Vonryn as Vaga over all the islands - even if it is as a figurehead in the previously held British ones. The way it's handled will make all the difference and of course there's their wedding to look forward to. Everyone likes a good wedding."

"Will Drystan step down as well?"

"I don't know," Michael sounded wary and Kathryn didn't pursue the subject, some things were better left unsaid on the telephone. "I've found us a place to live," he continued, "but only if you like the idea," he hastened to add. "Ruth is leaving politics and going back into law. She's moving to Mordeen to open a branch office for her previous firm and will let us have her bungalow at a knock down price on condition that we let her use the attached flat for the next six months whilst she's still an M.P."

"I love the idea, but why is she moving to Mordeen? I would have thought she'd have wanted to stay in St. Elizabeth where all her friends are."

"Another bit of gossip for you. She and Uncle Luke had a thing going for them years ago and it looks as if it might be rekindled."

"That's lovely," Kathryn smiled to herself. In her present euphoric mood she wanted everyone to be as happy as she was.

"I take it that we'll be getting married and not living in sin as my mother would put it."

"Definitely. Grandfather would go mad if we didn't. There's been enough scandal in our family lately to last a lifetime. How does a spring wedding in Mordeen Cathedral with Uncle Luke officiating grab you?"

"Very much."

"Warn your mother when she's out shopping for something to wear that our spring day is like a hot summer's day in the UK."

"I will," Kathryn said, "but I'd better ring off now. I dread to think what my phone bill will be, but it's worth it to speak to you. Goodnight Michael. I'll see you soon. Love you."

"Love you too," Michael replied, "counting the days until you come back."

Kathryn replaced the receiver. She was deliriously happy until she remembered the letter she'd posted earlier in the evening on her way to the club. Hastily she penned a short note and frantically searched the desk for a stamp before she rushed down to the postbox. Hopefully the second letter would arrive the same time as the first. In any event she'd phone her mother the following day and warn her never to reveal the contents of the first letter to Michael.

She lay awake for a long time planning her wedding. She couldn't wait to finish working her notice and return to the islands. Before then she'd try and spend the remaining weekends with her parents or get them to visit her in Bath.

Chapter 24

October

Dear Mum and Dad,

Last night's phone call must have come as a bit of a shock, but everything is moving along at a whirlwind pace. I know you expected me to work out my notice and then leave for the islands to get married, but Nadia wanted me to be her bridesmaid and I wanted to see Michael. I thought I might have to take unpaid leave or extend my notice to cover the week I intended to take off, but I had a big surprise waiting for me. Head Office have given me a year's contract to work in St. Elizabeth and open a small travel agency there. It will mainly specialise in people wanting to take holidays away from the islands, but I've also got to do a feasibility study with regard to mini cruises around the inner shores of the islands. As you know tour operators already bring in cruise liners to the outer shores. It's very exciting. I've been given a budget and have to find premises, buy equipment and employ staff - well at least one other person to work with me. I can't believe it's all happening. At the end of the first year, head office will take stock and who knows what will happen afterwards.

For the time being, I'm staying in Ruth's bungalow, soon to be my first marital home. Ruth spends most weekends with Luke in Innisver and is busy during the week, as am I, so we don't see much of one another. During the day, Michael is kept busy in the office and we meet up, either here or in the Governor's Palace. Nadia is back to her old cheerful self again. She confided in me that she had made up her mind to marry Vonryn and go into exile with him, even if it meant being poor together. It might have worked, but although I like Nadia, she has never had to work in her life, so who can say how things would have turned out. Naturally she's thrilled to bits that she can have Vonryn and her old lifestyle, who wouldn't be? The papers are full of the wedding, which is going to be in the cathedral in Christenbech. Nadia has had her dress made, but I haven't seen it yet. I'm meeting her tomorrow to discuss my bridesmaid's dress. We're cutting it very fine as the wedding is only a fortnight away. She has a beautiful, new engagement ring. It is traditional for the wife of the Vaga to wear a pure Envis stone. You'll love it when you see it. I'm quite envious, but the complete coloured stones are so rare that only the Vaga's wife has jewellery made of these. I'll treat you to a pair of earrings of the more common sort. They're just as pretty; but not so rare.

You mentioned on the phone that you were worried I might be caught up in a civil war once independence is granted in the New Year. You don't have to worry a referendum was held last week on the two British islands and there was a 97% majority in favour of having Vonryn as Vaga. All the islands are going to keep their own parliaments, so apart from having Vonryn has head of state instead of the Queen, people now realise that things are going to stay as they were before, and their fears have been allayed. The Islands' Council will remain, but as it didn't have any real power, no one seems bothered about it. Before, observers might be invited from the British islands to take part, but now there are to be two members selected by their parliament to participate at all meetings, and it has been agreed between all the islands that there should only be a maximum of twelve people sitting on this Council. Michael said his grandfather wasn't very pleased about that, but he had to give in. Enough of boring politics, but I thought it would relieve your mind that politically things seem to be stable here.

The next six months are going to be hectic. I can't see me getting home for Christmas. I'm really sorry about that as it will be the first Christmas I've spent away from home. After the independence celebrations there will be a general election in all the islands and as I told you before, Ruth is standing down. We thought that an election wouldn't be called until next September and Ruth was going to stay with us. If you recall, she let us have the bungalow at a knock down price. Michael and I felt awful about that and told her that we insisted on paying full market value for it as the situation had altered. Michael got a surveyor to tell us the full value and we offered it to Ruth, but she wouldn't take it. In the end we compromised and we agreed to split the difference down the middle. She said to count it as her wedding gift to us both. I won't say how much it is, but it is an expensive one, I can tell you. My wedding is on March 24th and if possible Mum can you come out a couple of weeks before then. I'd like your support. I'm sure Dad can spare you for a short time and then he can travel out with Tom and his family. Speak to you soon.

Love,
Kathryn
xxxx

P.S. I nearly forgot, but I'm enclosing a cutting from a magazine. Michael was telling me that there was a terrific storm over Envetta the other day and after when the sun came out the most beautiful rainbow appeared in the sky. This was reflected in Lake Iris and it appeared as if the rainbow formed a circle. This was just before the referendum as to whether Vonryn should be Vaga over all the islands. Naturally as soon as the journalists heard about it they all tried to see if anyone had taken a photograph of this phenomenon, as legend has it that when this happened the islands would be united again. They found one lucky villager who had taken a photograph and I wouldn't be surprised if he made enough out of the snapshot to retire. Pro unionists made much of this, but whether it influenced people in their voting it's hard to say.

Chapter 25

Kathryn's mother, Megan, looked around at the couples dancing in the ballroom of the state apartments and wished she were thousands of miles away. Her son and his family had just left saying they were going back to the hotel so that the children could go to bed. She turned to her husband, Ieuan, and suggested they should leave also, but Ieuan pointed out it was much too early for the bride's parents to leave. They at least had to wait until Kathryn and Michael left for their honeymoon. It was then that Justin had come across. He was bored he said with making polite conversation and would Ieuan like a game of pool back at Innisver Castle.

"Go on," Megan said, "I'll go and have a chat to some of the guests." She looked around for one friendly face that she knew, but in the crowd couldn't see anyone vaguely familiar. Ah well, she thought the day is nearly over. Absentmindedly she took a glass of champagne from a waiter and wandered out on to the balcony. There was a tiled bench against the wall and wearily she sat down. The tiles were still warm from the heat of the day and sighing with relief she slipped off her shoes. It had been a lovely day, although she hadn't really felt a part of it. She'd proudly watched her only daughter walk down the aisle, and said a silent prayer for Kathryn's happiness. However, after their turbulent courtship and the interference from Michael's grandfather, the future didn't bode at all well. All her parents could do would be to pray for the best and be there to pick up the pieces if the marriage should fall apart. Kathryn though had looked radiant with happiness. Her red gold hair had been swept up to the top of her head and was surrounded by a small tiara of pearls. The severe lines of the silk dress had suited Kathryn's slim figure to perfection, and Megan realised that Kathryn had been right to say no to the traditional white, the cream suited her daughter's skin tone much better. The bouquet had also been simple, made up of Lycaste Locusta orchids with cream rosebuds and stephanotis surrounding the deep green flowers. Her two grandsons hadn't wanted to be pageboys, and after hearing that the wedding was being video taped and was to be shown back home, they'd been adamant that they weren't going to dress up. They said their friends would never let them live it down. Their sister, Rebecca, however, was only too delighted to be a bridesmaid and it was a proud nine-year-old who walked up the aisle carrying a small bunch of cream rosebuds and wearing a lovely green dress that matched the orchids in the bouquet her aunt was carrying. Kathryn had laughed, when Megan had pointed out that green was unlucky and said that it was her favourite colour and she wasn't superstitious.

"I wondered where you'd disappeared to."

Megan looked up and saw Ria approaching.

"I needed a breath of fresh air," she said.

Ria sat down on the bench next to Megan.

"Kathryn will be fine Megan. I know what it's like to have a daughter thousands of miles away, but I promise you I'll keep an eye on her and I know Ilona will as well."

Megan smiled weakly. How could she say to Ria that it was her husband that Megan was worried about.

"Where will Ilona and Richard live after independence?" She asked.

"They haven't decided yet, but in the interim they'll live in Innisver Castle with us. There's plenty of room."

"I'm worried that Kathryn won't fit in," Megan said hesitantly. "Her background is so different from this."

"Oh she'll come across snobbery, especially in St. Elizabeth, but I don't think it will bother her too much. She'll make her own friends from the people she and Michael meet through their work. Some people will try to put her down, like they did to me when I married Drystan…"

"You!" Megan was amazed.

"Oh yes. I wasn't from the same social background as Drystan's first wife and when we attended social gatherings in the early days, I was nervous and frightened of making a fool of myself."

"I didn't realise."

"How could you? I soon weeded out my true friends from social climbers and those who only wanted to take advantage of my name and position and then laughed about how gauche I was behind my back. In the end I realised that those sort of people weren't important and soon I was so busy raising my own three children and my stepson that I didn't have time to worry about them. Anyway, Kathryn and Michael will have my husband's backing."

"But he tried to stop them getting married."

"That was nothing personal against Kathryn. He always liked her and thought she would be a good wife for Michael. He told me so. It was just that their marriage didn't fit into his grandiose scheme. He was determined that one of his descendants would be Vaga."

"If that was the case, why didn't he approve of Ilona marrying Morgan all those years ago. It would have made sense."

"You're right of course. It made sense to me, but not to my husband. Hallam Draymer was all for the marriage and that made Drystan even more against it. He thought it was a plot on Hallam's part to get Innisver from him. He was being paranoid of course. The main culprit was the centuries old feud between the two families. Surely you must have families back home who let old disputes linger on?"

Megan started to say no, but then she thought of her cousins who lived in adjoining streets in the village and hadn't spoken for years. No one in the family remembered the cause of the quarrel, but that trivial argument was being carried down the generations.

Trouble was likely to break out at any family gathering, and fist fights between some of the younger ones had taken place, especially after pints of beer had been downed.

Megan smiled at Ria. "Yes you're right, families are the same all over the world, rich or poor it doesn't seem to make any difference."

~*~

All day Kathryn had felt there was something wrong. She couldn't put a finger on it because the wedding in the cathedral had gone perfectly, with no one putting a foot wrong. The buffet reception, although not to Drystan's liking had also been a hit. There had been masses of food and plenty of tables, so that people didn't have to stand around balancing plates and glasses. Everyone had seemed to enjoy themselves, mixing with people they didn't see very often. As she'd mingled with the guests thanking them for their presents, she'd realised that quite a lot of politics and business was being discussed, and it annoyed her to think that her wedding reception was being used for such a purpose. This simmering resentment lasted with her all though the afternoon and it was when she was thinking of getting changed to go on her honeymoon that the thought crossed her mind that perhaps she'd made a terrible mistake. Apart from her parents and brother and his small family, the rest of her family and friends were back home. Oh the wedding had been video taped and there was to be an evening reception held in the local club later on in the month when her parents returned home. Two people though would be absent, the bride and groom. It wasn't how she'd imagined getting married, but it was too late now. She'd committed herself to living in a foreign country. She turned to look at her new husband and wondered if she loved him any more. He turned and smiled at her. "Let's dance," he said. He took her hand and she followed him meekly onto the dance floor. It was a slow waltz and Michael held her close to him. "What's wrong?" he whispered.

"Nothing and everything," she replied.

"That covers a lot," he said pulling away from her slightly and smiling down at her. "I think I know what it is. All these people and how many of them do we actually know and like."

"Not many," she agreed.

"The guest list was all about inviting the right people. Grandfather explained it to me."

Kathryn winced. "He did, did he?"

"Don't be like that Kathryn. We don't want to have a row on our wedding day. I've been stupid. I let everything go to my head. It wasn't so much the money, it was the power and the way people kowtowed to me. I'm ashamed to say I enjoyed it, but grandfather does know that it doesn't pay to offend important people, or those that think they're important. The situation in the islands is too delicate at the moment to make enemies unnecessarily." The music stopped and Michael led Kathryn off the dance floor. "We ought to go and get changed," she said.

"Let's have one more drink first. We'll go in the library; we can't get any peace here. I've got something to tell you. I've thought of something. It was to be a surprise, but then I thought no, there's to be no more secrets between us. I want your agreement and then everything can be arranged whilst we're on our honeymoon."

"That sounds ominous."

Michael fetched two glasses of champagne and they sought refuge in the library. With the door closed firmly behind them, it was a haven of peace from the noise and bustle of the ballroom.

"What did you want to tell me?" Kathryn asked.

"Our honeymoon was going to last for three weeks wasn't it, cruising around the islands? Would you be prepared to cut it short to say two weeks?"

Kathryn looked puzzled. "Not without an explanation," she replied. "I hope this has nothing to do with your grandfather."

"For goodness sake, forget grandfather. It has nothing to do with him. I don't want to start my job by asking for extra time off straight away. That would be taking advantage of who my grandfather is."

Kathryn looked interested. It seemed as though Michael was starting to grow up. "I'm sorry Michael. Tell me your plan."

"We'll cruise the islands for two weeks as planned. The third week we'll travel back to the UK with your parents and Tom's family. I thought we could have a blessing in the church you attended when you were small and invite all those people who couldn't come over here. You and Rebecca could wear your dresses again, although we'd have to get fresh bouquets. What do you think?"

"It's a lovely idea Michael, but there would be so little time to arrange it."

"Nonsense. Your mother told me that invitations had been sent out for an evening do on the Saturday after they get back home to see the wedding video, so surely a few phone calls will do the trick. Your mother has a list back home and someone there could pass the word around. Put a notice in the paper or make a few phone calls. You said the local grapevine worked better than a telephone."

Kathryn laughed. It was a lovely idea. "Do you think it could be done? What about the vicar, the church, the flights, oh everything."

"Leave it to me. I'll go and see our respective mothers and my grandmother. I'll leave everything in their capable hands."

Kathryn reached up and kissed him. "I do love you Michael."

"I hope so," he said. "I thought for a moment in the ballroom, you'd gone off me."

"Don't be long," she said. "The car is coming for us shortly and we still have to get changed."

"You worry too much," Michael said. "I can't see them driving off and leaving the Larn of Pendenny's grandson and his wife standing there. Can you?"

Kathryn sipped her champagne contentedly. Everything was going to be fine. Michael's actions had swept all her doubts away. The door opened and she turned her head thinking it would be Michael returning, but thought he'd been rather quick. To her disappointment it was Drystan Pendenny. He sat down opposite her and she thought back to Ilona and Richard's silver wedding where she'd almost been won over by his charm and then later found out he wasn't to be trusted. He came straight to the point. "I doubt if you'll ever forgive me," he said.

"Probably not," she replied.

"At least you're honest."

"What did you expect me to say?" All Kathryn's bitterness broke forth. "You tried to split us up and for what?"

"The Islands," he replied quietly.

"Oh no, not the islands. If you'd wanted the best for them you would have let Vonryn be Vaga even before you knew he was your grandson. He'd been trained all his life for that and no matter how much I love Michael, the people would never have accepted him."

"You come here, a foreigner, and tell me what is best for my beloved islands."

Kathryn stood up and looked down at him. She was married to Michael now and even though he was the powerful Larn of Pendenny, she wasn't going to take any more. "Yes I am telling you. Perhaps it is because I'm a stranger here that I can see things more clearly than you. The time has come to end all feuds. Maybe the islands aren't as united as you hoped, but at least they've all accepted Vonryn. Who knows one day in the distant future, the Islands' Council may be the nucleus of a Federal Government. From little acorns mighty oak trees grow."

"Yes, I do know the saying," he said wryly. "It's strange, but I had the same idea about the Islands' Council, that was why I didn't want it disbanded completely. Of course nothing will happen in my day, or Hallam's. I'm not stupid enough to think that. Once we die, it will be an elected Council and then who knows." He looked up at her and smiled. "I should have got to know you better Kathryn. It seems as if you're starting to feel the same way as I do about the islands. What do you say we bury our feud and start afresh?"

"Can you promise not to interfere in my life?"

Drystan grimaced. "The best I can do is to promise that I'll try to restrain myself."

"That will have to do," she said, sitting down again. She was silent for a few minutes, then she remarked. "Doesn't it seem ironic to you that the thing you fought so hard against all those years ago is now a reality."

"You mean Ilona and Morgan's son becoming Vaga?"

"Yes."

Drystan too was quiet for a moment thinking of all the wasted years of not seeing his daughter or grandsons. "I was bloody stupid, but I'll be serious for a moment Kathryn. I had no hand in Morgan's death, no matter what you may hear in the future. That was an accident pure and simple."

"I'm sure it was." Suddenly she no longer felt intimidated by Drystan and asked. What would you have done with the baby if you'd known about it?"

"Ah. I won't lie to you. I would have made sure he or she had a good home in some small village on one of the islands."

"Your own grandchild?"

"Yes. I would have sacrificed him so that James could inherit. Of course if Morgan had lived who knows what would have happened. The marriage was legal and I suppose in time I would have come around, but it wasn't to be. Fate stepped in and took a hand."

"As it did when the rainbow was reflected in the lake. That was a marvellous omen."

Drystan started to laugh.

"My dear girl, that strange phenomenon happens on a regular basis, only the people who live in that remote part of Envetta are so used to it they don't take any notice, and visitors rarely go there so they don't know about it. Hallam gave a camera to one of his tenants and told him to take a photograph next time it happened. He made a right mess of things the first few times, but eventually he got it right. We paid him well for the rights naturally."

"Naturally." Kathryn shook her head in amazement and she too started to laugh. It was thus that Michael found them when he poked his head around the library door.

266

Chasing The Rainbow

by

Patricia Thomas

.